THE HOUR OF THE WOLF

Thyri looked up. A pale wash of white hailed the coming of the moon. Her eyes opened wide as the silver orb broke the horizon, and her legs went weak. She looked down and watched the white coat of the beast sprout through her skin and cover her lower body. Her breasts caved in as the rippling white coat grew up to her neck. Claws sprang from her toes, and her bones wrenched, forcing her to her knees. Pain flared through her, clouding her vision until the transformation was complete...and the white wolf had come full into the world.

Don't Miss the Exciting Beginning of Avon Books'
BLOODFANG Series
by Michael D. Weaver

WOLF-DREAMS

NIGHTREAVER

Michael D. Weaver

AVON BOOKS NEW YORK

for Galadriel

NIGHTREAVER is an original publication of Avon Books. This work has never before appeared in book form. This work is a novel. Any similarity to actual persons or events is purely coincidental.

AVON BOOKS
A division of
The Hearst Corporation
105 Madison Avenue
New York, New York 10016

Front cover illustration by Rowena Morrill
Published by arrangement with the author
Library of Congress Catalog Card Number: 87-91453
ISBN: 0-380-75197-6

First Avon Books Printing: May 1988

Printed in the U.S.A.

K-R 10 9 8 7 6 5 4 3 2 1

Book IV: THE VALKYRIE

For three nights I have dreamed the same dream over and again. As I drift into sleep, I am joined by a cloud of leaves that swirl around me and catch in my hair. Beyond the leaves: eyes of red fire. My heart fills with hunger and I sing to those eyes, begging for them to feed me, to make me strong.

And then the world explodes in a blaze of bright, silvery light. Time slows, each moment maturing into a terrible forever before the shapes around me begin to steal back their forms from the silvery realm, and I recognize the feel of cold earth beneath my feet.

I open my eyes, and the leaves have settled, carpeting the forest floor. Before me, in place of those red eyes, she stands.

Her eyes still blaze; the red burns now along the edge of her sword. The silver world lingers around her, and she moves, carrying it toward me. She raises her sword.

Never have I seen a sight more beautiful, more terrifying.

I stand motionless; beyond her, around us, nothing seems quite real. *She* is the meaning behind every breath I take. Without her I am nothing.

She draws closer, and I embrace her. Above me, something flashes, and then iron bites into my neck.

Her sword.

Here, I wake. I have lost count of the times I have so wakened these three nights. And why do I dream this dream? The scene I know; I lived it first a month ago. The woman, of course, is Thyri, but I look out through the eyes of another, one who died by her hand.

Through my research into the life of Thyri Eiriksdattir, I lived this death. Since I last put down this pen, I have spent all my days looking into that part of Thyri's life of which I now must write. Rather, I have spent all my days in research but these last three, the three days of my dreams.

My task, it seems, will grant me no rest. And so I move on. I last wrote of Thyri's days in the new land over the ocean. An idea had propelled her there: the idea that she might somehow rid herself of the *were*-beast hidden beneath her skin. This had not come to pass. If anything, Thyri had grown more like her brethren of the wood; the beast had dug itself deep into her heart, her mind, and she had abandoned her battle against it.

Indeed, she had rid herself of the company of men, and she spent the winter after her victory over the warrior-king Aralak alone, sheltering in a cave from which she would venture only to hunt, or to challenge the occasional predator daring to test her control over her domain. She defended every intrusion into her hunting grounds fiercely, like an animal. Then, when winter lessened its grip, she left her cave and fared north, traveling without destination, letting instinct be her guide. In a dark sort of way, she was content, and she let the demands of survival fill her days and dominate her waking mind. This land had become her home, and she strove to gain peace with it. Thought of leaving seemed as absurd as thought of evading the wolf under the full moon.

Her past she had buried, and when she came upon the new land's people she would watch them from a distance and they would seem to her like strangers, even though she had dwelt with them the year before and they had named her a goddess. She was not a goddess, and they were not her people. Her past beyond that, she recalled only as one recalls strands of dream, the memories hazy and incomplete as if they rose to the surface of her mind like the final, weak gestures of a drowning swimmer.

One morning, a fortnight after she'd left her winter cave, she came upon the trail of a small boar. The scent was faint at first, but as she began to track, she lost herself in the hunt and morning passed effortlessly into afternoon. When the scent grew strong, she left the trail, skirting to the east, downwind of her prey. Approaching, she sighted the boar as he watered at a quiet pool. Under the heat of the sun, she slew her prey with a single arrow.

As she ate, she noted another faint, familiar scent: that of the sea. After eating, she swam in the pool, but the salty breeze made her restless and she set off again to explore the surrounding area. Near the sea, she discovered something that pulled up those old memories, teasing her mind, drawing her slowly up, out of the darkness:

Departure

The evening grew cold. It had not been spring for long, and after the sun turned its face away, winter was quick to reclaim the world. The sky was cloudy, and a light mist fell on the ground, glistening on the moonlit grass that covered the low mound. A great stone towered out of the earth at its foot. Thyri stood motionless before it; she had seen such sights before.

The stone was almost a megalith. It would have taken five men to set it in place. Moss had grown over it.

She stepped forward and scraped at the moss. Her labors bared the rune of the warrior and the rune of Freyr, Lord of the Vanir. There were other markings that she didn't recognize, marks of other gods; but Freyr's she knew. He was lord of more desolate climes even than those that had borne her. He was ancient, once the enemy of Odin and his sons. Thyri had known, and fought, many of his followers. They dwelt in jarldoms north of Hordaland.

How had they come here, and how long before? Grass and shrubbery had rooted in the mound. The moss on the stone might have taken one year or a hundred to gain the ground that it had.

Somewhere beyond the stone, under the mound, was a Viking warship.

The prince who had captained the ship—he lay buried with it. Had he perished of some accident or illness, or by the arrows of hostile Arakoy? Thyri stepped onto the mound. The prince had not died alone; she could feel the lost spirits of the dead in the earth and air, and a great sadness wrapped about her heart. The dead permeated the mist and caressed her like whispers of wind.

They had died far from home. With the name of Odin on their lips? If so, he had not heard them. He was too far away. They had sought new lands for their gods, and the gods had abandoned them just as Odin had abandoned her. Now they were trapped, cursed to forever live as shadows. If they had died in their homeland, they would now number among the ranks of Odin's host at Valhalla.

If Odin could not reach them, how did her curse reach across the Great Ocean to touch her?

The phantoms circled around her; the mist danced, and a dam suddenly cracked in her mind, a cascade of memories gushing forth to take form in the heavy air. She saw faces: her mother's, her uncle's, Pye's, Pohati's, Astrid's. Astrid gazed at her with hollow eyes.

Thyri rubbed her own eyes. These ghosts of her own making did not belong. She peered into the mist, concentrating. Her mother's features vanished. Pye turned, becoming a small funnel of wispy chaos before fading. A misty tear fell from Astrid's eye. Her lips quivered.

You have felt much pain, little one.

"Astrid?"

Do not mourn for them. They were not worthy. They ran from battle with Halfdan the Black, Harald's father. Only luck brought them to these shores.

The Valkyrie grew tangible. She began to glow, the mist now resting on silver armor, on gauntleted hands, on the fine wash of silky blond hair that fell down on her shoulders.

Then, behind her, Thyri heard sounds she had thought lost forever: a snort, and a steed pawing at the ground. She turned and saw Yrafax. He looked back at her thoughtfully and tucked his black, feathery wings against his sides. Astrid's steed, as immortal now as his mistress.

"Astrid!"

The Valkyrie smiled. *Time to go home, my love.*

Astrid's appearance chased all other thoughts from Thyri's awakening mind. She hadn't seen Astrid since that time she'd set to kill herself and Astrid had appeared to her to stay her hand.

So long ago . . . Now the Valkyrie returned. Astrid had not forgotten her. The darkness in Thyri's heart melted away, her old love for her cousin surfacing anew, turning back time.

"How did you find me?"

"I have never truly left you."

"My curse is over? You will take me to Valhalla now?"

Astrid looked at her sadly. "No. Your work is yet far from over."

"What work?"

"I—do not know. Have you not learned peace?"

"And forgotten it again. I have tried. I have known happiness, and in each case I have destroyed it. I know only misery now. I bear a burden of many lives."

"Your knots are forty-five now?"

Thyri nodded, her hand moving instinctively to finger the long braid behind her ear. Each knot touched recalled briefly its own set of memories, pieces of her past that Thyri had all but lost.

"Then you have learned," Astrid said thoughtfully. "I think, my love, that happiness is not ours to have. I have wondered if any of our people can gain it. We are desperate in love, desperate in war. We live, in the end, only to war with Loki and his forces of evil. And that, I think, is a war we shall lose." Astrid walked slowly to her steed. She reached its side and looked back to Thyri, holding out her hand. "You have with you all you require?"

Thyri nodded. "I have traveled lightly."

"Then come."

They spoke no words as Yrafax left the ground behind and carried them up through the clouds. The land below became patchy, indistinct shadows. In the distance Thyri recognized the teeth of Hagara Kohn jutting darkly up against the night starscape. She felt as if she dreamed. Being there, in the sky—being with Astrid, these things belonged in the realm of dream. She had left her sadnesses behind in the realm of the daylight; during that journey, Thyri was truly at peace.

They passed over a great flock of birds. Thyri looked down upon them, wondering how they all knew their positions in the wedge formation. The wind whipped her hair about. Astrid's hair blew back into her face, tickling her cheeks and neck. She moved forward, wrapping her arms about Astrid and fitting her body into the curve of her cousin's back.

"Balder is dead," Astrid said. "The omens of the Sibyl are coming to pass. I was there at Gladsheim after Frigg gained oaths from all things in all the worlds that they would not harm her beautiful son."

Thyri listened to her cousin's words. She absorbed them as if they were song, a beautiful melody unmarred by the darkness of the lyric. The lyric she all but ignored, though she would recall it later and reflect upon it with alarm.

"It was like a game to us," Astrid continued. "No pebble, no arrow, no sword could harm Balder. His skin showed no marks or evidence of any attack at all. I struck him, Thyri, through the mind-of-the-tyger. He did not even feel my touch." She paused, looking back. Thyri saw stars reflecting in Astrid's eyes, and she thought she saw tears.

Balder's death, spake the Sybil, signed the coming of the end.

"Hod killed him," Astrid said, looking ahead again. "Loki tricked him; he gave him an arrow of mistletoe—the one thing, I think, in all the worlds from which Frigg failed to gain an oath. The arrow pierced Balder's breast, and the God of Beauty died."

"But he's a god," Thyri murmured from her dream of peace. "An immortal should be . . . immortal."

"He yet lives in Niflheim," Astrid said, "if one can be said to live in that place. Hermod went for him. Hel appreciated his bravery and offered that, if everything in all the worlds would weep for Balder, she would release him.

"Frigg again petitioned aid from all things—all trees, all illnesses, all animals, everything and everyone except mortal man who *cannot* be involved in these things. All wept save *one*—a giantess who named herself Thokk."

"Could you not kill her?" Thyri asked. "Then all things would have wept."

"No," Astrid said. "*She*—Thokk—was the Trickster. Loki has disappeared. None have looked for him. All of Asgard mourns Balder."

Slowly, the weight of Astrid's tale forced the beginning of an understanding in Thyri's mind. *I meant you, Astrid,* she thought. *You are Valkyrie. You must have some power among the gods. Or are things so ordered, so set by the will of Odin, that you cannot stray from his tasks?*

"I stood at his pyre, little one." Astrid paused, gazing up to look at the gleaming, starlit outline of the serpent. "Among my brethren I am called Shield Bearer."

"And what shall I be called, Astrid, when I join you?"

"I am no longer sure you may do that."

"Am I to rank then among the warriors of Valhalla?"

Astrid pointed into the sky. "Do you see that star, my love? It was once whispered among the Aesir that the One God's son, the Christ, fell from there. The All Father desired to know, so he sent me to learn. I flew up, out of the sky and into the stars. Into the stars of the One God."

"Stars are but flaming embers from Muspellheim," Thyri said, "inlaid into Ymir's skull by Odin when he erected the sky over the Earth."

"No," Astrid said. "They are much more. This one was huge. Larger than the sun. And the leagues I traversed to reach it through open, glittering space—Thyri, you cannot imagine the beauty of it!

"But that is what I have learned as Valkyrie, little one. Of your destiny, I know nothing. I was there when they laid Balder on a pyre on his ship, Ringhold. I saw the throngs of Asgard gathered in sorrow, watching the giantess Hyrrokin heave Ringhold into the water with her great strength. I heard Balder's wife, Nanna, gasp as life fled from her out of grief. I watched Odin leap from the shore and lay the great ring Draupnir on his son's body.

"Since then the All Father has spoken but twice. First to the Thunderer, who grew enraged when he learned of Loki's masquerade as Thokk and desired his father's blessing for revenge. Second to me, to return you to nearer shores."

"Why?"

"I do not know. I have seen Scacath. She has taken counsel with Odin since my death. I spoke with her, but she would not tell me the reason for her visit."

"Where will you take me?"

"Where do you wish to go?"

"A battle," Thyri said. She crushed herself against Astrid's back. "A battle in which I might die. I'm so lonely, Cousin. I wish that this madness would end." She paused. "What did you find in the heavens, Astrid? Did you find the One God?"

"No. I found only a star, a fiery orb in an emptiness. It had no Earth. There was no life there but the star's own. I felt it, little one. Slow, churning thoughts. Strength. I have never felt such strength."

Little more passed between them during the journey. In the silent spaces, Thyri fell back into blissful half-dream. She couldn't imagine being unhappy in the presence of her cousin; she had yearned for her for so long.

Her wish to die was a wish to remain with Astrid. In the skies, all the tragic details of her life seemed far away. Only later would she place herself where she fit into the things Astrid said. Only then would she think it strange that Odin had handed her an undefined task, and only then would she curse him for it.

Astrid, however, knew where Thyri's thoughts would lead. As they neared the shores of Erin, she uttered one line. It was preceded, and followed, by silence. "It is because," Astrid said, "you are the wildfire."

Thyri was on the edge of sleep. The words carried her fully

into dream, and she would never actually recall them consciously. They entered her, rather, in a much deeper way.

They landed on a cushion of mist with grass faintly visible about three feet below the mystical horse's hooves. Thyri kissed Astrid and dismounted without speaking. Her feet stopped on a level with the steed's.

"Take care," Astrid said. "Yrafax will take your ground with him when we leave."

"Must it be so soon?"

Astrid nodded. "I am tempting Odin's wrath now. We were a night and a day in the crossing. We could have made the entire journey at the speed of thought."

"I will not say farewell, sword-sister," Thyri said. "We will meet again very soon." She turned and stepped down from the mist. When she glanced back, Astrid and Yrafax were gone.

Wildfire

The camp, smelling of fires, pork, and warm ale, was easy to find. After eluding the watch, Thyri strode boldly among the tents, her head held high, her hand on her sword's pommel. One man groped drunkenly for her. She kicked him and snatched the flagon from his hand. She went to his barrel of ale, filled his flagon, put it to her lips, and drained it. Then she filled the flagon again. She leaned against the barrel and smiled.

There was grumbling among them. All eyes fell on her. Her smile blossomed into laughter. The ale hit her stomach and its warmth coursed through her limbs. It had been so long since she'd drunk, longer since she had walked thusly into a band of male warriors who saw her as a woman, not a goddess. She never failed to get the same result.

"In whose bed do you sleep, wench?" one of them finally growled. He spoke Thyri's native tongue.

She drained the flagon and again refilled it. "My own. And I intend to be extremely drunk when I enter it tonight." She contented herself with drinking and watching them for a while. Her words had turned them to bicker among themselves as to who would share that drunken bed with her. They obviously thought her no more than a wench—one who had presumably dressed in some of her master's battle gear for a lark. She thought it funny that they didn't seem to care just *who* her master was. Were their fantasies true, and if she'd belonged to some officer, the winner of the argument would most likely have ended up dead the next morning.

So involved was their argument that they almost forgot about Thyri herself until she drew her sword.

Those who saw the weapon in detail gasped. One man told her to put it away. Others went for swords of their own. Another whispered, "Bloodfang!"

She glared at him. "Why do you speak thus?"

"Because," a voice came from behind her, "that is how you are known. A name given by he who bears the sister blade."

She turned.

"Thyri Bloodfang," he said. "The legend lives."

He was tall and broad, with a stiff blond beard and deep blue eyes. His hair was tied back, and his furs bore the insignia of a field commander.

"I am Anlaf Olafson. I fought against you once, battle-mistress. In the sea off the northern fjords. You captained a ship for Hordaland. You captured the vessel on which I served."

"I do not remember you."

"No," he said, laughing, "I doubt that you would. I worked an oar. You battled a man behind me. When I rose to enter the fray, you struck behind you with your elbow as if you sensed me, and I went over, into the sea."

She considered him, smiled and raised her flagon to him, then drank. "I am pleased to meet you, Anlaf Olafson."

"What brings you here, Eiriksdattir?"

"Where is here, my liege?"

His gaze grew scrutinous. "Lands of the Saxons, woman. Do you not know where you are?"

"There is to be a battle here?"

"A battle, yes, but not here. We await word from Ubbi Ragnarson, who brings ships and men. Then we march south and crush the Saxon kingling, Alfred."

Thyri reflected on his words for a moment but did not voice her thoughts. "Then," she said, "I now know where I am. I will add my sword to yours, Anlaf Olafson, if you will let me."

His smile returned. "Come with me, then. Partake of my ale. It is far better than the urine my men drink."

The remark drew mixed response. One warrior protested that he'd stolen *his* ale from Anlaf's brew. In fairness, it must be written that Thyri, in the end, could tell little difference between the two.

She followed him, and catcalls from half of Anlaf's men followed her. The other half, however, had already begun to spread whispered rumor among their fellows.

In Anlaf's tent, they rested on furs and drank. Thyri eyed him over the rim of her flagon.

"What do they know of me? Your men? That I slew my kin?"

He nodded. "They know that, yes. Some claim to know much more. Last summer I learned that Hordaland had lost the twin battle-maidens whose names had begun to invoke fear among all Vikings not under Ragnar's banner. It was said that Astrid died, and that you slew half your kin in your grief. You are *berserk*.

But wintering in a tavern in Jorvik, I spoke to a warrior who credits you with the downfalls of three Swedish kings."

Thyri grew thoughtful. They did not know of her curse—that much of her, at least, was safe. If they thought her *berserk*, they would think no ill of her at all. The battle madness was a gift of the All Father, and those who died before it were considered poor, hapless souls unlucky enough to be on the wrong end of the gifting. "I know nothing of Swedish kings. I have fought Swedes as I have fought Danes. None recently. Their king-slayer is another."

Anlaf laughed. "Dread of prophecies probably." He made a deep, growling sound, then laughed again. "The Swedes have not the strength of Danes." He looked at Thyri through his mirth. "Or Norwegians."

"What of Eirikson? He who gave me such—an unusual name?" *My brother,* she thought.

He frowned. "He is no longer a boy. He commands five ships under Ragnar. His blade, your blade, is feared. It is said that he calls out to you in battle."

Erik? Thyri thought. *You have tainted his blood, little one. As darkly as if you'd fanged him . . .*

"Who," she wondered aloud, "tends the fields?"

"Burned," Anlaf said. "Your house has no fields except those Ragnar will grant your brother when the whelp bothers to ask. Harald has grown mad—assaulting Hordaland last spring. All this war he brings—for the hand of a woman."

How many more of my blood dead?

"Gyda," she said blankly.

"Aye," Anlaf chuckled. "She whose name has spread as well. She yet denies him. Harald Tangle-Hair he is called now—he swears never to comb mane or beard until she consents to wed him. He has already gained much land. And burned more, mostly the land of his beloved. Or one of them. He already has thirty-nine wives."

"Enough," she said, draining her flagon. "I owe my people nothing now." She refilled and drank more.

"Well," Anlaf said, grinning and raising his flagon. "Here's to Loki's tits."

Thyri laughed and pushed thoughts of home from her mind.

As they drank, they traded stories. Thyri recounted the sea battle in which they had both fought. Another humorous thing had happened that day: a warrior had plugged a rent in Thyri's ship with his body in an accident involving a Danish arrow and a grappling hook that had ripped a section of hull out from under the port gunwale. He'd gotten wedged in, and they couldn't free him until the battle had ended. His bellowing during the fighting, however, had been louder than all others'.

Anlaf heard the tale with relish. He remembered the warrior's screams that day, remembered watching him squirm helplessly. He'd been in the water and seen it all. For Thyri, it was humorous only in retrospect. Her man had taken in a lot of water during that ordeal. He'd nearly died.

Later that night, Thyri's stories grew wilder. Near dawn, she made up a few.

Anlaf, however, told her much. Even the fraction she remembered when she woke to the call to arms was substantial:

He served under a King Oscetyl, who served in turn under the Danish Overking, Guthrom. They had been warring with the southern Saxon, Alfred of Wessex, for years. That January they had taken Alfred's capital from him. The Saxon had melted into the wood. He was somewhere south of them, rumored to be recruiting a new army. Guthrom was holding his forces back from further encroachment into Saxon lands until reinforcements could arrive.

Those reinforcements were expected under the Raven banner of the sons of Ragnar, on Ubbi Ragnarson's flagship. Ragnar's three sons were infamous among Vikings who sailed Saxon and Celtic waters. Thyri had encountered one of them, Halfdan, during her days under Hordaland. But she had heard little but rumor beyond that. Anlaf took particular pride in telling her their tale. He was related to them through a distant cousin who was brother to Ragnar.

Many years before, three young *berserks*—Ivarr, Halfdan, and Ubbi—had set foot on Saxon shores with a small invasion force behind them, the family Raven banner above them, and their aging, rotund father before them. Ragnar had been mad. He'd killed without mercy, spreading his forces over the land as if he'd expected the sun to stop rising, thus spoiling his fun. It is said that he had never slain more than a hog before leaving his Danish homestead. After a short, fiery campaign, an angry Saxon king had thrown him into a pit with a wild hog who'd torn out his insides with its tusks.

His sons, however, had fared better. They'd gone to Erin, eventually gaining control of most of the waters around the island. The son named Ivarr had made himself king there and reigned for a few years before falling to Norwegian reavers. Halfdan and Ubbi had survived him, controlling large tracts of land and sea for many years.

Halfdan had fallen in battle the past summer, about the time Thyri slew Aralak in that great battle in the new land. Ubbi, Anlaf thought, remained strong, and he was on his way to join Guthrom's army at that very moment. All expected to soon see the Raven banner—which had, amazingly, survived through all the years, passing from brother to brother—top the edge of the plain on which the Danes camped, then lead them all on a campaign through the forests that harbored Alfred.

The ironic undercurrent of the whole conversation was that Ubbi was already dead. Not even Guthrom knew it. This is what had happened:

A week before, Ubbi had reached England at a point farther south than he had planned—well inside Saxon territory. He had left his stronghold with a force of fifty ships. The seas, however, had been treacherous, and he'd arrived with only twenty-three ships in his command. Rather than risk more men and ships in traveling up the rocky coast, he'd landed upon first sighting shore.

He'd marched into Saxon territory with a thousand men lusting for battle. They'd laid siege to a Saxon fort. The commander of the fort, named Odda, had waited for nightfall before sending his superior forces into the field. Eight hundred Danes had died, the rest had fled to their ships and returned home.

Ubbi, and his Raven banner, had been among Odda's prizes that day. Alfred was quite pleased with the whole affair.

Despite Thyri's wish, Anlaf had not finished with his news of her homeland. Harald's skalds traveled throughout the North now, singing his saga and the plights of all others involved. Much was in these songs. Thyri herself was in these songs; her brother was in them as well.

Anlaf told Thyri that Erik had pledged to take Gyda for his own.

Warriors

The cries and shouts early the next morning pounded into her skull, forcing her awake. She looked around, tangling herself in her sables—she had passed out without disrobing for sleep.

Not far away, Anlaf still snored loudly. Thyri struggled to her feet and kicked him. He grunted. She stepped out of the tent, seeking first the nearest trough of water where she could purge the malignant taste from her mouth. Leaving, she dully noted the sounds of Anlaf awakening in a flurry of thrashings similar to her own.

The Danish camp was in an uproar. The cries came from messengers rousing the sleepers from their tents. There were many groans and curses—more than a select few had spent the idle night in ale. After drinking a great deal of water and splashing more on her face, Thyri grabbed one of the messengers by the arm and learned the details first hand: Alfred marched on them. He was, in fact, scarcely more than an hour away.

As this information sank in, Thyri snarled and threw the messenger away from her. She stormed back into the tent, colliding with Anlaf at the entrance and pushing him back onto the ground.

She glared down at him. "An hour away. The Saxons are an *hour* away! Half the warriors are still drunk. And you"—she pointed at him—"could very well die today due to the wisdom of your so-called leaders!"

Anlaf rubbed his eyes and looked up, still dazed. "Wh-what?"

"Go see to your men, Olafson. I require time to myself to prepare for the day."

The bewilderment in his eyes gave way to a brief flash of anger. But, for whatever reason, he rose unsteadily and left Thyri in his tent.

She sat down then, untied her braid of forty-five knots, and brushed the tangles from her hair. Slowly, she began the braid anew.

* * *

Despite her experiences in the new land, Thyri was not known to the Danes as a particularly capable commander. Given time, and perhaps feeding their idea that she was *berserk*, she felt she could mold at least a group of them into a weapon she could effectively wield. But she didn't have time. She had only her sword.

In the middle of an army, and still alone.

Her thoughts returned to Astrid—how it had been when they'd first entered battle side by side. Among the ranks, they had been as boisterous and insolent as any of their comrades, but none had ever quite understood them—only their competence.

Then, they had been alone together. Their aloofness had always gained them a cold sort of respect from Vikings they'd led. But even together that had always taken time.

"Thyri!"

She looked up from her meditations. Anlaf's voice had come from outside. She heard his footfall just before he entered.

"Thyri," he repeated, catching his breath, "we are to spearhead the left flank, beyond the shield-wall."

"Are we to have cavalry support?"

"I didn't think. You will want to go in mounted?"

"No," she said, smiling disturbingly. "I want to be in the middle of it." *I want to die.*

"Well, then." Anlaf smiled. "I want you to the left of me at any rate. In front."

"Your men won't follow me, Anlaf."

"Oh, they don't know they will." His grin broadened. "Ottar! Sokki, Horik! Enter!"

The tent flap opened and three burly young warriors timidly filed in. They stared at Thyri.

"These boys are brothers," Anlaf said. "Sons of *my* brother who died, entrusting them to me. They have brawled together since they were this high"—Anlaf motioned to his knee—"and they're not bad. Last year was their first season. The older warriors let them take the point of one formation last time out, thinking they would die. They didn't. They'll make formidable commanders one day, but they need experience. If you fight next to them, and they follow you, then the men will follow you. They won't take much convincing, fantastic stories of your past kept many of them awake late last night."

"If I am so infamous," Thyri said, "why haven't I been summoned by Guthrom? Doesn't he know I'm here?"

"No. He has sworn a blood oath with Ubbi against your people—against all people from the far Northlands. He feels, as do many of our kings, that too much blood has been spilled on our soil by Northerners too lazy to seek holdings in the South. I neglected to mention this last night."

Her eyes grew dark. "How, then, did you propose to keep me here!"

"I follow Oscetyl. He does not share Guthrom's hate for Norway. And we are left alone by the overking. He will not learn of you until battle, and possibly not even then."

"You talk as if this is a game, Anlaf."

He smiled, his teeth showing through his beard. "Combat is a game, Thyri Bloodfang. The only one." He bowed to her. "I must return now to the rest of my charges."

Anlaf left, and Thyri scrutinized the three Vikings who shifted nervously before her. Were they so believing of ale-soaked storytelling, she wondered, that they stood in awe of a woman they'd never seen before?

She did not like that prospect. "Which one of you is Ottar?" she asked.

One cleared his throat and nodded.

She frowned at him. His face and eyes could have belonged to any who had seen her as *akiya toyn*—as a goddess—in the new land.

Now she was elsewhere—relieved of that burden and glad of it; she had never asked for it. She suddenly felt free, and she intended to remain that way until death—until the Valkyrie—came to take her away.

She smiled at Ottar, then she kicked him sharply in the center of his chest with the point of her toe.

He doubled up in voiceless agony.

Thyri stood over him. "Look at me once more like I'm Aesir fallen from the sky and into your lap, and I'll kill you."

She threw them out of the tent and returned to her braiding. Thus began the training of the sons of Gunnar.

Ethandune

Misty rain fell on the plain. The sky was a uniform gray except where the distant sun turned a small patch of the cloud cover a dull, pale yellow.

Gusts of wind whipped her hair about her face and neck. The wetness had penetrated her hair, bunching it into thick strands that stung when they struck her cheek. She ignored it for the moment, forcing her attention to stay fixed on the thin, dark line of the horizon.

She stood at the point of Anlaf's left with the sons of Gunnar just behind her and to her right. She was vaguely aware of unease among the warriors in her ranks. But her thoughts had no room for them. At the moment, she was cursing Guthrom's choice of battlefields. He'd made hardly an attempt at defense—she supposed he knew no other manner of battle than direct, frontal assault hinged on the terror that Viking ferocity spread. And they were on ground that sloped away behind them. The slant was gentle, and she doubted that Guthrom had even noticed, but the rain had slickened grass and loosened mud. Footing would be treacherous. Their cavalry had more to fear in the way of broken legs than Saxon spears.

They'd probably get orders to charge as soon as Alfred's banners crested the hill.

Keeping her eyes on the horizon, Thyri tucked the wet mass of her hair behind her ears and bound it there with a leather band she wrapped around her head and tied in the back. She looked at Anlaf then. Sensing her gaze, he glanced at her and grinned. He, at least, knew something of battle tactics. His front line would act as a noose, with his wedge and Thyri's forcing attackers into the space between them, disorienting them and making them easy prey for the Vikings whose axes awaited. She would feed the sons of Gunnar many maimed, staggering Saxons that day. *If* she felt her own left and rear protected. She turned to Ottar.

"Who is the best among you?"

"Uh—I am, Bloodfang."

Sokki thumped him on the back. "Tell the truth, Brother."

Horik looked at Thyri and stroked his thin beginnings of a beard. "Sokki is, battle-mistress."

"Sokki," she said, "I want you on my right. Guarding my rear. You are the shield-with-teeth-and-eyes. You must tell me if our line fails on your side. You must tell me if the far flank begins to crumble. You will never stray more than two paces from me. Do you understand?"

He nodded and took the position.

Thyri turned from Ottar and Horik, who strained to catch her words as she began to instruct Sokki on the proper stance for his position and the most effective counterstrokes he could use. He picked up a little—more, actually, than she'd expected. It was a responsible task she'd given him. It contained within it attitudes and combinations of sword strokes that only she and Astrid truly understood. They had developed and perfected the tactic, so the martial techniques involved in it were peculiarly their own. In battle, they had been capable of switching the two positions without losing the tempo of the fight.

She couldn't count on Sokki for that. If he fell, she would be on her own. The prospect didn't worry her; she was there to lose herself in the clash of arms and the blood. In the back of her mind, she still wanted to die. If the Saxons could kill her, perhaps Astrid herself would return to escort her to Valhalla.

Shouts rose in the distance, and the Danes echoed them with their own alarms. Shady figures on horseback began to break the horizon. Banners fluttered above the riders as their numbers grew.

Thyri drew her rune-blade and tested its grip. She took a short battle-ax into her left hand, then the order came to advance. As the hosts drew together, she squinted. Over the center of Alfred's army flapped two banners. One was a prancing horse on a field of white; the other, a stylized raven on a field of red.

Ubbi's banner. The song of the sons of Ragnar had ended.

Angry shouts and disturbed recollections of prophecies rippled through the ranks behind her as the Danes recognized the banner and realized what Alfred's possession of it implied: Ubbi Ragnarson had fallen. It had been said that none under the Raven banner could enter battle and know defeat.

Thyri snarled and commended Alfred. For all that he was her immediate enemy, he showed canniness—he'd attacked the Danes already with weapons that cut far deeper than swords. The display of the captured banner would have the same effect on her comrades as her use of howling wolves had had on the Arakoy. She knew then that the battle was already lost.

Battle cries erupted around her and the Danish armies rushed forward. She cleared her mind of distractions, making herself aware only of the grip of her boots on the soggy ground, the feel of Bloodfang in her grasp, and the ranks of the men she would slay with it. There was no ceremony before the battle, no talk among the leaders. Shortly before her sword first bit into flesh, she realized that Alfred had somehow amassed a force far greater than Guthrom's.

Throughout the afternoon, the battle raged. For Thyri, it was a mechanical exercise in bloodshed. Sokki held his ground well, and Thyri's wedge suffered few losses at first. She was never aware of the awe her ability instilled among the warriors behind her; many of them were able only to watch her while waiting to fill breaches in the line. She never spoke to them, never had to rally them because she never faltered. She simply killed to her front and left and maimed to her right.

The Saxons faced her with a fire that almost made her weep. As her wedge cleared away rank after rank, the Saxons would charge anew as if they also wished to die. She wondered if their gods offered them the same glory Odin offered his fallen warriors.

As dusk neared, a command of Guthrom's to retreat reached Thyri. The overking's entire right flank had been crushed by a pincer movement executed by Alfred's cavalry, which had finally obliterated the weaker mounted units of the Danes. The shieldwall defending Guthrom's archers in the center had failed after that, and the bulk of the Danish host was in disarray and fleeing. And falling before cavalry spears.

Thyri ignored the command and fought on. The Saxons pressed against her and they fell before her in greater and greater numbers until their onrushing tide faltered against the rising barrier of dead. She began to wade through them when Anlaf's wedge collapsed. Behind her she heard Sokki pleading with her to stop lest they find themselves surrounded, one unit against the entire Saxon horde. The flank beyond him was fleeing.

She glanced back briefly to ensure that he remained with her, then she turned to press forward again. That was when Sokki brought the shaft of his axe down on her head.

When she awoke, the skies had cleared and stars dotted the roof of the world. The moon still hid below the horizon.

She groaned and heard voices in response. Ottar's: "She will kill you now, Brother."

She shook the ache from her skull. Sokki's face bent over hers. "Anlaf is dead," he said.

"So are you," said Ottar. "She was *berserk*. She wished to carve a path to Alfred, then die with his blood on her sword. She desired Valhalla."

Sokki's face twisted in rage. "Shut up, you fool!" He brushed the hair from Thyri's brow. His touch was light, his soft brown eyes full of concern.

"We are camped?" she asked wearily.

"Yes. Guthrom re-formed the shield-wall, allowing our escape. Many warriors died, but we would have been routed had we all tried to flee. He has found an ancient fort to the north. The armies are to regroup there in the morning."

Pursued, no doubt, by this upstart Saxon king. "You should have left me," she spat at him. "You have much to learn, young warrior."

Sokki grinned. "Had I left you, I would now have no one to teach me."

Thyri grunted softly, then sleep returned to her.

Ghosts

The second morning after the battle, a trio of warriors sent by Guthrom wakened Thyri and invited her to Guthrom's council. Grudgingly, she rose and followed them through the camp. Everywhere she looked, she saw the anguished faces of wounded and dying men.

Guthrom's warriors had little interest in speaking to her, and she thanked Odin for this small favor. As for the reason for Guthrom's summons, she didn't care. Whatever he wanted, it had to be pointless.

A large number of Vikings milled uncertainly about the entrance of Guthrom's command tent. None of these men bore wounds, and she wondered if they'd been similarly summoned. She stopped briefly, and one of Guthrom's men turned to wait for her. She studied his gaze; it seemed placid, but the corners of his eyes hinted at concealed desperation. Still, he said nothing to her.

She smiled weakly at him.

The other two warriors had continued on; now they turned. One of them barked back, rudely demanding that Thyri catch up. The Viking who had stopped with her tried to smile.

"They do not know to whom they speak, swords-mistress," he said softly.

She started forward. "And you do?"

"Aye," he said. "I have heard tales enough."

"And who are you?"

"I am Rollo Anskarson," he answered, turning away.

Shortly after they reached the others, all were ushered into Guthrom's presence.

Nothing decorated the inside of Guthrom's tent but the heavy, sharp odor of human sweat. Guthrom stood with his commanders at the far end. The overking cut an impressive figure; he possessed nearly twice the bulk of the average Viking. His legs were thick enough to be tree trunks.

If he'd been gifted with a competent brain, Thyri guessed that he would be quite dangerous.

No one present seemed capable of lifting the curtain of melancholy that had wrapped itself around the army's heart. Guthrom's eyes scanned over them with no emotion apparent in his thick features.

One of his lieutenants began to speak without ceremony, and Thyri learned what she'd begun to suspect: they had been gathered to receive appointments as field commanders, to be formally granted the tasks once executed by dead comrades. She wondered how she had happened to be considered for the position. Had someone conveniently overlooked the fact that she was Norwegian?

Her mind began to drift back to her days with Astrid. The gods had conspired to keep her alive, and she and her cousin were not to be soon united as she'd wished.

She heard her name called then, and she looked up at the speaker and nodded. Guthrom spoke, asking his lieutenant if the men would follow a battle-maiden. Oscetyl assured him that they would and said that several of Anlaf's men had told him that morning that they would follow no other. Guthrom looked for a moment at Thyri and nodded, then Oscetyl went on with his list.

Thyri paid them no attention at all after that.

When the meeting had ended, Thyri roamed out to the edge of the camp; Guthrom had led them to a hilltop that towered high above the plain below. The hill's crest was broad and wide, and it easily held the remains of Guthrom's once formidable force.

She walked along the outside embankment, staring down onto the plain. Alfred's horde approached—like an army of busy ants, she thought. She stood long in silence, watching the Saxons' progress.

It was noon, and the sun was much warmer overhead though the wind on the hill remained fierce.

She began to wish that she'd spoken out in Guthrom's presence, told him what a fool she thought he was. But still, she wanted nothing to do with him. She'd never even been sure that she wanted to war with the Saxon king; he'd merely been her first excuse for an enemy. He seemed a fine commander, and Thyri preferred now to watch him and possibly learn from the experience. Silence at the council had been her wisest choice.

At least Guthrom's scouts had found him an appropriate place to mull over his defeat. The hill fort was old, but its fortifications were adequately defensible. The slopes to the south and east were virtually unassailable. Doubled ramparts had been built around the entire perimeter by some king from ages past. Alfred, she guessed, would first skirt them to the west, then camp his men on the north side of the fort—the one position granting him relatively level ground.

Thyri eyed the barrow that stretched for fifty paces through the center of the fort. Guthrom had pitched his tents next to it in an attempt to allay fears among his men of the long-dead king buried there. She doubted it would help. The fears of the Danes were beginning to consume them. They had never known such defeat as they had suffered at Alfred's hands.

Slowly, she wandered through the camp to the barrow, then walked over the raised mound of earth. As she stepped down, she almost smiled as she realized that even this place would work ill for Guthrom.

She looked back to the barrow, wondering at the nature of the sorcerous presence awakening under its earth.

Two days later, Alfred had firmly entrenched his army on the north side of the fort. He'd gained the ground under cover of night and a siege was laid with all possible escape routes sealed after only another day.

Thyri spent this time mostly alone, though she eventually agreed to Sokki's pleas that she instruct him and his brothers in martial techniques. And in the evenings she would drink with her men, seldom speaking, but listening moodily to their tales. Many were of Harald—his power grew and the swords of his men drank deeply of the blood of neighboring Norse kingdoms.

She brooded, and she watched. The men began to dream strange dreams. On the third night of the siege, Thyri herself dreamed.

It began before she was truly asleep. She sensed its unnaturalness. It tried to draw her into visions of black death and snake-infested pits. It pulled her toward burning seas and malevolent, necrophagous mires. She fought it and woke.

Stepping out of her tent, she gazed at the barrow. Not far away, Ottar and Horik drank with a few warriors who yet remained awake, or who were afraid to sleep.

All over the hill, in fact, pockets of men huddled around fires, sleepless though dawn was but an hour away. And every few moments, someone would moan or yelp, breaking the stillness and the quiet drone of hushed conversation. From far away—from the Saxon encampment—she could hear pleasant laughter. She joined Ottar and the others.

"It is the kingling," Ottar was saying. "He has a sorcerer who plagues our dreams."

Horik began to answer, but he held his tongue when he saw Thyri.

She sat on a rock next to Ottar. "The Saxons have no sorcerer," she said. "At least none who does this." She threw her head back, indicating the barrow. "There is your evil. We desecrate hallowed ground. You have dreamed of evil, ancient death, have you not? Of skulls housing snakes and spiders? You hear corpses scream in the night, then waken to find the voice of the dead emerging from the throat of the man in the next bedroll. Who died here? How *many* died in this place long ago?"

And why? And how?

Ottar laughed. "The dead are dead," he said. "They do not dream."

Thyri ignored him. She drew her sword and inspected its edge, then rose and went to the barrow. Her men, including Ottar for all his bravado, did not follow her.

She had no trouble with the watch—it was far away and intent on Alfred. She circled the barrow, tapping it gently with the blade of her sword, looking for a weakness that would provide an entrance. She found none. She climbed to the top and knelt, driving her sword a foot, then deeper, into the soil. She felt the sorcerous presence ripple and intensify. She pushed her sword farther.

Why do you wound me?

The voice came from inside her head.

"I wish to speak with you," she answered.

Why?

"You harm my men."

They are not your men. This is in your heart.

"True. But you harm them. They are warriors. They fight a battle now, and you intrude."

They intrude. They disturb my sleep with their lusts and fears. I disturb them with mine. It is fair. Their battle, is it worthy?

"What is worthy?"

Do they war with demons, as did I?

Demons yes, she thought. Inside themselves. "No. They war with other men."

Then they fight without cause. They fight without enemy.

"Demons?" she asked. And he showed her.

Suddenly, the sun was setting again. The Danish encampment was gone, replaced by a sole group of fifteen tall, dark-haired warriors. The tallest among them spoke—words that Thyri could not understand but only feel: desperate, terrible words.

They were all beautiful, more like gods than men. And then from under the sunset came their enemy—black hell-spawn with leathery, oozing wings and large, watery red eyes. The things fell on the warriors.

They fought, they died. All of them.

"Two races of would-be gods," Thyri said.

Gods.

Thyri sensed deep contempt.

What are gods?

Thyri thought on that. The vision faded.

Now you have seen. Will you champion your warriors-who-fight-men against me?

Thyri grasped the hilt of her sword and drew it from the earth. "No," she whispered. She turned and started for her tent.

Changes

Over the next few nights, the atmosphere in the camp grew worse, heavier and more desperate. The warriors took to napping in the day and spending long nights huddled about their fires. The ancient king pounded into their sleep, and the Saxons began a game of answering with crude calls the cries that wafted through the night from the Danish camp. Guthrom seldom left his tent.

Over these nights, the moon waxed ever larger. Thyri observed this with indifference. The pathetic lassitude enveloping the camp disgusted her. Guthrom's own indifference disgusted her; it was all *wrong*. She—in returning to this place, this battle, this state of affairs—felt as if she witnessed the castration of her race, as if Astrid had delivered her unto subtle torture. Why had Odin allowed this to happen? Why had the swords of the North weakened and faltered?

As she thought these thoughts, the fact of her curse at first grew insignificant. Her acceptance of it had pushed its influence over her into that three-day cage toward which she now moved, if not willingly, then obediently. The familiar feeling of its inevitability almost granted her comfort in that it was certain, understood; it possessed qualities that stood in sharp contrast to the wrongness that had infiltrated the Viking army. Hearing the cries of the men at night, realizing that she herself slept in the arms of defeat, the edges of her new reality grew indistinct. She did not feel as if she had taken refuge among her own people any more than she had felt at home with the Habnakys in the new land. All were strangers, and none could connect her significantly to her past and thus susbstantiate her present. Anlaf had, but he was dead.

These feelings manifested themselves within Thyri and began to crystallize. In a way, this strengthened the beast because of its certainty, its reality, and with this strengthening came a vague desire to let them see her, let them know her for who she was—for *what* she was. Let Guthrom feel terror, experience true defeat: death, or a fate even worse.

And so she let the days pass and the moon overtake her. Only in the darkness after sunset, just before moonrise, on the first night of the wolf, did she think through the consequences of her inaction. The moon tugged at her already though it rested yet below the horizon. The bloodlust assailed her mind in waves, and terror gripped her as she realized that she had, over the past days, idly courted insanity; throughout her stay in the new land, she had kept the beast from human prey. She had made peace with her nature, but the cornerstone of that peace she had fashioned by forcing herself to seek sustenance from sheep, from deer—not from men. If she changed that now, if she stayed and let the wolf take Guthrom, she would make the overking's defeat her own. She would lose all the peace she had fought so hard to gain.

She should have left that day, escaped the camp and fled to distant forests. She would have left long before had she had a place to go, but among these men Astrid had brought her; beyond them, she had no apparent direction, no purpose. The land of the Saxons was not her own, and she knew little of it.

Nevertheless, she had to get away. She had joined Guthrom's army wishing to die, but not to die as a demon impaled upon the swords of her own people. As these realizations came to her, she looked across the space before her, into the real world: Sokki's grinning eyes gazed back at her.

They had just eaten dinner: a dilute broth that smelled of horsemeat. Supplies in the camp had run perilously low. Thyri smiled uneasily at Sokki. Why had she let things come to this? She had to get away!

"Battle-mistress?" Sokki asked, concerned. "You look ill."

Thyri rose unsteadily, looked desperately from Sokki to the horizon, then turned for her tent. She walked quickly, then ran, not looking back to see if anyone followed.

Inside her tent, she gathered her things, stuffing them into her sable cloak. Where was her sword? Where—

"Thyri?"

She looked up; Sokki stood in the entrance of her tent. Beyond him, on the horizon, a pale wash of white hailed the coming of the moon. She could smell the blood in him, and her mouth filled with saliva. She remembered how, long before, her mother had once stood thus in a doorway as the beast had taken her. She remembered the taste of her mother's blood in her mouth . . .

"Get out!"

"But—"

"Get out!" she growled, then turned back to her pack. Hurriedly, she took off her shift and her boots and stuffed them into the sables. Where was her sword! She closed her eyes, calming her thoughts, searching her memory for the rune-blade. She found it—resting on grass, next to where she had eaten.

Thyri leapt for the entrance, but once there, the moonlight pushed her back. Her eyes opened wide as the silver orb broke the horizon, and her legs went weak. She looked down and watched the white coat of the beast sprout through her skin and cover her legs. Her breasts caved in as the rippling white coat grew up to her neck. Claws sprang from her toes and her bones wrenched, forcing her to her knees. Pain flared through her, clouding her vision until the transformation was complete and the white wolf came fully into the world.

Then, she fought it. The smell of human blood outside was almost overpowering. But she couldn't let the beast out; she couldn't allow it even a howl. The battle raged quietly, interminably, until she collapsed to the earth, in control, but the hunger raged as never before.

Still, she had to get out. She rose. With a swipe of her claws, she tore open the cloth of the back wall of her tent; then she took the knot that bound her pack into her mouth, clamped down with her fangs, and clumsily tossed the pack up so that it balanced precariously on her back.

As she stole through the new exit of her tent, she saw no men, and without further thought she shot into the night, stopping only as she neared the southern rim of the hill fort. With Alfred camped to the north, the southern guard was sparse, but still present. Along the ridge, she could count five men standing watch. Two of those men slumped on their spears, asleep.

A small hare scurried past her, and she dropped her pack and dove on the hare, pinning it to the ground with her claws. Hunger surged anew, and she consumed the hapless animal greedily, thankful that Wyrd had granted her this one small meal—not much, but enough to give her strength for what she next must do.

Quickly, she licked clean her paws, took up her pack, and crept forward. She tried to remember the lay of the southern hillside. The grade was steep and laced with gulleys, but there wasn't enough cover to hide her completely from view. However, the two sleeping guards were separated by only one other. If she could take him out silently without alerting the others, she'd have a clear path down the center of the slope.

She neared the guard's back, then leapt forth over him. Retracting her claws in midair, she smashed one massive paw down on his head; she heard the dull thud of his fall as she continued to sail out over the edge of the hill. When she landed, she began to roll, and she didn't gain her footing until she'd rolled and tumbled down a full quarter of the hillside. After that, bruised and battered, she looked up and listened. No alarm had been sounded; no one had witnessed her change, or her escape.

She made her way more carefully then, keeping to what cover the hillside offered as she struggled to contain the wolf until she could reach the plain below and race for the distant forests where she could allow it to feed.

Sokki Gunnarson frowned as he looked around the bare interior of Thyri's tent. Even in the darkness, he could tell that she'd left nothing behind.

When he noticed the tear in the far wall of the tent, he stepped hesitantly inside. With this act, he grew uneasy; Thyri's presence still lingered heavily in the air, and thought of invading her privacy caused an aching fear to take root in the pit of Sokki's stomach. The battle-mistress did not take kindly to intrusions of any kind.

And yet his eyes told him that she had gone, that she had discarded this place and that she would not return. At the torn flap of the tent's wall, he peered out over the moonlit camp. She was somewhere out there—gone from his life. But why had she left? He thought they had grown close. For him, the battle with Alfred had bound their fates together for life.

True, she had never sealed their companionship in any overt way, but she *had* spent a great deal of her time in his company, and she'd always treated him with respect, even if she hadn't been as kind to his brothers. Over the past few days, she'd even spoken moodily to him, telling him tales, offering him advice on warfare and what she had named "the way of the warrior." She was ever detached, but he'd considered her detachedness an outgrowth of her experience, not an underlying aspect of her character. He'd not thought her actually uncaring—until now.

Tears welled in his eyes and he squatted down, idly brushing his fingers over the earth. A gust of wind blew open the flap, and his eyes fell on an ant struggling through a depression in the soil just outside. The insect labored under the weight of a small beetle several times its size. As the ant reached an upward slope its determination exceeded its talents; Sokki watched it gain two steps, then tumble back to the bottom of the slope and try again.

He resisted an impulse to crush the insect and end its excruciating labors. And then his eyes took in the nature of the ant's obstacle. He bent forward and examined the mark; the animal that had left it was huge—far larger than any of the dogs that scavenged throughout the camp.

He brushed his hand over the earth, smoothing it, smearing the print and burying the ant who struggled out from under the dirt even as Sokki watched. Sokki stood then, suddenly fearful that some nameless beast had stolen Thyri away. But she had taken with her all her things . . . And she had acted strangely earlier, a fact reinforcing the evidence for her voluntary departure.

A tear fell to Sokki's cheek and he reached up, unsure of the meaning of the wetness. The size of the paw print lingered in his mind, and he connected it with the tear. He was crying—had his tears caused the mark of a dog to grow? He stooped to examine the print again, but his careless defacing of it had made an accurate assessment of its size impossible. He crawled forward, out of the tent, searching for a similar mark, but the ground there was seldom passed over and remained covered with grass.

He stood again and stared off into the distance for long moments before turning away, going back through the tent, and walking slowly back to the fire he had earlier shared with Thyri. It seemed to him mere moments before that they had sat there quietly, eating dinner in each other's company. As he sat, he noticed Thyri's sheathed sword. As he rose to retrieve it, Horik approached.

Sokki looked briefly to his brother. "She is gone," he said plainly.

"Where?"

Sokki shrugged and bent, lifting the blade.

"She left her sword?" Horik reached out for the hilt of the blade.

"No!" Sokki jerked the blade violently away. "Do you so quickly forget the lore of these blades? They are sorcerous—they kill! Only with a gauntlet of silver may a Viking wield such a sword and live."

Horik scowled. "Do you really believe such stories?"

"I believe what I see, and I have seen a swords-mistress who might have proved a match for the entire Saxon army. Will you tell me now that she was not real?"

"Of course she was real," Horik said, dropping his eyes to the ground.

"Then the rest of her legend is real until proven false," Sokki said. He held the blade, hilt first, toward his brother. "Will you prove it false?"

Horik's hand started up, then dropped. "No." He paused. "I'm sorry, Brother. What will you do now?"

"I will keep this blade," Sokki said softly. "I will keep it, guard it, and wield it if I can find a way. For Thyri Eiriksdattir I will save it, and no man shall take it from me while I yet live." He sat, clutching the blade to his chest.

"We should tell no one, Sokki," Horik said, openly alarmed by his brother's oath. "If you carry that sword you should sheathe it plainly and show it to no one you do not intend to kill. If word spreads, Guthrom himself might test your oath."

"I don't care."

"But I do. Swear to me, Sokki. Swear this a family secret!" Horik spoke quietly but passionately, his eyes darting around nervously for anyone who might have overheard their words.

Sokki looked up. Tears had returned to his eyes.

"Swear!" Horik demanded.

Sokki looked down. "I swear." He set the sword between his feet. "Go get Ottar," he said. "And bring ale. If ever Odin intended a night for drinking, this is such a one."

Book V: THE SORCERESS

In my visions, time is a river and the past the infinite streams that feed it as it strains to spill into the sea of eternity. Looking upstream, one cannot rightly claim that the most meager trickle—the single drop—may have entered at any point other than that point where it did. Choice is illusion; all streams combine to define the present, and the placement of each drop embodies a unique significance. This I see clearly now, for no other view of the past can give substance to the present, else we all exist as part of a possibility, an imagined reality no more real than the imagined worlds of poets.

If only I could look downstream, to the future as well.

You will know that, after a fortnight in the ancient hill fort, Guthrom surrendered to Alfred. Seven weeks later, he and his lieutenants traveled south to Alfred's capital and accepted baptism by Saxon priests of the One God. Then the overking, and his followers, were sent back to the North.

The surrender ended the Danish conquest of my homeland. Thyri had no part in it. She wandered for a few months, then she surfaced in Danish Jorvik in late summer. I was there as well.

Guthrom's hall remained the center of affairs in the city for all that its lord had been defeated. In times past, a young Viking would have brought down the overking and assumed his place. As it was, all knew Guthrom's despair; the Norse bloodlust had been denied too decisively, and its thrust had turned back upon itself, leaving it free only to pervert the inevitable absorption of the survivors by the land of Arthur.

If anything, life in the streets of Jorvik was wilder than it had been since the Danes had wrested the city from the Saxons some twelve years before. The defeated Viking armies populated the inns and taverns, and nightly boasting contests often devolved into small, family wars. During daylight, affairs hardly improved:

crime against merchants flourished in the absence of a strong governing hand.

I was still quite young that year: twenty-one years to Thyri's twenty-four. My father was Saxon; I know little of him except that he died by Viking blades when the Danes took Jorvik, and that my uncle, who reared me, considered him a fine man. When I was twelve, my uncle died in an early, futile attempt to oust the Danes from Jorvik. A friend of my uncle had me sent south, where I studied for a time under Alfred's scribes.

Those years I still view as the worst of my life. The food was harsh, the discipline worse. A few years before Alfred's successful campaign, I denounced the son of Mary, whom so many peoples have accepted so readily, and I returned north to the wild lands of my birth. Life there always felt more real; perhaps it was the bleak power of the moors, perhaps it was that part of my blood I owe to my Pictish mother. Perhaps both—I don't know and it matters little. Alfred was a fine man and a greater king—to we Saxons, it seems, as great as the legendary Arthur was to the Celts. But he was never *my* king. My heart is lawless, and strong kingship mixes with it poorly.

So I lost myself among friends on the moors, faring into Jorvik fairly often during that time when Guthrom and his army chased Alfred around the southern realms. The city offered a great deal then to any man with a modicum of wit. The Danes were tolerant of those Saxons there still alive, and the Norsemen themselves were far from an uninteresting lot—drinkers and braggarts all. Yet still men, for all that my countrymen named them demons and reavers. They loved tales, the longer and more fantastic the better. For two years I braved the taverns where their post-raid ale fests would sometimes run on for days. With stories of hauntings and intrigues on the moor, I earned my keep. And I earned it well! It was nothing to pry from a Viking his most precious loot once he'd entered the glittering, hazed halls of Dionysus.

The small hoards I buried then . . . Probably all still there, overgrown now with heather . . .

Thyri had taken a room near the docks at the Harp and Sword, an inn run by a Saxon named Aelgulf who looked more bear than man yet still treated the transgressions of the Norse clientele with diffidence and great patience, the only way, really, that Saxons in Jorvik managed to stay healthily alive. One might put down one

Viking one day, and the next find his five brothers in no placable state of mind demanding blood for blood no matter what the circumstances of the original conflict.

The heat that summer was overbearing, and I seldom entered the city before nightfall because of the smell. I remember that I considered traveling farther north, but news of that region bespoke always small wars and the idea of forced conscription never appealed to me much. I might have gone anyway had the swordsmistress from Hordaland not become part of my story, and I part of hers.

Warriors

From her room above Aelgulf's tavern, she stared moodily over the crowded marketplace. The dull aching wake of the previous night's mead lapped at the edges of her vision; she was growing used to the feeling. She'd entered the city two weeks before, but she'd found little to interest her but the drink and the temporary release it granted her.

As the sun set over the marketplace, she grinned weakly. She wished that, somehow, she could make it *matter*. She thought idly of what it might have been like had she leapt from Yrafax's back as he'd carried her from the shores of the new land to the field of battle where she'd desired to die. Even there, the Norns had denied her. Some dark part of her contemplated killing Sokki for saving her. He had no right. He had no understanding of the nature of the beast he worshiped.

Nobody understood, Thyri thought. Not even Astrid—it seemed to Thyri now that her cousin had lost her own heart in her blind service of Odin. But that was the way of the Valkyrie . . . Perhaps it was really Odin whom Thyri couldn't understand. He was real; Astrid was proof enough of that. And *he* let her agony burn on. She worshiped him with her sword, and he shunned her. When the full moon came to call her, he granted her no haven. He would not grant her even an honorable death in battle; he'd let the Sokki's of the world save her so they could gawk at her, lust after her, and tremble before her sword.

Deep reds and purples scarred the distant, western sky. Over the new land, the land of Akan and Pohati. Thyri had known some freedom there before the darkness of war had stolen it from her. She'd even loved. And now the mere thought of love pained her because everybody she loved kept dying. Astrid, Akan, Pohati—for all Thyri knew, Megan was dead as well.

Her eyes turned to the street as an armed cadre of six men approached the tavern entrance. They were already drunk, and several wineskins passed back and forth between them. She recognized two of the men as members of Guthrom's personal guard.

One was Rollo, the guard who had spoken kindly to her on the morning of Guthrom's summons.

As the group drew close, they balked, and as Thyri's eyes turned farther beneath her, as she realized what fixed their gazes, she recalled the full extent of her actions the night before for the first time since her awakening late in the afternoon:

Posted on either side of the tavern's entrance, on stakes rising from the packed earth, two human heads spoke a silent warning to all desiring entrance.

Just before sunrise, still possessed of a drunken rage, Thyri had pounded those stakes into the ground herself. The men to whom the heads had belonged had confronted her late in the evening to inform her that the tales of her battle prowess had spread and that Guthrom had decided to take a royal interest in her at last. They had come to escort her into his presence. She'd declined; they'd drawn their blades and then died.

As Thyri had carved the stakes from the building's rafters, Aelgulf had feebly attempted to dissuade her, citing the fact that rotting, decapitated heads outside his door would attract only flies, not customers. She vaguely remembered asking him how he felt business might fare were his own head placed such that it might greet every customer without exception.

He'd backed off. She was surprised, however, that he'd left the heads. She must have presented a fairly convincing argument. She decided to tell him he could dispose of the sentinels whenever he wished; they *were* below her window, and the smell of the city was already bad enough.

And her actions had already served their purpose: she could see it in the faces below. She had no doubt that the men had either heard of their comrades' fate or had come to look for them. Whatever mystery had remained, the sight greeting them had dissolved. Guthrom's message *had* been delivered to Thyri Eiriksdattir, and she wasn't listening. Maybe the realization would save their lives.

One of the leaders nudged the other, and the group proceeded single file into the tavern. Thyri looked again to the darkening sky. Unless Aelgulf told Guthrom's men where to find her, she would meet them downstairs soon enough. Perhaps they would even manage to kill her.

She looked over to the sword by the door; she had stolen it from Guthrom's smith—a fitting act since her own rune-blade probably hung now among Guthrom's arsenal. Perhaps it would kill him, as it had Akan . . . as it had her own father . . . She choked off the onset of tears with a crackling, dry fit of laughter.

Once she would have confronted an army of demons to regain her blade; now it hardly seemed to matter.

As her laughter died in a hoarse croak, another sound—a strange, clacking *whoosh* from somewhere out in the dusky sky—grew audible. She peered out, fixing on a speck too near to be a star and too light to be a bird. Slowly, the clacking grew more distinct, and the speck drew closer.

Thyri forgot Guthrom's men downstairs. Something new was amiss; she could already sense the odor of sorcery infiltrating the omnipresent stench of the city.

The speck took on form—a bird. Or what was once a bird. Nothing but bones, it landed on the sill of her window, its skeletal wings still twitching, its empty eye sockets gazing at Thyri over a cracked beak. A thin silver tube hung from its neck on a golden thread.

She reached out for the tube. As her fingers brushed against its guardian's wing, the creature twitched away from her touch, then crumbled into a pile of white dust on the windowsill. A light breeze began to scatter it back out into the night. Within moments, Thyri was left only the tube on its golden thread. It was unadorned, perhaps the diameter of the finger of a small child, and it was sealed at both ends. She shook it, and something small rattled inside.

Rising, she retrieved her sword and placed the tube on the floor. Testing her aim once, she brought her sword down and sheared off one end of the tube. Inside, she found a scrap of parchment and a small aqua gemstone. Scrawled on the parchment, in Latin, was a short message: *Crush the gem in a place of power and wait for me there*.

She rose, testing the feel of the gem in her cupped hand. She knew it; she had felt it thus before. She smiled.

She knew only one possible explanation for a skeletal bird bearing such a burden: Megan of Kaerglen Isle.

Gerald had entered the city shortly after midday. For the past month he had lived a leisurely life in the country as the guest of Othar Farfirson, an elderly Dane who had retired from battle young, modestly wealthy, and wed to the daughter of a Saxon merchant. The marriage had satisfied all involved: Othar had gained an alternative to warfare, and the bride's father had gained acceptability, and thus a profitable living, among the Norse settlers, for Othar had been a feared and respected warrior in his day.

In his later years, Othar had become an expert at *hnefatafl*, a game on which Norsemen were often inclined to gamble. Gerald had accepted his friendship hoping to gain enough skill at the game to supplement his income during his forays into Jorvik. At one time, Gerald had himself been expert at dice, but he'd given up that pastime after a band of rogues had accused him of cheating, stolen his money, and all but blinded him in the left eye.

And that explains why Gerald favored that side of his face as he sat in the Harp and Sword, drinking mead and occasionally laughing at one of Aelgulf's jokes about the heads staked outside the door. Often he would scratch at that scar as the heat made it itch. He scratched at it as Guthrom's six guardsmen entered the crowded tavern.

Aelgulf, at the time, was filling Gerald's flagon. Earlier, before business had gotten out of hand, Aelgulf had put away a large quantity of the mead himself while explaining to Gerald the tale behind the heads and how he feared they would be the end of him. Now, with the tavern nearly full and the clientele notably unswayed by the gruesome spectacle outside, Aelgulf was quite boisterously drunk. As the six men entered, Aelgulf winked at Gerald and hailed them, "Come, brave warriors, you are pale! Have you seen ghosts?"

At that, the entire tavern burst into laughter. One of the leaders of the six looked at Aelgulf, snarling. "We have seen no ghosts, man, but we shall see yours if you do not serve us obediently as a Saxon maggot should."

Aelgulf muttered under his breath and scurried off to his casks. Gerald sat back and looked over the tavern, which was indeed nearly full though the sun had just set. The night promised to bring the Harp and Sword more customers than it had housed all summer. All due, of course, to the same severed heads that Aelgulf had feared would chase business away. Rumors of the previous night had spread like fire through the city. It had even been said that Guthrom himself would enter the tavern to exact revenge for the deaths of his men.

And these rumors had attracted Gerald as well. He had already heard something of Thyri. Few hadn't, as many survivors of that last battle with Alfred claimed that she had slain more Saxons that one day than most Vikings might hope to their entire lives. Gerald had felt it worth an evening to see this woman for himself.

When she descended the steps, when he did see her, he had no idea of the impact she was about to have on his life. She did not even strike him as beautiful at first; he'd expected a giantess, muscles packed in shining armor and rivers of flowing, silky hair.

The woman Gerald saw was short, her blond hair tangled and

matted, her armor naught but a brown cotton shift and a skirt. Her gaze was thoughtful, distant. If not for the sword dangling from her belt, Gerald would have taken her for a tired servant. He could not see through to the pains she felt; he could not picture her at the front of an army confronting a giant Arakoy warlord. He had no comprehension of the strength in her sword arm or the skill hidden behind her hazel eyes. He did not know that she, of all living warriors, had received the training of a goddess. And he would never have guessed in a century that, for three nights each month, all that skill could not hide her from the curse of the *were*-wolf that burned in her blood.

He saw only a woman, no hint of anything more, until her eyes focused on the tavern and he noticed how intently they scanned the crowd, how they paid particular attention to Guthrom's six men, and how they passed confidently on, making him feel as if, somehow, she had seen through to each of their souls and knew already who would confront her first, who would shy from battle, and how each would fight. And that intensity in her eyes cast her face in a different light, as if, when he'd first seen it, it hadn't been fully alive.

And then she looked at Gerald and started toward him. During those moments, something came alive inside him; he could feel it rise like a vine up his spine, sending icy fingers of sensation over his skin. The stale, smoky air suddenly tasted clean, and he couldn't shake off the impression that summer had magically fled and that it was spring now that clutched the earth to its breast. Spring, the flowers and festivals of Beltane, the season of making. And what had inspired this feeling? A woman. Not the warrior inside the woman, but the nearly palpable completeness—the wholeness—of the woman's presence. This he hadn't felt since the death of his Pictish mother some years before. He had come to think that he would never again feel it. Power, and the power of creation.

She stood a mere arm span beyond the far edge of his table. That was when she smiled down at him and seated herself before him.

He looked at her, unable to speak. He realized that she hadn't had the choice of drinking alone; nearly all seats in the house had occupants. From the tales he had heard, he imagined that she could have easily demanded, and received, a table of her own, but she seemed to possess nothing of the primal bloodlust that the tales of her tended to suggest. He supposed that she could yet demand that he leave her, but she only looked passively past him, her smile contained, secretive. He found himself now failing to believe that this woman had taken two heads off the shoulders of Guthrom's handpicked guard and displayed them for all to see outside the door of the tavern in which she had committed the crime.

"I am called Thyri," she said. She was speaking to him, and her words . . . they didn't break the spell of her presence, they expanded it and yet freed him from it, inviting him to enter, to become a part of it. And when she looked at him he felt as if she were giving him those hazel eyes like a lover would.

"I am Gerald," he said.

"I greet you, Gerald," she said. "Pardon my rudeness, but I need a guide. You are familiar with this city?" Her eyes strayed back to survey the contingent of Guthrom's men. She had spoken to him in the Saxon tongue; her words had been peppered with a curious hesitation, as if she struggled absently with the language.

"Yes."

"Then I can pay you well."

He watched her face; at first glance it remained unremarkable, almost boyish. He wondered whose weapon had given her the scar under her left eye. It was the way her expressions flowed, one into the other, that captivated him. Every blink of her eyes, every slight motion of her lips, was natural, marked with amazing fluidity.

"Where do you wish to go?" he asked her finally.

"You must escort me to a place of power."

As she'd entered the tavern hall, seen the looks on the faces of Guthrom's warriors, and felt the tension in the air, Thyri had felt a sudden urge to laugh, like it was all part of a dream deposited on her windowsill by a delicate, flying skeleton. Gone was the dark, brooding cloud that had engulfed her heart for longer than she cared to remember. She had found Megan, or rather, Megan had found her. The sorceress was alive, and she still cared. This one act, this act of seeking, made Thyri feel loved as she hadn't since the death of Astrid. Not even the love of the Habnakys, the love of an entire race of people, could match this gesture, for of all she had met since the fangs of the wolf had tainted her soul, Megan alone had understood her. When she had sailed blindly from the shores of Hordaland, when the sea had overwhelmed her, Megan had saved her and given her life again. When Thyri had later, desperately, sailed west in hopes that she would thus purge the curse from her veins, she had sought Megan's companionship, but Megan had refused. Only now, with the promise of the sorceress burning inside of her, did Thyri realize how much that refusal had hurt her. And that pain now but sweetened the promise.

Eventually, she focused on Guthrom's men, and the blades they carried reminded her that she did not dream. *Crush the gem in a place of power . . .* She needed to get out. By herself, finding such a place presented no problem except time. Her senses were easily keen enough, but she felt impatient, and wandering without apparent direction in and around the city could only get her into trouble. She felt no desire at the moment for swordplay or death. *Megan,* she thought, *we can set each other free.*

She began to sift through the faces in the crowd, disregarding the Norse, concentrating on those of darker hair and skin. Most sat in rowdy groups; only one sat alone. Still thinking of Megan, she started toward him.

Rollo Anskarson was twenty-nine that night, and he had served Guthrom for more than twelve years. His sword had first tasted blood when the Danes had overrun Eoforic and named it Jorvik. Since then, he had lost count of his victories. And yet, for all that he had great confidence in his prowess, he couldn't dispel the terrible fear that there, in that very tavern, a greater warrior drank. He had no real stomach to face her though he had sworn to the old man that he would escort her, dead or alive, to his hall that night. If he did not succeed, Guthrom would very likely take his head.

Rollo looked around at the others, seeking some clue in their eyes that might tell him that his doubts about facing Eiriksdattir were not his alone. But whatever they had felt at the sight of their friends' severed heads had now turned to anger; vengeance, he knew, burned in their hearts. Somehow, he could not summon up the same emotion within himself. His growing respect for Eiriksdattir's prowess made the heads outside a simple matter of fact, not tragedy.

As Rollo watched Eiriksdattir descend from her room above, Thorolf, next to him, cursed under his breath: *"There she is, the witch!"* Her eyes fell on them; Rollo wanted to look away but found that he couldn't. She looked at him, and he knew then that he could not cross his sword with hers. To his amazement, the realization did not make him feel a coward. He had no *reason* to fight her. True, Guthrom had ordered it, but the old man was truly king no longer; he had lost that right to Alfred. Rollo could not see even how Odin could fault him. Guthrom had, after all, forsaken the All Father in accepting the One God's baptism. Even if he'd done it to save his kingdom, he'd done it nevertheless. And,

Rollo reasoned, if his lord could do such a thing, so could he.

No, he would not fight her. He would live to see the morning. When she sat with Gerald, Rollo found within himself a real desire to join them. He continued to watch her while listening to the conversation among his companions grow more brave, more adventurous with each passing moment. When Erling, one of the youths, started to rise, Rollo reached over and put a gauntleted hand on his shoulder.

"*I* will go," Rollo said. They were the first words he'd spoken since entering the tavern.

As he approached Eiriksdattir, he noted how casually her hand fell to the hilt of her sword. She did not watch him directly, but he knew she was aware of his every movement. Slowly, he raised his hands to rest them on his breast. The position felt awkward, but he hoped she would read in it his true feelings. She didn't turn away from the Saxon, nor did she remove her hand from the hilt of her sword, until he stood over her.

"Guthrom sent you," she said.

"Yes."

"I will not go to him, Rollo Anskarson."

She remembered him—remembered their brief encounter in the Danish camp. He did not let his surprise show, but he chided himself for supposing that one such as Thyri would consider any meeting inconsequential. "I know."

"You will fight me now?"

"I will not. The others might."

She looked past him, then she looked at Gerald. "You agree to my request?"

The Saxon nodded.

"Go back to them," Thyri told Rollo. "Tell them I will accompany you, but I must go first to collect my belongings."

Rollo nodded, and Thyri rose and went for the stairs; the Saxon followed. Rollo returned to his table. "She will come," he said as he sat. "She saw our swords and knew that Guthrom's will cannot be denied."

He looked at Thorolf, and his fellow veteran grinned wildly. "She is ours then," he whispered. "Let's take her, Rollo! Let's lay that Norwegian bitch in an alleyway—" He paused, tilting his flagon to his lips, pouring a large quantity of the mead over his chest. "Let's take her," he continued, "and let her feel the fires that burn in Viking loins."

Rollo grinned back, striving to keep his betrayal hidden. "We shall see," he said. In Thorolf's eyes, he could see the scene just suggested played out. The idea was absurd, repugnant—unworthy of one named a Viking. With these thoughts, Rollo's uncertainty about Guthrom—for the overking was ultimately responsible for the attitudes of his men—began to turn to hate.

Still, Rollo kept his grin steady while his hate and disgust extended from Guthrom to Thorolf as well.

Magic

Upstairs, Gerald discovered that Thyri's room bore no marks of the riches he'd been sure she'd possessed. Other than a broken silver tube on the floor, the only evidence that the room even boasted an occupant was a large makeshift pack fashioned out of a sable cloak. Wordlessly, Thyri lifted the pack, tossed it to him, climbed out the window, and disappeared quickly onto the tavern's roof.

He carried the pack to the window and held it out. She whisked it from his hands, and he climbed out after her.

Standing on the roof, he looked out over the city, seeing it in a way he'd never seen it before. Rows of buildings snaked up and down hills like crazy, directionless rivers. For a moment, he forgot the reason for his lack of experience; when he remembered, he motioned for Thyri to crouch low. On the roofline of Jorvik, a man was a thief, and Guthrom's archers would not hesitate to fill them with arrows without ever seeing their faces.

Thyri maintained her crouch as she led him quickly away from Aelgulf's tavern. She reminded him of a cat, so easily did she pass over the most treacherous stretches of wood, carrying her pack as if it were weightless. After she'd stopped, it took him a full minute to reach her side.

"Well?" she said.

He bent next to her, panting. *Places of power* . . . If she meant the stone circles where the countryfolk still practiced the old rites in defiance of the orders of the One God, he knew of several, but most would be unattainable before morning without good horses. He knew of one in the city, on the property of a wealthy merchant, but it would be guarded heavily by the cult that practiced its rites there. Then there were the ruins, south by the river. The city dwellers never dared enter them; they had even built their roads around them. The ruins were said to be haunted, but Gerald had passed them several times and noticed fires within. An old woman once told him that Brigid was strong there and that the goddess had put the fear of ghosts in men's minds to protect her sanctuaries within.

Places of power . . . It suddenly stunned him—how easily he courted the thought, how easily his mind turned to places shrouded by tales of demons and other unspeakable horrors that awaited the uninvited intruder: the aching consumption of the Morrigan that could suck up the unwary Christian traveler, leaving no trace but the echoing wail of a devoured soul; the vengeance of neglected, forgotten gods; the sacrificial knives of the druid . . . It was *she*—Eiriksdattir—who allowed him these thoughts without fear. She, fearless herself, would protect him. He felt this with a certainty he had never felt before.

Rising, he decided the ruins a lesser risk than the merchant's circle of stones. Taking a final, deep breath, he motioned for Thyri to follow.

The buildings there, south by the river, must once have been grand. Now no roofs remained, and only a few walls stood here and there. The river had laid its silts over the area, covering any traces of floors. In places, huge intricately carved columns of stone rose out of the ground, some as thick as the chests of the mightiest of warriors. Those walls still standing were cracked at their base by the roots of nearby trees. Vines also dug into the cracks of stone once raised to the glory of Apollo and Mars and those other gods of the dead empire. More primal forces had since claimed the terrain: Thyri could feel them, their terrible strengths lacing the air, bringing to life her sixth sense.

Gerald stood next to her. She handed him her pack. "This place is Brigid's, you say? I know that name."

"She was life to the people of Arthur," he said. "There is a rhyme of her that my mother taught me as a child: *Born under roof without walls, fed with the milk of a white red-eared cow, she hangs her cloak on the rays of the sun, and the halls of her house blaze with its fire*."

"She is not a cruel goddess?"

He shrugged. "All of the ancient ones are cruel. All have lost great power in the shadow of the One God."

Thyri started forward. When Gerald took a step, she spoke without looking back. "Stay," she said. "Await my return."

She stopped as she neared the river. The ground where she stood was marked by charred grass, burned in circles and other patterns. The power of the place swamped her senses. Rougher stones than those hewn by the Romans lay scattered around the patterns in the grass.

Sitting before the centermost stone, she closed her eyes, and the wind began to whisper to her. She tipped the aqua gem from its pouch into her palm. Starlight glittered at the edges of its facets. A tiny yellow flame burned now in its center. She placed it on the stone, whispering, "I would make you an offering, Brigid of flaming halls, but I know not how."

"Your wish is offering enough, daughter of Chaos," the wind whispered back.

The reply awakened a deep mourning in Thyri's breast. *You are alive,* she thought, *yet you wither. Like Odin, whose sons have learned defeat at the hands of the One God's people. Whose sons have taken baptism and turned their backs on he who gave them strength.*

"I have strength enough, moon-cursed, though I have been named a saint of the One God. In time that will kill me, for I will not change. Perhaps it is your Odin who changes. Has he not abandoned you?"

Moon-cursed, Thyri thought. *I have been named that but once, and by my own pen. Is my pain so visible?*

"To those who may see it, yes."

Is there no escape?

"From all the pains of life, there is but one certain escape."

Death, Thyri thought. *But Death will not have me. Had it desired me, its chances have been many.*

"Then live. Work your magic and go."

Thyri recalled Tana, princess of Kaerglen, whom she had told to seek knowledge of Brigid. The power in the girl was very strong. *"Wait, goddess,"* she whispered. *"Perhaps I can offer you something. There lives a princess, on an isle the far side of Erin. She is very young. She seeks you."*

"Do not fear, she has found me. I am no dead saint yet. Work your magic. We shall meet again."

"Tana," Thyri said, crying now as she felt a grief she did not try to understand. "Tana, goddess, her name is Tana."

The wind, this time, brought no reply. Thyri looked down at the gem, and the yellow flame at its heart faded and then was gone. Still crying, she unsheathed her sword and brought its hilt down on the gem, which shattered almost effortlessly, laying rays of fine blue powder over the surface of the stone.

"Come to me, Megan," she whispered. "Come heal me again." She cast about for the slightest hint of Meg's presence. "Come to me, lover, I call you from the haven of your goddess. I call you with the heart beating in my breast; I call you with my eyes, my lips. Come to me, and let our love burn so brightly that eyes not our own must turn from it. Let us join and cause mountains to tremble. Let the thought of us breathe fear into the hearts of men. Let our love scorch the earth. Let the gods see our strength and know despair!"

First, a small, shimmering circle of silver and gold suspended in the air: Megan's ring. Thyri's hands ran over the surface of the stone. Minute shards of the gem dug into her palm; she pressed down hard against the pain and closed her eyes. *Come to me, Megan!*

"Hello, white-hair."

Thyri opened her eyes and let Megan's beauty steal her breath away. Before her, cascades of black hair framed a face so serene and refined that the most masterful artisan of porcelain could never hope to match it. A plain dress of black silk wrapped her body from shoulder to hip, then flowed down with the breeze to tease the ankles over her bare feet. Her nipples pressed hard against the silk, thrilling with the ecstasy of the sorcery. Almond eyes shone through the night like stars. Rouged lips moved slowly, sensually, into a wide smile. "Oh, Thyri," she said. "I thought you dead!"

Thyri rose. "I have wished it, Megan."

"So my bird found you at last? I cast that spell a mere week after you left me."

"I found a great land over the ocean."

"Too far for my magic to travel—I had guessed as much."

"But not too long for your magic to last. Even after flesh abandoned your messenger, the sorcery survived."

The sorceress smiled sadly at Thyri. "You did not escape the moon?"

"No."

Megan stepped forward. "You must tell me all that has transpired." She reached Thyri and took her into her arms. "Why do you cry, little one?"

"I—I do not know. I have missed you."

"I too have missed you. I was wrong to let you leave alone. I'm no longer even sure why I remained on Kaerglen. Only after you had left did I realize what I had done. Now we are together, and my heart is healed." She looked down into Thyri's eyes; Thyri saw a tear streak down her lover's cheek. "Shall we leave this place?" Megan asked.

Thyri sighed as she felt the sorceress shift in her arms. She let her hand fall lower to rest on the curve of Megan's hip. She reached up and tore at her shift, ripping it down between her breasts and spreading it open so that her own nipples stood free and aching in the air and magic of Brigid's haven. Slowly, she eased her body back against Megan's, sliding her nipples over the silk, inviting a white ecstatic fire to grip her body and consume her mind. And then she felt Megan's hands gripping her breasts, nails digging into her skin, then one hand sliding around to the small of her back, and the other pushing her down onto the grass. "Not yet," she heard herself sigh. "Let's not leave yet."

She felt lips dancing lightly on her neck, then moving down over her breast, the ache in her nipples suddenly fired anew by the grip of teeth. And then she felt the sorceress everywhere, sliding over her, silk setting her body effortlessly on fire.

Gradually, she forced her hands and her mouth into motion, slowly returning every caress she received.

From high above, the waxing moon shone down, lighting their bodies and the grass and stones around them. In four nights, it would be full.

Avalon

For centuries, the void had consumed her tortured cries, returning her naught but silence. Silence from which her only escape had been sleep—dreamless, as formless as the void.

Still, she'd slept. In sleep, she didn't remember. In sleep, she would allow a generation of Man to pass, then she would wake to test the void anew, to strain futilely against unseen chains, to curse the darkness she had once served, the darkness that now trapped her.

Sleep without thought. Yet now, she woke, and the void stretched out before her.

"Merlin! Release me!"

Silence; the wizard was dead, but his spell remained.

She cried out again, calling upon agents far darker than her captor.

Warriors

"Odin's beard, man," Thorolf bellowed at Aelgulf. "What do you mean, 'She disappeared'?"

"Jus' what I said," the taverner slurred back. "Sh'ain't there. Go look for yourself if you want. Naught there but this," he said, dangling the silver tube before their eyes; Rollo snatched it quickly from his grasp.

Thorolf leapt to his feet and reached over the table to clutch at Aelgulf's shirt. "You drunken lout! I'll kill you!"

Rollo reached up and grabbed the Viking's arm. "Sit down, Thorolf. It isn't his fault."

"Who's fault is it, then?" Thorolf seethed. "Yours? You let the bitch escape us!"

"If so, I probably saved your life."

Thorolf let go of Aelgulf and turned on his companion. The taverner scurried quickly away. "What are you saying?" Thorolf roared. "That a wench with a sword is a match for Thorolf Godfredson?"

"No," Rollo said, anger exploding inside him. Under the table, he unsheathed his long knife and placed it on his thigh. "I'm saying that Thorolf Godfredson is a fool to think that Guthrom still wields power enough to command warriors who owe him loyalty no longer."

Thorolf's face went red, and his hand began to fumble at his sword hilt. As the blade began to slide from its sheath, Rollo gripped his long knife and buried it in Thorolf's chest. The Viking stood up straight, blood beginning to stain his hairy chest. Rollo pushed him back, then jumped up, drawing his sword.

The four young Vikings with him stared dumbly at Thorolf's limp body. "It is a sad day," one mumbled, "when a Viking kills a Viking over mead."

"It is a sadder day," Rollo said, "when a Viking kills more than one Viking over mead. Leave me! Go tell Guthrom that Eiriksdattir has abandoned Aelgulf's tavern and that I, Rollo Anskarson, will seek her. Tell him that if she desires him, I will bring her, but tell him also that she will not desire him, and tell him that Rollo Anskarson wishes that Thor would piss in

Guthrom's flagon to teach him the folly of the One God's baptism."

The four looked on, still stunned. Rollo waved the point of his sword before their eyes. "Go!"

Fumbling, the four rose and scrambled out the door.

Rollo sat, glaring about in defiance of the stares of the other customers. "Aelgulf!" he shouted. "Quick! Another mead. I cannot remain here long."

Sokki made an effort to maintain the confidence in his stride as the four guardsmen came toward him. Still, his hand fell discreetly to his belt, and he casually flexed his fingers inside the gauntlet lined with thin silver links. He kept his gaze on the four steady, steeling himself for a confrontation, but they passed him by with scarcely a glance.

Puzzled, Sokki walked on toward the tavern that rumor said housed Thyri. After a few steps, he paused and glanced behind him. Guthrom's men had already rounded a turn; they were nowhere in sight, and Sokki realized that the anxiety he'd felt that afternoon for Thyri's safety had been unnecessary. She had vanquished already her foes of the evening—at least the first wave of them—and she'd done so without the rune-blade. Not that this minor detail mattered much: the perfection of Thyri's mystical weapon could only enhance her ability, it could never define it.

His hand fell onto the hilt of the sword, and he felt a brief flash of envy. For him, the blade had been a heavy burden. Not that he'd have done things any other way, but the temptations had nearly torn his soul asunder. Though he possessed a legendary weapon he could wield it only in secret, and he could tell no one but his brothers of its lightness and perfection of balance. He had not had the chance to use it in battle, but now he was glad of that fact. Even without the attachment that battle would have brought, it had taken him all afternoon to overcome a persistent, nagging desire to keep the sword, to discard the opportunity he now had to return it to its rightful owner. He'd finally forced his hesitation to dissipate by reflecting long on that experience they'd shared on the field against the Saxons. In his memory, his respect for Thyri could only grow, and, searching his heart, he'd realized that he'd do anything to regain her companionship, a prize next to which her sword was a trinket of no real value. *She* was the legend, while he, though skilled, was but a novice. And after her, he knew that he could accept training under no other warrior. His mind already dwelt constantly on the past, dissecting every memory of her words, her actions.

Sokki eyed the tavern's sentinels only briefly before pushing his way inside. The chatter of excited conversation enveloped him, but most present were Saxon, and he could understand few of the words. As he looked around for Thyri, he noticed the body of a Viking sprawled on the floor. Near the dead man, another Viking sat, calmly belting down a large flagon of mead. Both men bore the colors of Guthrom's personal guard.

As Sokki tried to fathom the meaning of the scenario, the living guardsman rose and brushed roughly past him and out the door. The Viking's brusqueness confused Sokki more than angered him, and this confusion grew as a drunkard claiming to be the innkeep staggered up to him and forced a flagon into his hand.

Before the innkeep moved on, Sokki grabbed his shoulder. "Where is Eiriksdattir?" he asked softly.

"Dissapea'd," the innkeep said, grinning wildly. "Gone! Poof! Dissapea'd." He laughed, breaking out of Sokki's grasp and gesturing wildly at the other customers. "Poof!" he declared loudly, and the tavern burst into laughter.

Sokki stood still for a moment, then glanced at the dead man on the floor and suddenly realized that the Viking who had just left might be his only hope of a straight answer. He turned and dashed out the door, but the man had already vanished from view.

Sokki sighed and fingered the hilt of the sword before setting off for the room near the docks that he shared with his brothers. Inside him, turmoil raged. Had he not wavered in his decision that afternoon, he would not have missed Thyri. But even if he had found her—what then? She had abandoned him once already. At least now, he still had her sword . . .

So ran his thoughts, around and around, throughout the duration of his walk.

Rollo searched through his mind, trying to recall details of the village off the north edge of the city. He wished he'd drunk less. The roads between the dwellings had surely changed . . . Why, by Odin, wasn't there enough light for him to see? His fingers felt cramped; he realized that he had hardly eased his grip on the small silver tube since he'd found it on the floor of Eiriksdattir's chamber.

Now if he could only find Fandis—she whom the Saxons named "the river witch." He knew she dwelt nearby. Exasperated, he slammed against the door of the nearest hovel and felt the latch crack under his weight. He burst into the one-room shack and thought he saw a figure moving on the far side. Instinctively, he drew his sword.

"Don't kill me! Please don't kill me!"

It was an old man's voice. "I won't kill you," Rollo said. "Tell me where I can find Fandis!" He decided to leave his blade bared, hoping it would persuade truth from the man.

The old man spewed out a stream of directions, and Rollo had him repeat them more slowly. When he felt sure that he had the directions memorized, he sheathed his sword and fared back into the night.

Gradually, the shadows grew less menacing, more familiar. Around each turn, a memory seemed to linger, a memory waiting to catch him up and carry him back to that night years before when they'd plundered the village on their way into the city. He'd been young then, with a young heart. He'd seen his companions laying into the villagers as if those armed with broomsticks were warriors. He'd spent most of the night staying the hands of others. That was the night he'd found that part of himself that could command men. He'd been foolish: if the nascent leader within had not been strong, he would surely have died.

He wondered now that he had survived this night. Before that battle with Alfred, he could never have defied Guthrom. No Viking could have done so. To Guthrom and Odin they had pledged their very lives. It was Guthrom who had betrayed that trust, not Rollo Anskarson. His anger swelled; under Guthrom the Danes would become like their enemies. They would cease to be free. They would be turned back from the gates of Valhalla.

So why did he not call on that leader inside of himself? Why did he not raise the call to arms anew?

Because it was too late. Because *she* had not done so, and if she hadn't, then that dream—the dream of Norse rule over the Saxons—had ended. If she would raise her banner, then Rollo would follow her.

Fandis did not sleep. When Rollo entered her hut, she moved not at all, and her eyes stared blankly past him. She sat, her back straight, her head held high and tilted back slightly. She looked much older than he remembered her. She hadn't been young then; she could almost have been his mother, but she'd still been beautiful. Now her painted cheeks bore the lines of age, and the skin of her neck sagged, folding in grotesque flaps. Three candles, two black and one white, burned on a small platform before her. A small frog squirmed under the light where she had pinned it with slivers of iron.

The smell in the hut, and the sight of her, made him gag. Over the years, he had thought of her often as he'd drifted into sleep. Over the years, she'd grown more beautiful in his memories, not less. Now he felt his loins shrivel, recoiling from the fantasies, the many thoughts of her that had once set them on fire. Two dreams now had the night taken from him.

"Fandis!"

She stared past him. He thought that she began to smile.

"Fandis!"

Still, she did not respond. He started forward; then, slowly, she raised her hand. He paused; when her palm fully faced him, he felt something grip his mind. *Wait,* he heard a voice say. It was a voice he'd heard but once before in truth, and countless times in reflection. This time there was but the one word; before there had been many. That night he had saved her . . . that night when five Vikings had held her pinned to the ground, and he'd preserved her virtue with his sword. As he'd lifted her from the ground, he'd heard her voice: "My thanks, man," she'd said, "but I never thought I'd be thanking a Dane. Return to me when I am well, and one boon I will grant you. One boon alone, for I owe not your people much." With that, she had swooned, and he'd returned her to her hut where he'd discovered the tools of her trade. From a villager outside, he had gained her name, then he'd gone on to the city . . .

As her grip on his mind relaxed, he began to wish he'd forgotten her. But no—he would have his boon. Her hand had dropped, but her eyes still stared past him.

He looked around the hut; it hadn't changed much. In one corner was her dingy cot; everywhere lay scattered the talismans and other wares of her witchcraft. Opposite the bed, a bag of grain lay on its side. He watched a rat scurry from the shadows into the bag. There, he kept his attention, preferring the shadows and the sound of the rat's scratching to the decaying ghost of his fantasies working her magic on the floor at his feet.

"A new power has entered the land this night," she said as she came out of her trance.

He grunted, still listening to the rat. "I care not of that," he said.

"Look at me, Dane," she said. "I must see your eyes."

He turned.

"Ah!" she said. "I remember you now!" She smiled; his stomach churned again as he saw the rotting mass of her teeth. She burst into laughter. "So! You've come for me at last, have you?

Here, on the floor? Or can you contain your passions long enough to reach the cot?"

He felt his face grow red, and his hand gripped the hilt of his sword. "I do not desire that, witch!"

Her laughter subsided into a cackling, rheumy cough. "But you once did," she forced out between spasms. "I can see it in your eyes." She paused and spat into the dirt next to her. "The years have not been kind to me, my young savior. Why have you come to me?"

Slowly, he bent forward and placed the silver tube in her hand. "A woman abandoned this thing this night," he said. "She hails from Hordaland, and she is called Eiriksdattir. You must help me find her."

Fandis stared down at the tube, then looked to Rollo, amazement kindling new life in her eyes. "You came by this? Were it not you asking, I would slay you." She sighed. "But I am no longer young, and I owe you one boon, and the river witch keeps her word."

"So—where is she?"

Fandis closed her eyes and fell silent again. Rollo waited; two rats now milled about in the grain. After a time, he began to feel his own weight dragging on his shoulders, and he sat, resting his back on the creaky framework of the hut's walls.

"She moves," the witch said finally. "I can give you no direction this night."

He stared at her.

"If you wish," she said, "you may sleep here. Perhaps on the morrow, I can aid you."

He started to protest, then grunted agreement. Even if she could have told him where to go, he wouldn't have been able to make it there. Sleep already clouded his mind. He slumped over onto his side, and he listened to her rise and shuffle to her cot. She still mumbled to him, he strained to hear her words: ". . . there are powers so bright they burn, my young savior.

". . . let not the hunter become the prey . . .

". . . beware her fangs . . ."

Wildfire

At the edge of the ruins, with Thyri's pack for a pillow, Gerald drifted into and out of a fitful dream. In this dream he was lost in the heart of a blinding snowstorm. A roaring, bitter cold wind pounded ceaselessly against his aching ears. He could feel nothing in his feet, even his legs, but looking down he could see them moving relentlessly, propelling him forward, against the wind.

Cold—such as he'd never felt before. Cold, stinging his face, his eyes, biting through to his heart.

And the wind . . .

A woman's voice, distant, urged him on.

The wind—something terrible hid in the wind. It twisted the swirls of snow into faces, demonic images: a cat-faced warrior with five arms; a hideous, shapeless mass of flesh with a thousand eyes; a monstrous wolf with fangs of ice.

Nightmares in the wind.

A woman's voice . . .

. . . a strange tongue. Familiar—his mother's?

He opened his eyes. Thyri emerged from the ruins, a dark shadow at her side. She spoke—that strange tongue; the shadow grew.

Gerald sat and shook his head. When he focused again on Thyri, the shadow next to her had taken form: another woman, draped in dark fabric. From a distance, the woman's figure brought thoughts of his mother rushing back into his mind. As the pair drew closer, the woman's beauty swiftly brushed away the wisps of memory. She stood half a head taller than Thyri, and her light skin almost seemed to reflect the starlight beaming down from the heavens. She walked with the carriage of a goddess, and Gerald wondered if Thyri had done nothing less than persuade Brigid to enter into the world.

They approached him. Their speech grew clearer, and he grew certain of its alien familiarity. It *was* his mother's. Or close.

Had this night suddenly thrust him into the affairs of the gods?

Did he still dream? Would that snowstorm arise from the ground without warning to again engulf him in its fury?

For a moment, he felt sure that Thyri and the woman would pass him without a glance. Their conversation seemed absorbing enough to shut out all else, but then Thyri drew next to him and stopped. Her companion, upon closer inspection, appeared no less fantastic.

"Gerald," Thyri said, "this is my friend Megan."

He felt his head bob in acknowledgment. Meg raised an amused eyebrow in return.

Thyri smiled and spoke to him again. "She's a witch," she said. She bent for her pack and threw it over her shoulder. "Is there a place nearby where we can eat in peace?"

"A bed would also be nice," Meg added in Gerald's tongue.

Gerald cleared his throat. "Country tavern?" he forced out. "Probably no Danes though."

"Perfect," Thyri said. "Shall I pay you now, or will you lead me further, Gerald of Jorvik?"

He almost told her that she need pay him nothing at all. "I will lead," he said, turning for the road quickly in an effort to hide his confused smile.

As they neared their destination, Gerald's thoughts, ironically, turned from the wild gods of his mother's people to tales he'd heard at Othar's of increased wolf-kills in the local flocks. The country people thought it an ill turn in the land, and many whispered of coming famine and pestilence. A few, he'd heard, had even invoked the ancient idea of evil man-wolves in explanation. Such talk was common, and Gerald knew that it could occasionally lead to persecution and death of strangers. For a moment, the thought alarmed him; then he recalled the near legends he'd heard told of Thyri's sword. Farmers with pitchforks would present no threat to his companions. Still, he would have felt more comfortable entering the tavern with Megan looking a little less—conspicuously sorcerous.

And little did he realize, as he opened the tavern door for the women to enter, that she with the sword was the source of the countryfolk's fears. For two months she had hidden in the nearby forests; for two moons she had dined on the local flocks.

A wicker talisman in the shape of a wolf's head—folk magic to ward off the curse of the *were*—hung over the tavern door. Thyri passed under it, Megan followed, then Gerald entered and swung shut the door.

Inside, Gerald counted ten customers, but only a few looked

up at their entrance. Most of the others sat captivated by the peaceful meditations of a lutist working his trade on a raised platform in one corner. The night was no longer new, and the movements of all present seemed lazily slurred. One of the customers lay collapsed over the table before him; as Gerald led Thyri and Megan through the tables, this tableau didn't change. His fear of some sort of confrontation began to ease.

They had taken seats before Gerald became aware of the change in Megan's appearance. Gone was the black garb of the witch. Gone was the flowing, black-as-night hair. The witch now sported a disheveled brown mop, and her clothes were also plain brown and covered with the dirt and grime of the fields. He blinked, and Thyri too changed. She looked older, her sword transformed into a walking stick, which she propped against the edge of the table next to her. He looked at Megan and her eyes smiled knowingly back at him. She was a witch . . .

A tavern wench brought mead. "A leg of lamb," Gerald said. He smiled up at her nervously, hoping that she hadn't noticed the sudden changes. When he smiled, a look of disgust spread across her face.

"Filthy old man," the girl said, backing away.

Gerald looked down at his hands and saw that they were wrinkled, bony, and covered with warts.

Thyri giggled. "Careful, Meg," she whispered. "Too much and they'll refuse us beds."

"That could easily be fixed," Meg said.

"Yes, but why waste the effort?"

Gerald sat back, watching them, awed, again wondering whether he sat in the presence of a goddess. Or goddesses. But he felt no fear. With Thyri especially. She had been kind to him all evening. Even now, though she seemed preoccupied with Megan, she did not shun him; she hadn't bade him leave. And until she did, he had no desire to stray from her presence. She was, after all, the reason he'd entered Aelgulf's tavern that afternoon.

Over the lamb, the two women fell to conversing in their strange tongue—Irish, Gerald later learned. He'd begun to feel nervous that his part in the affair would soon end when Thyri looked at him suddenly and asked, "How well do you use that sword?"

For the first time since watching her descend the stairs, Gerald remembered the blade he wore at his own side. He looked down to see it; it had transformed into a cane. The sudden shock of it all made him laugh. He smiled at Thyri. "Well enough," he said.

"But I daresay my blade is no match for yours, swords-mistress."

"Call me Thyri," she said.

He nodded.

"I have been called many things, Gerald, least among them demoness and kin-slayer. Do these things scare you?"

He looked into her eyes; he could see nothing of those names in them. "No," he said.

"Will you serve me? Follow where I lead?"

Anywhere, he thought. He felt a cool tingle slide across his scalp, a sensation he related to the taste of a rare, fine wine, or the first hesitant touch of a repentant virgin. He felt very wise, but he was still a child.

The Warrior

The smell of boiling pork lured Rollo from a vague, uneasy dream of misty waters and the haunting voice of a songstress whose body hovered distantly in the mist. He rolled over, and his cheek bit into dusty, packed earth.

"Good morning," Fandis said behind him.

He turned and looked at her. She was slumped over, tending a small caldron over a fire of coals. In her other palm rested the silver tube he had brought to her. "I thought you would sleep through breakfast," she said. She looked up. In the morning light, she simply looked old, or perhaps it had been his fantasies laying a veil of revulsion over her features the night before. Those fantasies seemed less real now in daylight. He remembered Thyri. Had she been unreal as well?

No. The question couldn't be asked. She had brought him here. Over her, he had slain Thorolf.

He grunted and sat up. "Smells good," he said.

"I knew the pork would get you. Never knew a Norseman who could resist it." Fandis smiled weakly, then looked down at the silver tube.

He sighed and rested back against the wall, letting the aroma of cooking revive him slowly.

"I have performed your casting," she said flatly.

"What did you learn?"

"Many things. The winter is coming."

"What winter?"

"*The* winter." She gave him a curious smile. "Your winter. The winter that will end all things."

She spoke of the *fimbulwinter,* he realized. When the gods would battle on the Plain of Vigrid. "How soon?"

"Not soon," she said, tossing him the tube and taking two bowls from a shelf behind her. "But not long either."

"Did it—did the vision scare you?"

"No. I will be already dead." She paused, holding the bowls in her lap. "Did you know," she said distantly, "that with the stone that vial once contained, I could have spelled myself young again? Why could you not have come into it a mere hour before you did?"

He didn't answer; he felt his stomach rumbling and restrained himself from grabbing for Fandis's caldron. His impatience made him rub his back roughly against the wall. "Where is she?" he asked gruffly.

Slowly, she began to ladle her broth into the bowls. "South of Jorvik," she said. "A small inn where Guthrom's men can't find her."

"Can you tell me the way?"

"Aye," she said, holding one bowl out to him. "But first you must eat."

His stomach reminded him that he hadn't eaten since noon the day before; he hadn't lingered long enough at Aelgulf's to dine. He took the bowl from Fandis's bony hands and tipped it to his lips, pouring the hot broth down his throat, pausing only occasionally to chew the small chunks of pork that slid onto his tongue from the bottom of the bowl. When he finished, he handed the bowl back and nodded for more. Eiriksdattir could wait a little longer.

The blazing sun rose higher in the sky as Rollo walked south, skirting the city. The heat had already begun to coax moisture from his skin, causing the woolen shirt he wore to stick and itch. He thought of the *fimbulwinter,* idly welcoming it if it would bring the summer to a rapid end. Most Danes preferred the climate of the Saxon lands to that of their homeland; Rollo, however, often found himself wishing for the vast expanses of snow and ice that he'd known in his youth. Even during the depths of Jorvik's winter, such sights were rare. His father had once told him that it was the winter that gave a Viking his strength; perhaps that explained Guthrom's failure. Perhaps that explained all the failures of the Norse in southern lands . . . failures presaging the end of all things.

His mind raced, whirling back to the oracle of the river witch: *fimbulwinter.* Three years of snowstorms descending like armies on all lands, north and south. Warfare possessing all, pitting father against son, brother against brother. Women deserting their men for the spawn of their own wombs . . .

Loki freed from his chains . . . But did the Trickster not first need to be fettered? Had this already come to pass? Had Balder already fallen?

Rollo tried to discard the questions. Were Fandis's words true, no power within his own mortal grasp could break the final, fatal threads of fate's tapestry. And if the terrible wars were indeed coming, he could think of no master he'd rather serve than she whom he now sought. Whatever she would command of him . . . His every thought of her came tinged with mystery, legend.

As he passed a field where goats grazed, a small swarm of flies discovered him. He stripped off his shirt and flailed it about to discourage them. The sun bearing down on his bare back, he left the flies behind.

Ghosts

Gerald rose midmorning as was his habit. He went to the window and relieved himself, then drank a portion of the water he'd brought up in a pail the night before. The last of the water he poured over his head, soaking his long, black hair.

He left his room and went down the hall to the door of the chamber Thyri shared with Megan. He listened, hearing no sounds from within. After a moment, he backed away; he'd almost reached the stairs when he remembered the spell Megan had cast to conceal their true features. He looked down at his hands; they were clean, young again. For him to wander freely in the inn, they needed to be diseased and gnarled.

He scowled and returned to his room. He sat on his cot for a while, wishing for a quill and parchment though he had no clear idea of anything to write. After he conceded the fact that wishing would achieve nothing, he lay back down, stared at the rafters, and slowly drifted back into dream.

Fandis felt the riders' approach before she heard the hooves in the distance. She knew they would draw closer. She *knew*.

So soon, she thought. She hadn't expected this so soon . . . Still, the night before, when she'd looked up at Rollo, death had lurked beyond his shoulder. Just as death had intruded into all of her castings of late, watching her silently, patiently.

She rose and went to her chest, taking out a small, neglected mirror covered with grime and dust. She polished the metal with the cloth of her robe, then peered in, at her face. The sight made her gasp; she had grown so old. She raised a bony hand and ran her fingers over the creases in her skin. So this was what Rollo had seen the night before: this old, decaying face. Where had her beauty gone? Stolen by the lonely years . . . and the magic.

She had been a fool. The warrior who had come to her—she could have had him; she could have lived out her life with him, in the arms that had saved her. Perhaps she could even have used her talent to maintain her beauty.

After that night long ago, she had so often wondered how long it would take him to return to her. After a year had passed, she'd begun to regret the harshness and brevity of her words to him. Still, she'd waited; her pride would not let her seek him out herself. If only she could turn back time.

"You're a fool," she muttered at her reflection. "An old fool."

She had chosen magic over love. She had sacrificed her body for power—the power to see into distant places, into the future. It was the only real power she had. It had shown her Guthrom's defeat. It had shown her, the night before, the entrance of Megan Edain into her world. It had heralded her own death.

So be it, she thought. If one could not accept one's own demise, then wasn't one living a lie? Yet truth could bring such sorrow. Her savior *had* returned—far too late. And his life had bound itself to another's. Not hers.

She had seen truth in Rollo's eyes. Truth: the secret love he'd bore her all these years. Truth: the horror of her appearance, the horrible cost of her sorcerous dealings.

After it had seemed that he would not come to her, she'd given herself to the power greedily. She'd often thought that, if she would not court a man, then she would court death. Death was a lover ever faithful once won.

And now death returned her affections. How ironic that the man had shown death the way.

The pounding hooves had grown ever closer. Now, even as she eyed her reflection, they stopped. She heard boots on the earth, the crack of wood as someone burst through her doorway. A hand on her shoulder, whirling her around to gaze into cruel eyes, the same cruelty she had seen over and again the night she'd been raped.

Yes, raped. Rollo had been too late. He'd merely halted the last of three assaults.

Now, as she looked deep into the cruel eyes, she saw something else. Death again, but not her own. That death—her death—hung in the air. She smiled.

"Where is he?" the Viking demanded.

"Death," she said. "You do not want to know."

"Where is he?" The man shook her.

She smiled again.

"Beat it out of her, Einar!" came a voice from outside.

She looked deep into the Viking's eyes, past his glare, into the impish, mischievous glint of death. She closed her eyes for a moment, seeking the death's nature.

A heavy hand smashed against the side of her head, and she

fell to the floor. She struggled to sit, but the Viking pushed her down, thrusting his face in front of hers. "Where is he?" he seethed.

She smiled at the death in his eyes, then she told him where to find Rollo.

Ahead, a cart approached, laden with barley; perspiration streaked the driver's face as he fought to keep his unruly mules on the road. His daughter, next to him, held on to her seat, frustration creasing her forehead.

Rollo acknowledged the mules' protests with a wry smile. The day before, he'd been no better than they. No, he'd been less: they cried out; he'd wanted to, but instead he'd shied from the bite of Guthrom's reins and obeyed in silence, in shame. On that day in spring, in that battle with Alfred, Rollo had lost something, become like a living ghost: the ghost of the already-dead, the listless spirit of lifeless motion, Guthrom's tame mule.

No more. He laughed, softly at first, but his mirth grew, blossoming into a sound that rang out over the fields. As he passed the cart, he noticed that the girl had relaxed and now took the jolting ride as a simple matter of course. She gazed at him in soft-eyed amazement; he didn't fully realize what that look meant until the cart had passed. On another day, he could have stopped the cart and taken the farmer's daughter at sword point and she would have thanked him later and offered herself to him as a wife. She would have loved him and followed him anywhere; he could see all this now in his memory of her eyes. She had young eyes, eyes that had not yet lowered permanently to the level of the ground just beyond the edge of the milking pail. Her eyes could see dream in the daylight; they could turn a man on the road into a hero with the power to give the world itself as a gift.

The look, directed at him, felt strange; it wasn't a thing he'd experienced often. Perhaps she'd seen through his laughter, seen through to the rebirth of that thing he'd lost in the world of Guthrom and Alfred, his awakening at the gateway to a new world, the one *she* offered.

Could the girl have seen him even more closely, she would have seen that he was like her. What she had seen in him, he had seen in Eiriksdattir. His mind turned, picturing the girl abandoning her father and racing back down the road in search of the laughing hero who had passed her by. The absurdity of her chasing him while he chased Thyri made him laugh again. He forced her back into the cart, next to her sweating father. She would stay chained to her life, thinking of him in the darkness of night much as he had long dreamed of Fandis. Or perhaps she would remember him only briefly one summer morning years hence when the sound of his laughter would ring anew through her mind. And she would wonder what it had been that had made him laugh. And she would long for him again for a moment before bending down under the cow and reaching for a teat . . .

Maybe the farmer had been destined for Jorvik. Maybe Rollo had gifted the girl with the strength to test her chains, to escape into the city.

As Eiriksdattir had gifted him with the strength to escape . . .

Rollo stopped suddenly, realizing that ahead, just off the road, sat his destination. His walk was nearly done; within the wooden walls of the distant tavern, Thyri would be. The cart in his mind had fueled his journey, consuming the miles. He strode forward.

And then, behind him: pounding hooves. The sound grew rapidly, and Rollo cursed, throwing himself into a patch of bushes at the side of the road. He looked back and counted twelve riders. Einar Godfredson, Thorolf's brother, rode at their head. Rollo knew all of them; the day before, he had been a leader among them.

Cursing again, he prayed that he'd hidden in time. The riders drew near and he steeled himself, but then they passed, reining in their steeds only when they reached the tavern. He watched a figure step out into the yard, a woman with hair like the sun and a blade raised high over her head. *Thyri!* He crawled closer.

The riders remained mounted and circled her. They produced a net and stretched it out. She went for one of the riders, but the net caught her, and he saw her sword fly out of her grasp as the net battered her to the ground. And then six of the twelve descended on her, forcing her, still netted, into a large burlap sack, which they lashed around with many lengths of thick rope.

"Rollo!" Einar bellowed. "Where are you? Where is the maggot that killed my brother!"

The words stung Rollo's ears as they stained the air that he had filled with laughter. He wanted to lunge out and call Einar to him; he wanted to free Thyri, killing them all if he had to. All twelve . . . *Twelve swords, mounted.*

Seething, he stayed hidden. The ghost of the already-dead cackled in his ears.

Guthrom's guard milled about outside the tavern, then eight came back toward him. They passed, Eiriksdattir still bound, her cloth cage attached by rope to three of the horses and bouncing along in the rear.

Einar had stayed at the tavern, had started for its door. He had with him now only three others. With surprise, Rollo could take them . . . *But they were killing Thyri!*

Abandoning everything but his sword, Rollo leapt to his feet and raced toward Jorvik after the riders.

Thyri ducked underneath the edge of the window and giggled up at Megan. "That was beautiful! How long do you think it will take them to open the sack?"

Meg eased down next to her, starting to giggle herself. "Probably not until they get where they're going. They're dragging you with three horses, so they'll never notice a sudden loss of weight."

Thyri choked back her laughter at the thought of Guthrom's guard proudly dumping a heavily bound chicken at their ruler's feet. She looked over at Meg, but a distant glaze coated the sorceress's eyes, and shadows still danced around the ring on her finger. Not all of the riders had departed, and Meg yet worked her magic.

Thyri rose slowly and went for her sword.

Einar Godfredson grinned as he stooped, lifting the blade from the dust. He tested its grip and smiled. With the witch's blade, he would kill Rollo.

Motioning for the others to follow, he kicked in the door of the tavern. A room empty of all but tables and chairs greeted him. He ordered two of his men to the kitchen and waited until they emerged with three people, an old couple and a young girl.

He started up the stairs. "Rollo! The Valkyrie lust for your blood!" He reached the top and smashed in the first door. Gerald looked up out of his dream and saw Einar, a hulking shadow that filled his doorway. The shadow backed out.

Einar knocked down the next door—and there, before him, impossibly, stood Eiriksdattir. He struck at her with the sword in his hand even as the blade disintegrated into a shimmering mist.

Thyri allowed the Viking time enough to draw his own, real blade before she killed him. She stepped out to confront the last three who tried to assault her in unison. They attacked wildly, swords biting into the wood of the restricting walls. She reacted mechanically, and each fell within seconds.

Gerald emerged from his room and looked down at the bodies littering the hall. Blood still ran down the edge of Thyri's blade. She glanced up at him briefly before walking back into her room.

Warriors

It took Rollo twenty minutes to reach the city. Along the way, he found several short strands of hemp—twists of the rope with which the riders had bound Thyri. He carried the strands in one clenched fist; in his other hand was his sword.

Thyri was dead.

Among the last stand of hovels before Jorvik's south gate, he stopped, panting heavily, a wildness burning in his heart. His lungs drank in the air and begged for more. The blade at the end of his arm twitched, and anger flared through his mind in waves.

Thyri was dead! She had to be; she couldn't have survived: The rocks on the road had splintered every bone in her body.

She would be avenged!

He would slay the riders, and Einar when he returned. And Guthrom. Especially Guthrom, for it was he who held the reins that commanded all the mules, ruly and unruly alike; all but the one who had broken free.

And Rollo would find Thyri . . . She deserved the burial of a queen.

As he caught his breath, he realized that some instinct had stopped him short of storming the gate. Caution hadn't occurred to him. He felt strong enough to defeat Guthrom's entire army with his sword. He felt like trying, but something deep inside him, beneath his thoughts, had remembered that the gate guard had arrows in no short supply. That something had saved his life. If only it could have saved Thyri's as well.

Slowly, he grew aware of the people around him. Most were women whose husbands slaved away in the city for a day's worth of bread for their families. He spotted a couple of old men in the crowd, and small children ran everywhere in packs. He looked around; if Jorvik were ever assaulted, these people would be completely at the mercy of the attackers. But they had nowhere else to go; the city was already overflowing the walls built a short ten years before.

He knew the people watched him, though they turned their

eyes when he stared back. He shut them out again. Sheathing his sword, he moved along the face of the last building and looked around:

His eyes grew wide in horror, and again he almost stormed Jorvik in *berserk* fury. High on a stake next to the gate was another human head, one with dark hair, one he recognized with certainty even at a distance. His vision blurred with tears, and he slumped to the earth.

Two deaths played through his mind: Thyri Eiriksdattir's, and now—Fandis's. Guthrom's men had done to the river witch what Thyri had done to their comrades-in-arms. Why? Because Rollo had gone to her. He couldn't believe that he had been followed. More likely, they had learned of his movements from those who had seen him pass. The old man who had directed him to Fandis? He would have been all Einar needed.

Before she died, Fandis must have told where she'd sent him and that Thyri would be there. And then they'd staked her head outside the city as if they thought it a game that they could win against Eiriksdattir. As if they thought they could defeat someone such as her.

But they had been victorious . . . Rollo cursed Odin for these cruelties—all dispensed in less than a full passing of the sun. As the curse passed Rollo's lips, he realized that all that had passed had its cause in him. His actions had led to Fandis's death. *He* had led Eiriksdattir's killers to their prey.

He looked up, and the stares of the people suddenly accused him and condemned him and his betrayal of the two women. In one child's eyes he thought he saw Thyri's gaze cursing him for his meddling.

Guthrom had won.

No.

She lived, and she would have her revenge. As long as he could wield his blade, she could not fully die.

As he rose, his anger consumed his mind, forcing his thoughts down to where reflection and introspection cannot follow. His senses sharpened; in a way, he became much like the beast that took Thyri under the light of the full moon. Low, menacing growls escaped through his teeth as he turned toward the river to seek a more accessible path into Guthrom's city.

"We need a ship," Thyri said softly, twisting a blade of grass absently around her fingers.

Gerald watched her. A beam of light filtered through the leaves above had caught in the thin scar under her left eye. Thyri looked as if she cried, and the sun itself was providing her tears. Gerald found his hand moving automatically to touch the scar below his own left eye.

"I know little of the sea," Megan said. She stood under the low boughs of the old oak. Gerald and Thyri rested on the grass near the trunk. Beyond Megan, the afternoon sun scorched a heavily grazed grassland. Against the light, Megan seemed little more than a dark, shapely shadow.

She turned and looked at Thyri. *Except that the sea brought you to me*. She smiled and looked away again.

Gerald did not hear Megan's voice. Thyri heard it in her head, as clearly as if it had been spoken. Gerald did not yet suspect that the two women could communicate without words. "I know nothing of the sea, either, swords-mistress," he said. "But I do not fear it."

"That is good," Thyri said, smiling at him.

They had left the tavern within minutes after Einar's death. Megan had given the old couple who ran it a gold coin to compensate for the trouble of the corpses.

Gerald had had no idea of their next destination (beyond the oak tree) until this talk of a ship. "Guthrom has many ships," he said, trying to present an idea that would justify his place in the odd trio. Already, after seeing Thyri in action but once, he found it difficult to consider himself a swordsman. And what had he to offer on the level of Megan's sorcery?

And it certainly didn't seem as if he could offer either of them anything as a man. Only a fool could see them together and not *know* . . . Only a fool would dream that he could somehow give Thyri what Megan could not.

And yet, deep within Gerald, that fool lusted. Gerald refused to acknowledge this, but it made him no less insecure.

"Precisely what I was thinking," Thyri said. "Guthrom has more ships, in fact, than he needs."

Avalon

"Arise, little sleeper!" *answered the void.*

"Merlin!"

"No, Morgana, I am no mere wizard. I am the binder of light. I have sired beasts with the power to crush this earth. I am Balder's bane, and I am the darkness. I am the ending of that which you began."

"Me? Then you are *my* son, and I command you to free me."

The void laughed. "You do not command me, and I will not free you. I will remove but one layer of your prison, and you must do the rest. I return to you your sorceries as well; you are no good to me without them."

"No good for what?"

The void laughed again, then it smashed down upon her, thrusting obscenely through every defenseless pore of her being. She felt icy fire ignite within her; the laughter crawled up her spine and into her mind, possessing her, filling her as no man, mortal or demon, had filled her before. She growled, struggling against it even as the fire spread and grew hot, burning her. Waves of ecstatic pain crashed onto her, into her, through her.

"More!" *she screamed.*

"Free yourself!" *it demanded, vanishing, leaving her achingly unfulfilled.*

"More!"

Silence, but the void turned gray and laced itself with seams. Rays of light streaked across the gray . . . stone. Sunlight—no, the light of the moon. Hesitantly, she moved, gritting her teeth as a painful creaking sound split the air. She sat, brushing the dust from her white, fleshless limbs. Bone clacked against bone.

"I live!" *she shrieked. She held her skeletal fingers before her eyes and laughed insanely.* "I live!"

She crossed the chamber to the window and gazed out at the moon. Below her, surf pounded against the cliff at the foot of her tower. It made no sound; she yearned to feel the freshness of the sea breeze, but the air around her was still.

She turned, her hollow eyes falling on the pedestal near her altar. A patch of darkness spread out from the pedestal's center. She approached it. From the center of the darkness, a black orb beckoned to her as if it were alive. She approached it hesitantly, watching her reflection on the orb's surface grow more distinct.

The orb of Babd? Had Merlin been fool enough to leave it within her grasp? Or had he used its power to trap her? No, such humor was not in his nature . . . Nor would he have left it for her in the tower. Had she known of its presence, she could have freed herself. And she had tried that aeons before.

No, the presence in the void had returned the orb to her. She owed much to whatever wizard or god had freed her. "Free yourself," *he had told her. One layer of her prison now was gone. Through her sorcery, and the power of the orb, her spirit could be free, outside the tower as well as in. Merlin's curse on her physical form, however, was more permanent, unbreakable. Should her body ever leave her tower, her soul would perish. She knew the spell well. Of course, if her spirit found a new home . . .*

She picked up the orb and let its power surge through her. In her thoughts the void assumed a form of masculine perfection; she had been given no hint of his physical shape, so she shaped him in her mind: a muscled, golden youth with eyes of fire. She twisted the vision carefully until it resembled her son, Mordred. She began to feel a terrible aching for her flesh.

Her mind filled itself with the memory of the presence's laughter. She looked down at the bleached nakedness of her bones and imagined the laughter the moon's.

She sneered. The moon would not laugh long; nay, it would lust for her!

She turned to seek out the darker chambers of her keep.

Vishnu and Ra lay curled around the pedestal of her scrying stones. She set the orb of Babd among the crystals and stooped, lightly touching the leathery, shriveled skin of the hounds. A dark brown substance came away on her fingers.

"We shall be free, my pets," *she said, reaching up for the orb. Over Ra's head, she squeezed it, conjuring tendrils of darkness that oozed out between her fingers and flowed over the hound's mummified form. Beneath the black magic's caress, Ra's hardened flesh began to grow supple. As it darkened to its natural black, the orb's magic spread to Vishnu as well.*

"Free," *Morgana muttered as Ra's eyes fluttered open. His irises were orange, like fire.*

She reached between his legs and he growled at her. She dug her fingers into his scrotum, pressing her palm down hard against his penis. She felt it harden, and she stroked it until its semen spurted out and up, along her arm—where her arm should have been. The white liquid hung suspended in the air, an inch from her bones; as she watched, it began to flow slowly down the imaginary curve of her flesh.

Chuckling, she reached for Vishnu and awakened him as she had his brother. When she was finished, she stood and spread the semen over her body until her own flesh began to take form under her fingers. Then she took the orb and held it over her head, bathing herself in its magic, completing the spell.

She lived.

She returned to the chamber of the moon with a silver mirror and sat on the stone platform on which she had slept for centuries. In the mirror she gazed at herself, using the orb's magic to adjust her features until she became satisfied with the perfection of her own dark beauty. She grew thick, black hair until it reached to the pale smoothness of her thighs. She let it dance there, reveling in the feeling of her flesh, her fingers slowly probing between her legs as she sought to quell the ache that the presence in the void had left her.

Vishnu and Ra watched their mistress. Vishnu tried to force his snout between Morgana's legs, but she kicked him away.

Screaming, clawing at her breasts with one hand, she brought herself to orgasm. When the waves of pleasure had subsided, she still felt the ache.

She sighed and went to the window, the hounds padding along behind her. The surf was still silent, and her hair hung limp; the air about her remained still.

Ghosts

A place known as Reaver's Haven stretched from the south wall of Jorvik to a point midway between the city and the ruins to which Gerald had led Thyri for her summoning of Megan. It was a lawless place where Guthrom's ruling hand was seldom felt. Merchants could avoid tariffs by dealing there, and thieves, beggars, and whores lay in wait for these merchants in every dark corner and alleyway. Dwellers of the city proper were likewise considered fair game by the Haven's denizens.

The name might suggest that it was a safe place for Norsemen; it was not. In the Haven, the Saxon still ruled. It gained its name from the thieves who plied their trade there. They named it thus to goad the Norse to enter.

Guthrom, of course, could have eradicated the problem with a single, crushing blow. He hadn't done this because he'd had other problems, one of which had been Alfred. But even if Guthrom had been an unambitious ruler, it is doubtful that the Haven would have had much to fear. Too many of the overking's men had been captured by the women there. The Vikings were the first to take the thieves' bait, and the first to swear on the Haven's innumerable, exotic virtues, even though most who braved the Haven's paths exited significantly less wealthy than they had been upon entrance.

Such a place is not unique; any city of modest size has its own Haven, its place where the generally understood, established order of things does not apply, where one can witness the depths of human pain and cruelty, or experience pleasures unimaginable in safer surrounds. Sometimes, it is a small place; at other times it spreads itself like a disease over entire countrysides. In Jorvik, it took the form of an outskirt that rubbed up against the city wall like a playful bear.

In Reaver's Haven, Rollo Anskarson had fulfilled, from time to time, some of the fantasies he'd built around Fandis over long, sleepless nights. The fact that he'd sought such fulfillment in the arms of nameless whores had often bothered him. For hadn't Fandis been waiting for him to ask his boon? Couldn't she have been his for the price of an evening's walk? And yet, deep inside, he'd understood his inaction: Fandis had been his promise of perfection, a mirror in his mind into which he could gaze to judge his own thoughts and actions, to measure himself as a man. And into this mirror, Rollo would often look and despair. Even before Guthrom's defeat, Rollo had felt somehow *wrong* in doing the bidding of this man whom he saw as just that—a man. But he was a warrior, and warriors served leaders. He had had no other leader, had known of no other way to live.

And so he'd felt unworthy. And with that feeling, he could not shake the fear that Fandis would reject him, even laugh at him when he approached her. After all, he was Norse, and she'd made it painfully clear that she bore no love for his people. And if she'd—if his *perfection* had laughed at him . . . No, it had always been better to leave the mirror in his mind unblemished, uncracked. At least until he'd felt worthy.

Now Fandis was dead. If Rollo had not been consumed by grief and anger that day he last entered Reaver's Haven, he might have sensed something significant in the way that Thyri's entrance into his life had erected a new, more polished mirror in his mind next to Fandis's. But Thyri was dead as well.

Fandis, before she'd died, had been old. Now, in his memory, she was young again, forever youthful and beautiful. Thyri had never been old. Both their mirrors blazed behind his eyes, they had become twin beacons urging him forward on his mission of revenge. Somehow, despite the knives that the day had buried in his heart, he had never felt more alive.

As dusk gave way to night, the beacons in his mind began to burn more brightly still. Some weak but victorious fragment of his wisdom had urged him to stay in the shadows until the sun could no longer betray him, until he could count the night his ally. He had hidden in an abandoned shed, but now the night called him out, and he followed.

On the streets, he set himself on a course for the city wall, to a section that he knew would be unguarded. Beyond the wall, he would find Einar and Guthrom and the others. On the way, he dimly realized that the beggars were letting him pass, as if they sensed in his gait that he would cut them down out of his path before proffering a coin. The whores were less empathic, and he had to brush them aside. Several times, however, his eyes unwillingly met theirs. Each time, he found the ghosts of Thyri and Fandis staring out at him, demanding blood for blood.

As Rollo stole over a dilapidated section of wall into Guthrom's city, Thyri, Megan, and Gerald entered Reaver's Haven from the south. The women had donned long, black capes with hoods that hid their features. The capes were real, woolen; they had bought them on the road from a traveling merchant. Megan had provided the money. She'd also offered to provide disguises again, but Thyri had cautioned against it, pointing out that hoods would achieve the same objective, and abuse of Megan's sorcery could likely place them at added risk. If Guthrom had enlisted the aid of a sorcerer or wizard—and the fact that they'd been ferreted out at the country tavern hinted at just that—then their very disguises would give them away.

That thought had sobered Gerald somewhat. He'd found it quite easy to lose himself in a sort of numb-minded euphoria in Thyri's presence. He couldn't picture her failing at anything, and in a way he felt just as safe with her as he had as a boy with his mother. Talk of a sorcerous opponent, however, had rekindled the feeling that he was suddenly in over his head, involving himself in a conflict in which he would have never imagined himself on his own.

With this thought, he entered the Haven. He had enemies there; their faces passed briefly through his mind as boisterous singing reached his ears from the first inn they passed. There was the high-priced harlot who called herself Ramona; Gerald had once cheated her of a night's pleasure by posing as a Frisian prince (he'd not known the language then, but neither had she). But hers was the most attractive of the remembered faces, and she posed no great danger to his life. Ogbert and his organized band of thieves and mercenaries was another matter entirely.

Years before, he'd been foolish enough to play dice with the uncrowned lord of the Haven. Ogbert had only just begun then to consolidate his power, and he'd still spent much of his time on the streets. Fate had brought Gerald in contact with him. Fate had blessed Gerald with an impossible run of luck that night.

He'd been lucky to get out alive.

Now he felt naked, acutely aware of the fact that he wore no disguise and that he hadn't had the presence of mind earlier to take his past into account.

Here he was, without even a hat, looking exactly as he had when Ogbert had slashed his face with a knife. Except now he had the scar... He tried to convince himself that Ogbert and his friends had probably forgotten him. After all, they had known him for but a night. And the number of small-time hustlers they'd stepped on over the years was surely vast.

As they passed a band of about ten men and women holding an impromptu party in the street, Thyri asked Gerald if the Saxon people always enjoyed life so thoroughly, or if Guthrom's defeat still contributed to their high spirits. He told her that Reaver's Haven didn't care who controlled the city as long as there was a city off which it could feed.

Thyri laughed at that, and her laughter chased his fears away. Suddenly, he found himself hoping that he would find Ogbert and that the thief would confront him. With Thyri, Gerald could gain his revenge.

So strongly did this feeling grip him that he changed his plans. Thyri wanted a ship, and for a ship they'd need a crew. He'd flirted with a vague notion of picking up men in the city on the strength of Thyri's reputation or Megan's sorcery. Upon reflection, effort expended in that direction directly under Guthrom's nose was likely to attract the overking's attention. And there was an establishment in Reaver's Haven where one could engage in such an activity as manning a ship and go quite unnoticed. Besides, Thyri had said that they didn't really need a crew until they started downriver for the sea. She hoped to remove a vessel from Guthrom's harbor without his knowledge, and that would require slow stealth, not the speed afforded by a dozen oarsmen. If they could hire men to meet them downstream, they would be better off. And in Reaver's Haven, they were already downstream.

The establishment which Gerald had thought of bore no formal name. It was called, simply, Ogbert's.

He had never been there; it hadn't existed two years before. But the place was almost legendary, and he'd heard that word of it had spread already to the ends of the earth, even to the far south to the ears of the descendants of the dead empires. It was a gambling house, and it was a brothel, and a menagerie. In it, he'd heard, one could see creatures the likes of which one could see nowhere else. And the women—some were said to have skin the color of night, others the color of the sun.

Ramona probably sold her wares there now as well.

Thyri stopped abruptly as she reached the end of the entrance hall and took in the view. The building was circular, built in three tiers with an open center. The ground floor was crowded, and the noise of human voices was almost deafening. At the banister of the second tier, a row of women garbed in colorful silks motioned and moved seductively for the men below. On a raised platform opposite, a dark-skinned woman danced erotically with a serpent. Those men not caught up in drinking or gawking at the spectacle of female flesh were gathered around a railing in the center of the floor, looking down; there was some sort of pit at the building's core.

Megan drew next to Thyri and gasped. "Incredible," she said after a moment. "I never thought such sights existed in this world."

Thyri smiled; she didn't share Megan's wonder, yet the nature of the place excited her because its pleasures were tainted, attracting the cruelest and most heartless of men. Within these walls, she could sense the demons that lurked in the darkest corners of the human spirit. She did not necessarily enjoy the company, nor was she wont to seek it out, but experiencing it provided an ironic comfort. Here, in such a place, she could almost feel clean.

Gerald led them to a table near the pit and ordered mead. Thyri asked him what the pit was for.

"Cockfights," he replied, hoping that what he'd heard was true. He started to look out over the crowd, searching for people he knew from the city as well as those faces from his past. He didn't see Ogbert; it seemed sensible that the proprietor would spend his time managing the finer details of his business in a place removed from the noise. In this Gerald felt relief. His boost in confidence had begun to wane.

As Gerald looked around, Megan glanced at Thyri, rose, and walked to the edge of the pit. A young girl with circles cut in her shift to reveal her nipples stopped briefly at the table to deposit three large flagons. Thyri took up one of the flagons and drank, eyeing Gerald over the rim.

He started to speak, then felt a hand on his shoulder. Ogbert! he thought, his hand moving to the hilt of his sword.

"I thought you didn't like this place, my friend," said a thickly accented voice.

The voice made Gerald jump. He turned and looked up into an exotic, olive-skinned face with a flat nose and dark, almond eyes. "Rui! I thought you dead!" The sight of the familiar face swept away Gerald's unease; he laughed, rising to embrace the newcomer.

"I have often thought that myself," the man said, smiling warmly. "May I join you?"

Gerald looked to Thyri, who nodded almost imperceptibly under her hood. The man sat, and Thyri pushed Megan's flagon toward him. Gerald signaled for more mead, then turned to Thyri. "This is an old friend, though I hardly expected to find him here. His name is Rui; I cannot pronounce his surname."

"Taichimi," Rui said.

"He's a merchant."

"No, just a traveler. I no longer have anything to sell."

"Are you elven?" Thyri asked suddenly.

Rui looked at her, openly surprised that the voice coming from the hood had been female. "No," he said uncertainly, "if you mean Fairie as Gerald's people call that race. I was born in Nippon, the land of the sun." He turned to Gerald. "Who is this woman dressed like a man in the company of harlots?"

"Thyri Eiriksdattir," Gerald said.

Thyri pulled back the rim of her hood, revealing her face to the traveler. He could see restrained fire burning behind her eyes.

Rui laughed. "Eiriksdattir? I did not intend my words to insult you." He paused, looking at her carefully. "I am honored. It is said that you deny the lord of the city."

She nodded, then retreated into her hood. "You are a traveler? That means you know ships?"

"I know them enough to stay alive on them. If I knew them well, I would not now be so far from home."

"Rui," Gerald said, "I have brought Eiriksdattir here with her companion to find men like you. They plan to steal one of Guthrom's ships tonight."

Rui raised a dark eyebrow. "Companion?" he asked after a moment's silence.

Gerald tilted his head in Megan's direction. Rui looked. Megan's back faced them; her slender ankles and bare feet were just visible in the shadows beneath her. And then she turned, starting back to the table. She sat.

"Who's this?"

"Rui Taichimi, friend of Gerald's," Thyri said. "He says he is not an elf."

All fell silent then, and it seemed to Gerald that even the noise around them backed off into the distance. Rui could not see Megan's eyes, but he nevertheless felt the weight of her gaze.

"He isn't," Megan said softly.

Rui smiled. "I hope not." He indicated the pit. "Did you enjoy the game?" he asked.

"No," she said. "It seemed cruel."

"It is cruel," the traveler said, "but so is life at times."

"We seek a crew here," Gerald said.

"That can be arranged. You have money?"

Megan reached across the table and dropped a handful of silver coins into Rui's hand.

He tested their weight and began to stand.

"Wait," Gerald said. "Pay them half, and tell them to meet us at the first landing south of the ruins."

Rui nodded, then disappeared into the crowd.

"He can be trusted?" Thyri asked.

"As well as any," Gerald said before he realized that Thyri's question had been directed to Megan.

"He seems a strong, honest man," the sorceress said. "Very calm inside."

Gerald asked them if they'd like to see more of Ogbert's. Thyri considered the idea briefly; exploration hung implicit in the air, such was the nature of the place. Falling prey to the temptation, however, was not a part of the strange comfort she'd found there. She declined.

After that, they drank in silence. Gerald began to feel foolish that he'd ever feared confrontation with the master thief and his minions. He watched Thyri, realizing that this old fear of his—this defeat by Ogbert that haunted him—no longer carried weight in his reality. Thyri had carved him a new reality, one that could free him from his fears and make him whole. In her, he saw no trace of fear. He saw now that he and other men cherished fear and labeled it caution to justify their cowardice. The caution—the cowardice—chained men as surely as the strongest iron, but beyond these chains, didn't death lurk? Were the chains not necessary? A week before, he would have answered smugly, fatalistically, in the affirmative. Now the fact of Thyri's existence proved him wrong.

He threw back his head and drank deeply, trying to drown the convoluted contradictions in his thinking. To his relief, Rui returned, providing reason to turn his mind to the matters at hand.

The traveler sat. "It is done," he said. "Eight men, though I would not stake my life on their worthiness."

"Can they work oars?" Thyri asked.

Rui nodded.

"Then let us go." She stood.

"Eiriksdattir?" the traveler asked hesitantly. "May I join you now? I would much like to see how you do what you plan, and I am no novice at battle."

She paused, then nodded silently. They rose and started for the door. Rui stopped them there and retrieved a large bow and its quiver from a nearby storeroom, then they exited into the streets beyond.

Nightreaver

Thorir Ulfson wearily dismounted and stamped his feet on the packed earth, trying to shake the ache from his legs. He had been riding since shortly after sunrise.

Painfully, he led his steed to the water trough and cursed loudly when he found the trough empty. Still cursing, he went to the nearby well, brought up two bucketfuls of water, and dumped them into the trough. He tied his steed where the beast could reach the water, then he started for the barracks.

He would stable his mount later, after the muscles in his legs unknotted.

Starting up the barrack's wooden steps, he smelled smoke and stopped in alarm, standing motionless until he realized that the smoke emanated from his own clothing. He stank of the day's business. Behind his eyes, the country tavern ignited again and the flames reached up to the heavens. So would Einar Godfredson's passing be remembered forever.

With this thought, Thorir entered the barracks. Buri and Askold, two of his fellow guardsmen, looked up at his entrance from the table where they had just dined. A half-devoured leg of hog sat on a plate in the table's center. Thorir silently went to the table, tore off a chunk of meat, and started to eat even before he had sat. When his behind touched down on the wood of his chair, new spears of pain shot up his spine. He winced and tore into his dinner with new vigor, trying to ignore the pain.

"Eiriksdattir is still free?" Buri asked him.

Thorir looked up impatiently. "Had I found her, do you not think you would have known before I entered this room?"

Buri averted his eyes. "Einar should never have slain that Saxon witch. If she could find Eiriksdattir for Rollo, she could be finding her for us now."

Askold slammed his fist down on the table. "Buri! You tempt evil omens by speaking the name of Thorolf's slayer without cursing him in the same breath!"

"Evil omens have found us already, Askold. Seven of us dead

in the space of two days. We used to be called Guthrom's best. We used to be feared, but now we are laughed at.

"And I tire of your talk of evil omens. You said it would be an evil omen if we untied Eiriksdattir before we reached Guthrom. You said it might free her! If we hadn't done what we did, if we'd presented Guthrom a chicken, *he* would probably have slain the rest of us!"

"How do you know that we didn't free her? Perhaps she worked some sorcery upon us!"

"It was a dead chicken, Askold!"

"Then perhaps Eiriksdattir is dead. Perhaps—"

"Tell us who killed Einar and Erling and Gorm and Haki Fjolnirson then! An evil omen?"

"The maggot-spawn, Rollo!"

"And how do you explain the report that Eiriksdattir was seen in a field south of the city early this afternoon?" Buri scowled. "Rollo's sorcery?"

Askold grew distant. *"Fimbulwinter,"* he said softly. *The Saxon witch had spoken of fimbulwinter*. . ."Evil stalks all the Norselands now."

As the room went silent but for the sound of Thorir's jaws, something heavy smashed into the rear wall of the barracks. A low growling came to their ears from outside.

Buri jumped up. "Dogs," he said. "Now we have dogs trying to get to our food. Is there no end to this madness!" He rose, unsheathing his sword. Askold followed. Thorir started to rise as well, but Buri told him that two of Guthrom's best swords ought still to be a match for hungry hounds. Thorir shrugged and tore off another chunk of ham.

At the bottom of the steps, Buri stopped, then he signaled Askold around the other side of the building. He waited a moment before he himself prowled down the building's edge.

At the corner, he looked around and saw nothing. At the same time, he heard Askold scream.

His heart suddenly beating in his ears, Buri raced toward the sound. He turned the far corner to find Askold curled on his side, his fingers clutching at his chest where a stream of blood still poured out onto the ground.

Then something bit into Buri's leg. He jumped back, agony flaring in his mind. Dimly, he saw a blade retreat under the building. On that side, there was almost a two-foot gap between the earth and the barracks floor.

"Eiriksdattir!" Buri thought, desperately trying to limp farther away.

Rollo snarled as he crawled, blade first, from under the building. He locked his gaze on the wounded Viking and stalked forward, wild power surging through his limbs.

Buri's face contorted in a soundless scream as Rollo drove his sword into Buri's heart.

And then Rollo turned back for the barracks, running until he reached the steps. He started up. The door was ajar, but he kicked it violently open. Inside, there was only one to face him. Blood dripped from his blade onto the floorboards as he moved to face this last opponent.

Thorir stood, his back to the far wall, his eyes wide in disbelief and horror. Once, he had called Rollo friend . . . "You!" he said. "Rollo, you've gone mad!" He tightened the grip on his sword and wished again that the pain would leave his legs. With the threat of death before him, the throbbing only grew worse.

Growling softly, Rollo closed the distance between them. From ten feet away, he began his charge, smashing his blade down upon Thorir's.

Thorir felt the hilt of his sword disappear from his hand, then heard it clatter to the floor. As Rollo brought his blade down again, Thorir closed his eyes. And that is how he died. He had been twenty-six that day.

Rollo backed away, then slipped silently from the barracks and started for the hall of Guthrom.

As Thyri's small party passed along the edge of the grounds of the royal hall, a scream split the night's silence. Thyri commanded Gerald to halt, and she led them slowly toward a breach in the wall. At the breach, she stopped and looked in.

Guthrom had taken residence in ruins much like those south of the city, though these remained largely intact; the central structure possessed a quiet grandeur unequaled by that of any building Thyri had looked upon during her travels. To those ancient dwellers of Ebaracum, it had been a temple, a monument to the dwellers of Olympus, and a sanctuary dedicated to reflection. It yet radiated its architect's desire for unity; its pillars mirrored the heavenward thrust of the trees growing in its garden, and its strong, subtly curving lines granted an illusion of growth from the very rock of the earth.

Even so, motion in the garden gave its serenity a menacing, indistinct cast: shadowy figures moved away from Thyri across the grounds; she could see the needles of their swords shining in the moonlight.

Thyri needed to move on to the docks, but there, at the breach, she hesitated. Guthrom claimed ownership of all she saw: the ruins, the bushes, the trees of his garden. These things he did not deserve, and she possessed the power to take them away from him. And yet, his death had not been part of her plans . . . Events had moved too quickly, and were she now to seek Guthrom's downfall, she would place the lives of those who accompanied her at grave risk.

Still, she had almost stepped through the breach when she heard Megan's voice in her mind:

We need a sentinel here, white-hair, said the voice of the sorceress, *and I am the one most suited to the task. Call to me when you have secured your vessel. I will hear you.*

Megan's clipped seriousness surprised Thyri. She could find no words with which to reply as Meg brushed by her into Guthrom's garden. The sorceress looked back; her eyes told Thyri firmly that her friend understood what Thyri had been considering, and she was not going to allow it. There remained the threat of a wizard now working evil at Guthrom's side.

Thyri turned away, quickly leading Gerald and Rui on. As Gerald passed the breach, he looked in to see Megan moving cautiously toward Guthrom's hall. He paused then, watching the sorceress. After a moment, Megan seemed to turn and melt into the air, leaving Gerald's eyes naught but the moonlight glinting off the garden's grass and trees.

As they reached the docks, Thyri took cover and scanned the harbor, quickly choosing a slender oceangoing Norse vessel with a deck and cabins. The ship would require twenty oarsmen to attain speed in still waters, but she would worry about that later. For now they needed only to drift downriver. After that, Rui's crew of eight would give her oarsmen enough for a time.

As for Guthrom's guard, Thyri could see but four lone figures along the docks. The task would be easy.

A ridge composed of rigging provided her ample cover as she led her party to a point behind the guard nearest her target. From there, she moved forward alone, drawing her knife and flipping it so that she held it by its point. Ten paces from the guard's back, she stopped, raising the knife.

She paused, studying the guard's back—she knew the man, and she could not bring herself to kill him for all that she had cursed him the night before. After a moment, she stamped her foot on the deck and the guard turned.

"Sokki Gunnarson!" she whispered loudly, pulling back her hood to reveal her face.

Sokki's eyes widened. "Thy—" The greeting was cut short as his eyes took in the raised knife. He stepped forward, lowering his sword. In the moonlight, Thyri recognized the blade. "Thyri," he whispered excitedly. "What are you doing here!"

"Stealing that ship," she said, pointing with her knife at the vessel beyond.

Sokki glanced over his shoulder, then his eyes returned cautiously to Thyri. "You were going to kill me?"

She nodded. "I may still, unless you join me. But I do not desire your blood on my hands."

Slowly, Sokki fell to his knees. "I have failed you, Thyri," he said. "Through my own inaction, I failed to return to you what is rightfully yours." He looked up into her eyes, nervously turning Thyri's rune-sword in his hands so that he held it out to her hilt-first. "I have kept this blade for you these months. Please take it back."

Thyri smiled at him, shifted the knife to her other hand, and took the sword. As she gripped the weapon, she felt a part of her old self returning, as if the blade gifted her by Scacath now made her whole. "Thank you, my friend," she said softly. "I did not expect this." She looked down at Sokki, seeing in his eyes a reverence that once offended her. Now she understood how much she owed him. He had saved her life once, and now he willingly returned to her one of the few possessions she'd ever truly valued. When she had given up hope, this man had taken that hope into himself and provided it a haven.

She studied him silently. "You will remain in Guthrom's service?"

Memories of that day on the field against Alfred rushed through his mind. He could almost feel Thyri next to him, feel the power of her battle fury surging through his own veins, making him feel invincible. And invincible they had been until Guthrom's retreat . . . "No," he said. "I will follow you."

"Where are your brothers?"

He pointed to his left.

"Call them," she demanded.

"Ottar! Horik! Come quickly!"

Thyri looked right long enough to be sure that she knew the men approaching through the night, then she turned left to watch the approach of a third figure, the guard whose identity she did not yet know. For a moment, she thought the Viking would not stop before he reached her.

"Thyri!" Horik Gunnarson exclaimed behind her.

At that, the fourth guard stopped, fear spreading across his face. Thyri watched his sword start to rise, then fall again. This one would not fight her alone. He started to turn to flee. Before he could turn his face away, Thyri threw her knife, burying it between his eyes. The Viking still moved, his legs turning him back in the direction from whence he'd come before he fell face-down on the dock.

She turned back to the sons of Gunnar, glancing over their shocked faces. "I'm sorry," she said, "but I have a friend who must soon join us. I will not risk her life unnecessarily by allowing an alarm to be sounded." She fixed her gaze on Sokki's while signaling behind her for Rui and Gerald to join them. The two emerged shortly from the shadows.

Briefly, Thyri closed her eyes. *Megan!* she called in her mind. *Join me now!* She waited for a reply, but none came. From the direction of Guthrom's hall, however, a war cry suddenly erupted, and Thyri's enhanced senses picked up a distant clash of arms.

An intense fear wrapped itself around Thyri's heart, and she fought to keep it hidden. Megan was all right. Megan *had to be* all right.

"Just do as she says!" Sokki whispered to his brothers. Thyri opened her eyes and glanced at him again as she stepped by him for the ship.

"Come," she said. "We have much to do."

During the same moment that witnessed Thyri, knife poised, realizing that friends, not enemies, stood between her and her goal, a sixth man, a Viking named Arnulf, fell by Rollo's sword. Rollo, however, was not keeping count. An army stood against him; numbers didn't matter. The only thing that mattered was victory, victory and Guthrom's death.

He had fought his way onto Guthrom's grounds. Silence filled the night around him, but he knew they were out there, hunting him now. But they were mules hunting a fox more deadly than the fiercest of wolves. They could kill him, but first they'd have to catch him. And that he could not allow until Guthrom's blood had stained his sword.

He heard several sets of footsteps approaching, and reason forced him to melt into the shadow of a tree next to the wall of Guthrom's hall. The overking would be somewhere beyond that wall. Rollo could almost smell him; in his mind he could picture the unworthy ruler lounging in the luxury of his governing chamber, being tended by a stream of Saxon servants while reveling in his defeat of Eiriksdattir. Perhaps Guthrom now displayed Thyri's head at his side.

The footsteps of his enemies receding, Rollo scaled a pillar and reached the stone roof above. In the center of the ancient building, adjacent to that room centered on Guthrom's throne, was another small garden; Rollo had seen it often, though Guthrom's guard was forbidden to enter it. All close to Guthrom knew that the overking often spent hours alone there, and Rollo had heard, during one such time, the overking's voice imploring Odin not to forsake his chosen conqueror.

In places, crosshatched boards patched holes in the roof; Rollo fought the *berserk* madness inside himself, forcing his body to its hands and knees to crawl carefully along the seams of the roof toward the central garden. After what seemed an interminable time, he reached his goal safely, then dropped down to the grass.

Immediately, he sensed movement. A hulking form behind him shadowed the ground at his feet, and he spun around in defense. But the form was a statue, a rendering of the god the dead empire named Jupiter. Again, he sensed movement, and this time he dove. The singing sound of an iron blade split the air behind him.

Rollo landed and rolled, raising his sword. A human form now blocked out the moonlight from above. Metal clanged against metal; Rollo's grip held, and he kicked up at his attacker, rolling again after his feet connected with flesh and the shadow backed away.

He gained his feet then, and he glared over his blade at Guthrom. The overking stood in Jupiter's shadow. For a moment, the two Vikings did not move, then Guthrom stepped out into the moonlight and relaxed his stance. He wore only a wrap of fur about his waist, and a sheen of sweat coated his skin with a silver glaze. He stood taller than Rollo, and the muscles of his arms and chest rippled as he shifted his grip on his blade.

"You," Guthrom growled softly. "You disappointed me, Rollo. I have waited for you here."

Rollo didn't reply; he flew at Guthrom almost before the last words passed the overking's lips. His attack pressed the larger man back, and Guthrom thudded into the statue's base. Rollo attacked again, but Guthrom moved quickly, and Rollo's blade bit into stone. He jerked it free and turned in search of his opponent.

Guthrom stood under the moonlight again. Blood streamed

down his sword arm where Rollo's last attack had grazed his shoulder. The overking bellowed, his battle cry shaking the night. Rollo returned the bellow with one of his own and braced himself to turn back Guthrom's charge.

The overking's weight crashed into him, and Rollo felt the force of the attack surge down through his legs. He stood his ground, and threw Guthrom back. Guthrom fell, and Rollo let him rise before he charged anew, his sword whirling in the night, forcing Guthrom's retreat with each blow. So consumed by the fury of the battle was Rollo that he scarcely noticed that Guthrom had backed out of the garden and onto the pillared landing that edged the throne room.

Within the throne room, a growing audience—ten already of Guthrom's guard, Rollo's former peers, and an equal number of Saxon servants—watched the two combatants. Still, Rollo pressed the attack into the throne room, oblivious to the presence of all save the sweating, faltering Viking he had once sworn to serve with his life.

In the end, Guthrom said nothing of great note, and for all the overking's power, Rollo's *berserk* fury never allowed him even a weak counterattack. Methodically, Rollo pressed him all the way to the far wall, and Guthrom's guard watched, dumbstruck. Halfway to the wall, Rollo's sword bit deep into Guthrom's stomach, tearing it from side to side. At the wall, Rollo buried his blade into Guthrom's heart.

And then he turned. The rest of the guard moved uncertainly, their faces a mixture of awe and fear. Rollo glared at them, not recognizing any of the faces, seeing only enemies whose leader's blood still dripped from the point of his blade. Slowly, his enemies spread out, cautiously drawing their swords.

During that moment, Rollo Anskarson could have commanded the allegiance of the Danes of Jorvik, and none would have opposed him. He could have taken Guthrom's place, and he could even have taken the battle, once again, to the southern lands of Alfred if he'd wished.

Instead, Rollo attacked again, and ten expert blades rose up against his one. He killed one man, then another, but as he felled the third, he felt iron bite into his thigh, cutting through flesh and into bone. He looked down at the wound, stunned that he could feel no pain. He raised his blade against the man who had dealt the injury, then a blow of incredible power smashed into him, knocking him back, to the ground, into darkness.

* * *

Thyri grew tired of inspecting the ship's two cabins and stepped impatiently back out on the deck. *Megan!* she thought loudly. *Answer me!*

She looked anxiously toward Guthrom's hall. The clash of arms had ended. Horik passed in front of her, carrying supplies to Ottar, who packed them into the ship's small hold.

Rui appeared at Thyri's side. "She is strong," the man said strangely, as if he understood her thoughts. "She will come."

"Did you learn much, traveler?" she asked sharply, recalling his request to join her and reacting against his invasion of her anxiety. "Did you learn much from my capturing of this vessel?"

"Certainly," he answered.

She looked at him. "And?"

"I learned that you know what you're doing." He smiled at her curiously; the expression intensified the alien set of his features. "It would be unfair to your friend if I assumed that she does not." His smile faded before he turned and went to help Sokki and Gerald load the rigging.

Thyri looked up at the waxing moon and felt like screaming. If she had to endure the moon's curse again, without Megan awaiting her in the morning, she didn't know what she would do. The sorceress had given new meaning to her life; thought of losing her so swiftly terrified her. Guthrom had his wizard, and they did not know his power . . .

White-hair!

Megan! she replied uncertainly, fearing now that Meg's call could be an illusion of the night. *You're okay?*

Fine. But I'm not alone.

Thyri sighed relief. She wanted to ask Megan why she had ignored her earlier calls, but she'd known that all along: with Guthrom's wizard nearby, *any* exercise of Megan's powers—necessary or frivolous—placed them in danger. Rui had been right; she'd been wrong to speak harshly to him. On the other hand, Thyri knew Megan, and she knew that the sorceress had seldom, if ever, had to fight for her life. Powerful she was, but power was worthless against the unexpected; Astrid's death had been proof enough of that.

White-hair! You must concentrate deeply on a flat hard place near you.

She looked around, then raced by Gerald onto the dock. There, she stopped, looking down the planks before her. After a moment, the air ahead shimmered as two forms began to take shape in front of Thyri's eyes. Thyri restrained herself from leaping into Meg's arms until her nose verified the sorceress's complete materialization. Next to Megan, the second form collapsed onto the dock.

"Odin!" Thyri whispered. "I thought I'd lost you again. Did you clash with Guthrom's wizard?"

"I saw no sign of him at all."

"Perhaps he has fled." Thyri dug her fingers into Megan's back before she stepped away and looked down at the limp form at her feet. She nudged it with her foot, bringing its face into the moonlight. The slow but deliberate motion of the man's chest assured her that he lived.

"He slew Guthrom," Megan offered, "but he would have been slain himself had I not intervened. He seemed a great warrior, and I could not bring myself to leave him."

The man moaned and coughed, then kicked one leg spasmodically. Blood seeped slowly from a slender gash in his leg. Thyri bent and gripped him under the arm.

"Be careful with the leg," Megan said. "I did not have time to heal it fully. It was a dire wound."

Thyri nodded, then lifted the man from his wounded side. His eyes fluttered open, and he looked at her dully as his other leg uncertainly tested the deck beneath him.

"Eiriksdattir," he said softly. "So this is death?"

"No, Rollo," she said. "Not quite." Patiently, she helped the Viking onto her ship.

Magic

Rollo tried to sit and winced as pain flared up from his wounded leg. "I *am* alive," he said emphatically, then he collapsed back to the deck and looked at Thyri. "I saw you captured! You could not have survived that ordeal."

Thyri looked at him oddly, slowly realizing that he must have witnessed the events that morning at the country tavern. She should have suspected something then, what with the leader of the riders calling out Rollo's name. "That wasn't me they captured," she said simply, looking at Meg and glancing at Rollo's leg. The sorceress nodded and went to bend over the man.

"What of Fandis?" Rollo asked. "Is she alive as well?"

"I don't know that name," Thyri said. "How did you find me this morning?"

Rollo propped himself up on one elbow while Megan examined his wound. Wincing occasionally under Megan's probing fingers, he told Thyri how he had sought to find her, how he had gone to Fandis for aid, how she had directed him to her, and then how he had seen her fall. And then he told how Guthrom had hung the head of the river witch at Jorvik's south gate.

The images Rollo painted with his words sobered Thyri; she couldn't help feeling that she was the source of all that had transpired. At least Guthrom had died . . . She glanced at Megan, who returned her gaze.

So here is Guthrom's wizard, the sorceress said silently.

Thyri nodded, and Megan looked down into Rollo's eyes. "I can heal your leg," she said, "but you must sleep." She passed her hand over his eyes, and the reflections off her ring fluttered about him, then began to steal away his thoughts. He didn't fight the magic.

As the ship drifted downriver, and as Guthrom's harbor receded into the distance, Megan remained bent over Rollo and began to sing. Gerald and the sons of Gunnar still worked, readying the mainsail, but the sound of Megan's voice stopped them with its beauty. Almost in concert, Sokki, Horik, and Ottar abandoned their task and sat back against the port gunwale; Rui and Gerald sat on the starboard side, balancing the load. And Megan sang.

She swayed over Rollo, unaware of how her lyricless, soaring song of healing enchanted the entire crew. Ottar heard in her voice the simple, pleasant comfort of childhood, and Sokki thought of tales he'd heard of the One God's angels. Megan's voice transported Horik to the shore of a moonlit lake, and Rui to a place half the world away where he'd once contemplated the beauty of a single drop of water on a blade of grass.

For Gerald, it was as if the song became part of the night, and the night the song, with the stars themselves dancing off each note, each phrase.

And when she finished, Megan looked up at Thyri as if time hadn't passed, as if the song that had passed her lips had been as natural and unremarkable as breathing.

"Do we yet require Rui's crew?" Megan asked.

"To man the ship," Thyri answered, "yes. Actually, we'll need more than that. This was one of Guthrom's best ships, and we'll need thirty oars in battle to handle it."

Is that all? You've not been thinking of building a fleet? Raising another army as you did across the water?

No, Megan. Where is the use for that?

"What if I could provide enchantments to make this vessel obey the commands of four oars, even two oars?"

"Then we would not need the crew."

"But you have already paid them!" Rui spoke out.

Megan turned to him, reaching into one pocket of her cloak. She withdrew a handful of corn and held it out for Rui to see, then she passed her other hand over the corn. She smiled; five pieces of silver now rested in her palm.

Rui creased his forehead and reached into his own pocket, withdrawing a handful of coins. Megan touched his hand, and two of the coins shriveled into golden grains.

Rui laughed. "Brilliant! But dangerous—you risked mutiny."

"Mutiny," Thyri said softly, "requires the demise of the ship's captain."

Megan looked at Rui. "Had we the money, we would have given it gladly. But we are not rich. They would have been paid in the end, just as you shall be, if that is what you desire." She took the grains of corn from his hand.

Sokki chuckled. "So where do we go?" he asked.

"Let's go back, depose Guthrom, and make Thyri queen!" Ottar offered excitedly.

"Guthrom's dead. Rollo killed him." Thyri pointed to the deck where the Viking snored softly.

Ottar dropped his eyes, feeling as if his mother had just admonished him for failing to strap up his boots.

"Then it will be that much easier, Thyri," Horik said, "to make you queen. We can make the Danes follow you! We can take the war again into Alfred's lands!"

"Do you not think, Brother," Sokki said to him, "that the Danes would have already crowned Thyri had she wanted that? Any true Viking who witnessed—"

"Enough!" Thyri said. "I do not want that. I do not feel like a queen."

"Then where shall we go?"

"Anywhere."

"And what shall we call this vessel bound for anywhere?"

"Nightreaver," Gerald said. It was his first word since they'd pushed off the dock, and even as he said it, he wondered what had inspired the sudden utterance. But since they'd shipped, he'd felt incredibly at peace with the night around him, and Megan's song had carved the atmosphere into the stony cliffs of his memory. And reavers—that was what they were: Norsemen, reavers—at least five of the eight of them. Reavers of night.

Thyri grinned. "*Nightreaver.* So be it."

Thyri had indeed chosen one of Guthrom's best vessels. *Nightreaver* was a war boat, crafted in Vestfold where Harald had collected the most talented shipbuilders in all of the Norselands. Guthrom had come by it as a battle prize, and he would have made it his flagship if he hadn't abandoned the sea for the conquest of land.

Under normal circumstances, Thyri should have had a crew of sixty-odd. As it was, the six men on board faced a near impossible task in manning the sail in rough winds. The ship stretched seventy feet from stern to bow, and it could achieve speeds, under sail, exceeding ten knots.

With only eight people on board, Thyri could almost picture them as ants bent to the task of managing a horse. But the presence of Megan added her sorcery to their strengths. And if they picked up a crew of nameless faces, men whom she did not know, as she had not really known the crew of the *Black Rabbit* . . .

That slaughter came back to her, acute in every detail: the

screams, the blood . . . The hunger, and Elaine's pleading eyes . . . She would not allow it to happen again.

And so they drifted south down the river. Ottar and Horik retrieved a keg of ale from the hold, and Rui told all a long story of a warrior of his homeland who had once challenged the fire-breathing god of the mountains and lost. It was said that when the molten rock spilled out of the earth near the warrior's village, the warrior's face could be seen in its surface, twisting in pain as it flowed slowly down the mountainside, destroying all in its path.

Midway through the story, Rollo wakened. He felt dazed, and the strangeness of his company, and the fact that his leg bore not even a scar, fueled a nagging doubt that he yet lived. But if this was Asgard, then Rui might be Aesir, and Rollo did not care to interrupt a god's tale to ask where he was. Groggily, the Viking rose and went to the cask of ale, keeping his silence.

As Rui finished his story, Megan took a small leather pouch from her cloak and tipped its contents into her palm. Two small gems—twins of the one she had sent Thyri for her summoning—fell onto her skin; from where Gerald sat, he could see little beyond a faint blue glow until Megan took one of the stones from her palm and held it up under the moonlight, where it became, for the others, a glittering new star. When the sorceress lowered her hand, the gemstone remained fixed in the air before her. She closed her eyes and began again to sing.

This time, the others could *feel* her song; it became part of the night. Megan's ring began to sparkle, then shine, its light brighter even than the moon's, its beams reaching out to engulf the ship. The aqua gem's brilliance grew to rival the ring's; sparks flew from it, streaking the ring's silver light with scintillating greens and dark blues.

Gerald felt the deck become like clay beneath him while Megan's song and the light wrapped about him, holding him. And the clay beneath him flowed and stretched. Behind the sorceress, the deck rose up and two additional cabins began to take shape. Near the bow, benches for oarsmen began to melt under the ring's power, and the prow stretched out, a ghoulish shape wrapping about its length like a demon caressing it in the night.

The little gem exploded in a blinding shower, and then the night itself fell on the ship, painting it black from bow to stern. Megan's singing abruptly ceased. No one moved until she opened her eyes. She smiled weakly.

"Odin!" Rollo gasped. He *was* dead.

Gerald wiped his forehead and gazed in amazement at the sorceress, only dimly aware that the wood beneath him was solid again.

Megan reached down for her ale-filled cup and brought it up to her lips. "Now," she said, "I can relax and enjoy this." She looked at Thyri. *The talismans of power you gave me, my love, are strong, are they not? This last one we shall keep for the future*. She tipped the remaining gem back into its pouch.

Thyri smiled at her, but concern lurked at the corners of her smile. *You look pale, Megan. You should have rested first.*

Megan chuckled, smiling warmly. *I am always pale.*

Thyri scolded her briefly with her eyes, then Sokki moved, capturing her attention. The man rose and went to the prow, his hand hesitantly reaching out to touch the hindquarters of the beast Megan had shaped. Thyri followed his actions. *You cannot escape it,* she heard Megan again in her mind, *but now you command it*.

The beast shaped around the prow—the sight that would first confront any enemy they approached—was a huge, black wolf. It had only to move to seem alive.

Throughout the remainder of the night, the only thing that felt real to Gerald was the ale. Drunkenness was not normally his habit, but that night he welcomed it. The others were in a similar mood; this became apparent when Ottar and Horik launched into a series of drinking songs without considering the presence of two women in their midst. Rui and Gerald soon added their voices to the noise.

Thyri didn't mind; she drank quietly, said little, and felt simple contentment inside, as if she dreamed a pleasant dream that no longer threatened transformation into nightmare. Her only concern was Megan; the others couldn't notice, but the sorceress had expended much in her last casting. Megan's ever-erect carriage slumped when its mistress grew careless, and fatigue lingered behind her eyes. What concerned Thyri was not so much that her friend was exhausted, but that Megan tried to hide the fact and did not seem of a mind to sleep it off—a small thing, perhaps, except that they did not know what dangers might lie ahead, nor how soon they would have to confront them.

Still, all was peaceful. And the sorceress, after all, had embarked on a new adventure of her own. Thyri guessed that the present circumstance had summoned up the child within her, and this suspicion was confirmed as Megan began to pick up on the choruses of the others' songs and join in, adding her voice without inhibition to the otherwise raucous cacophony.

Gerald watched Megan also, finding the joyousness of her expression difficult to believe. He did not yet know that she had spent her life on a relatively small island, among people who either loathed or feared her. She hadn't been treated casually since she'd been a girl, and the ale and the night and the songs had brought something to life inside of her that had not lived in years.

As dawn began to tinge the eastern horizon, Thyri staggered drunkenly to Rollo's side. The Viking's silence had gradually come to disturb her, and she'd slowly come to guess at its causes. She took his cup, went to the keg to slosh more ale into it, and returned it to his hand. "Look at me," she said firmly.

Rollo's eyes met hers; she searched his expression, finding both tenderness and fear. It was the fear that she meant to dispel. She took his hands in hers and squeezed. "You are alive," she said. "And so am I. This is not Asgard. If you don't say you believe me, I'm going to start punching you."

A faint smile spread across his lips. "I believe you—I think."

"It's true, Rollo. When you die, are you not to go to Valhalla, to Odin's hall?"

"So it is said."

"And does this ship seem to you like a hall?"

"No."

"And how does one get to Odin's hall?"

"The Valkyrie."

"Have you seen Valkyrie this night?"

"No," he acknowledged.

"Listen, Rollo! While you slept, while you healed, these Vikings suggested I return to take Guthrom's throne. That throne is rightly yours, and you have but to ask and I'll turn this ship and we'll go back and make you king. If we do this, all the Vikings, these included, will be yours to command." Thyri nodded toward the sons of Gunnar. Ottar had collapsed against the gunwale and already snored softly. Horik bent over his cup, all but asleep himself while Sokki was slurring something in the direction of Rui, Gerald, and Megan.

Rollo followed Thyri's gaze and laughed. He looked back into Thyri's eyes. "Last night," he said, "I swore my sword into your service. If you will not be queen, then I cannot be king."

Thyri smiled at him, squeezed his hands again, and went for more ale.

Megan had gifted *Nightreaver* with two extra cabins—enough space for all on board to live comfortably. This night, however, the ale tarnished her magic in its way, and sleep claimed all of them where they sat.

Avalon

In her tower, she dreamed, the orb of Babd clutched to her breast. Her physical form shook under the dream's violent intensity, and the beauty she had crafted in her face faltered, her features contorting into horrible grimaces, her fingernails cracking against the unyielding surface of the orb.

And yet, in her dream, she refused her body's limits. She pushed it, commanding its lungs to take in more air, commanding its heart to beat faster and faster, pumping its strength into the flight of her soul.

She had soared over the seas, seeking a means of escape. Her quest had taken her to the eastern shores of Arthur's kingdom. On a river there, she had found a vessel that had given her hope, and it was coming her way, into her waters, into the reach of her powers.

All on board possessed great strength, but it was Edain who had first attracted her attention. Or at least, the woman had felt like Edain.

Though she had been pressing herself on her quest for nearly a full day, Morgana refused to return to her body. Not yet . . . She couldn't yet; she needed to know more, and she needed to be sure that the craft would not dock before it reached the sea. Through the mortal hearts on board, she sought the answer to that question, and she felt a dark joy as she learned that all thought themselves bound for the sea.

Into the immortal hearts, she could see little. The one felt like Edain, and then not like Edain. If she were Edain, she possessed power greater than ever in the past. Morgana had little desire to confront such strength, but if it could grant her freedom . . .

In the next immortal heart, she found the darkness that she truly sought. This heart Morgana could persuade; this heart she could use. She studied it long.

When she finally left, she did not do so on the demands of her body, but on a growing fear that Edain would discover her presence.

She would learn of it soon enough, but not now . . .

Nightreaver

Throughout the morning, the crew of *Nightreaver* woke, shook off the ale, and made their way to the cabins. The sons of Gunnar elected to share one amongst them; Gerald found himself bunking with Rui, and Rollo had a cabin to himself. Thyri and Megan shared the captain's cabin.

Before she retired, and against Thyri's protests, Megan cast a simple spell to keep *Nightreaver* centered in the river, and then, for a few brief hours, none on board was awake to guide the ship. After she woke again, Megan took pains to shield the vessel from the eyes of those on ships traveling upriver for Jorvik, but during that time while all slept, *Nightreaver*'s dark, black lines and its wolf's head prow impressed observers as a demonic vessel; other captains on the river steered well clear.

In the light of day, Thyri couldn't bring herself to scold her friend for dispensing again her powers, even though Megan's fatigue had grown more apparent, and she looked as if she'd slept not at all. Upon reflection, Megan's spell did seem a wise one. Pursuit by Guthrom's armada could not be discounted, and in such an event, the invisibility Megan granted the ship could save it. And, after all, Megan *was* the sorceress and, as such, knew best her abilities. And Rui's scolding kept returning to Thyri's mind; against her better judgment—and her understanding of Megan's lack of combat experience—she kept silent.

Later, after all had risen, they ate from the ship's stores. They were wanting for nothing—Horik and Ottar had packed the hold full, and it was capable of providing for seventy men for ten days. With only eight mouths to feed, they could survive on the water for months without setting foot on land.

After eating, the sons of Gunnar and Rollo took up the ship's oars, and all were amazed at the speed they quickly attained. Thyri called Rui into her cabin, leaving Gerald to help Megan look ahead for danger. The sorceress perched herself on the small foredeck she'd created the night before, and Gerald stood next to her, feeling useless again as he couldn't imagine his eyes being more effective than those of the sorceress.

The cabin Thyri shared with Meg was, like the others, black inside as well as out. On one side, also like the others, a table extended out of the wall, and there were several chairs fixed to the floor about the table. In the center of the table was an oil-burning lamp, while brackets around the walls held several other lamps.

Unlike the other cabins, Thyri's boasted a large table for charts and one large bed instead of wall-bunks. This last fact did not surprise Rui; rather, it affirmed what he'd suspected about Thyri and Megan during those times he'd seen them together. In this way, the archer was much like Gerald.

One other item marked Thyri's cabin uniquely: over the bed, a large painting covered the major part of the wall. It was a scene of woodlands, with mountain peaks reaching toward the sky in the distance. Above the peaks, a full moon cast an eerie glaze over the landscape. Rui had never seen a work of art rendered with such realism; he assumed that the painting had decorated the cabin before Thyri had taken the ship. This was not so; Megan had created it as part of her sorcery the night before, and none of *Nightreaver*'s crew could have guessed at the purpose which it served.

Thyri sat at the table and had Rui sit across from her. She'd brought a bottle of wine in with her from the hold, and neither of them spoke until she'd uncorked it and poured two glasses. Rui drank with her; the wine was good, but after the night before he would have preferred a less potent brew.

Thyri stretched back in her chair and truly surprised the traveler for the first time since he'd first heard her speak. The surprise came in the form of a question, and the question was this: "You said you came from the land of the sun, Rui. In this land of the sun, does the sun still set and the moon rise?"

"Of course," he answered. "Does the moon not rise over all lands?"

"I suppose," she said distantly; then she smiled sadly and looked into his eyes. "That is not why I called you here. I wanted to ask you of your travels; I have been no farther south than the Frankish lands. I have heard of lands beyond—are they interesting?"

"Yes," he said. "There are places where winter does not come. Many strange sights. In one land, there are temples the size of small mountains, and no one knows who built them. In another, the people are wild, and they have skin the color of night. There is much to see in the South, if seeing is what you desire."

Thyri had grown distant again. "At the moment, my friend, I can think of nothing else."

"You seem troubled," he said. "You should not be so. I have done many interesting things in my years, but the most interesting of all was joining you last night. You are a woman, but you carry yourself like the bravest of men. I've seen enough of your skill to know that I would never dare cross arms with you, and yet you are not arrogant. You are a mystery, more so than those temples, because you are alive. Are you a goddess?"

She laughed. "Please, not again!" She paused and filled her cup. "I am not a goddess, Rui."

"Is Megan?"

She looked at him curiously. "I do not know. Perhaps. Perhaps we are all gods in our way. What makes a god a god?"

"Immortality."

"Then there are no gods," she said flatly. She fell silent for a while, and when she spoke again, she told him to go, to tell the others to fare south when they reached the sea.

After he'd left, Thyri sat long in thought, staring into the painting over her bed, into the eye of the moon.

In two nights, the moon in this world—the real world—would be full.

They could be far from land at sunset.

She prayed Megan's magic would work.

Water

Later that evening they reached the sea; they raised the mainsail and fared out, away from the coast, and headed south. Then came the storm.

It had been a peaceful, starry night when clouds suddenly darkened the sky and the first giant spear of lightning streaked across the heavens. Thunder crashed, and just before the rains fell, the four Norse crewmen joked that, somewhere above, Sif had just accused her husband, Thor, of infidelity and now the Thunderer was breaking his hammer against her head (Sif's head being the hardest substance in Asgard). Rollo chuckled at the joke (it had started as Horik's, then Ottar had expanded the theme), but Fandis's prophecy of *fimbulwinter* darkened his mirth, suggesting more insidious objects for Thor's wrath.

Such was the banter as they lowered and secured the mast and stowed the sail; then the rains came and the sea rose up violently against them and all became more concerned with staying on board than with jokes and dark prophecies.

Thyri and Megan were in their cabin when the storm hit. Megan immediately sat up on the bed and fell into a trance; Thyri rose and exited, running to help Sokki and Rollo, who were struggling to close the hold. After that, she made sure that the crew all safely reached the cabins.

When Thyri returned to Megan, the sorceress opened her eyes, and Thyri saw fear now mingled with fatigue. "This storm is not natural!" Megan shouted. She closed her eyes again and grimaced, as if she struggled with some powerful, sorcerous foe.

Thyri stood in the doorway and glared up at the sky, heedless of the pelting rain that stung her cheeks. At that moment, the ship lurched violently, throwing her into the cabin, toward Meg. For a moment, it was as if the sorceress rushed straight at her. She twisted in midair, narrowly missing her friend, but now Megan moved as well. The sorceress's head cracked loudly against the bed's headboard.

Thyri braced her own collision with her hands, then scrambled to Meg's side. The sorceress was unconscious, but still alive. Thyri placed her hand under Megan's head and it came away beaded with blood. Anxiously, she turned Megan onto her stomach, took a knife, and carefully began to cut Meg's hair around the wound, revealing a large, oozing bruise. She tore off a piece of sheet and pressed it against the wound, then rolled Megan over and lay next to her, trying to brace both of them against the continuing, violent jerkings of the ship.

Across the room, the cabin's door flapped loudly against the wall several times before the ship lurched once in the opposite direction and slammed the door shut.

Nightreaver's crew had all gathered in Rollo's cabin and braced themselves against the walls. Conversation was difficult, and little was said (or shouted) until Rui protested that the storm should be no match for Megan's powers. This thought began to consume them all until Sokki finally volunteered to rise and check on Thyri and Megan. He went out, returning minutes later with the news that Megan had been hurt. After that, each fell into his own thoughts as they struggled to ride out the storm.

Gates of black iron, their portals shaped of intertwined serpents, rose up before the sorceress. Machinery ground beyond, and the metallic rumbling grew deafening.

Megan raised her hand over her head and called forth her ring's magic: that flame from the fires of creation gifted her by Fand of the floating gardens and bound into the metal by Andvari the dwarf. The power came in spurts; she had tapped it too often of late. And she was tired, and a numbing pain threatened to blacken her vision. Where was she? What had happened to the ship?

She gritted her teeth and commanded more energy from her ring. The pain's grip tightened on her mind, then the power surged, and she forgot all else as she struggled to save herself from the fury of her own magic. The silver flames fought against her, and cackling laughter penetrated through to echo malevolently between her ears. A sibilant voice came in the wake of the laughter, its whispery hiss invoking names unspoken since the fall of Danu's children. They were old names—weak names—but even as Megan cast them out they tested her strength, forcing her to draw further on her reserves until the voice retreated into its laughter and then was gone.

Megan stood alone then, cloaked in her flames. Her anger swelled; her attacker had toyed with her with weak magics, and she had almost faltered. She took part of her fire within herself, soothing her pain, bracing herself for the next assault, but none came. For a moment she stood, eyeing the black gates solemnly. She took one step forward, then raised her magic high over her head and smashed it against the gates. Again, the effort sapped her strength; she could feel the straining tendons in her neck and hear the blood pounding in her temples. She sensed dark clouds lurking beyond the edge of her mind, swirling, prowling, seeking a weakness, a way in. The laughter lurked there, among the clouds.

As her magic spread out over the gates, the sorceress screamed, focusing the negative energy of her rage. She stepped forward again, and a resounding crack split the air.

The gates flew open, and Megan's silver surged through. The laughter rushed at her now with the roar of an aural army; she quickly drew back her magic to shield herself from the overbearing sound, then, slowly, she walked between the opened gates. As she stepped through, the laughter faded and the voice returned. "Welcome to my world, child," the voice hissed.

Megan retained her shield and said nothing. She did not know her attacker's voice, and its mystery nagged at her. She would ask of the voice its name, but to do so would show her ignorance, her weakness. She had been named a child. Young she was, but no child. And a match for her opponent? Time would tell . . . She had not lost yet; she yet lived.

The hiss fluttered a moment into laughter. "I am Arthur's bane," the voice said as if it knew her thoughts. "I am Morgana, child. And you have already lost. Death is not the only defeat."

Megan heard the gates slam shut behind her. She whirled then to see them shimmer and dissipate into wispy nothingness.

The voice laughed again, then left her in silence.

At dawn, the storm fled as quickly as it had risen. Thyri was first to gain the deck, and first to gasp at the scene that greeted her eyes:

Straight ahead, a dark granite tower blocked out the rising sun as *Nightreaver* drifted slowly into a quiet harbor. The island out of which the tower grew was small, almost impossibly so, but it was the tower that claimed Thyri's unswerving attention. Anger burned inside of her; Megan's last words rang continuously through her mind: *This storm is not natural.* She thought of her friend, still prostrate in their cabin; she seethed. She had no doubt that the tower's resident had sent them that storm, no doubt that the storm had drawn them there. If Megan died, she would bring that tower crashing into the sea before she would leave.

Rollo was first to reach her side. "Odin!" he exclaimed.

Thyri looked at him a moment before going to her cabin for her sword. As *Nightreaver* eased up to the sandy beach, she strapped her blade to her side.

"I will get the others," Rollo said, starting to turn.

"No!" she commanded. "I will go alone. Stay here with Megan. Guard her with your life." She turned without another word. *Nightreaver* ground to a halt, and Thyri jumped down into the waist-deep water and started for shore.

Fire

Off the beach, a path to the tower's door invited Thyri as if it were carpet laid at her feet. She stepped upon it, her anger forcing each step without caution.

As she neared the tower, she thought briefly of Castle Kaerglen, the only other structure she'd seen of similar, forbidding construction. The tower looked hewn of solid rock. High above, a solitary window looked out to sea. At the end of the path, a massive wooden door broke the seamless expanse of stone. Her sense for sorcery went wild. While she looked at the door, it swung open as if her eyes had pushed it in.

She never reached it; near the tower's foot, a mist rose up and enshrouded her, and her next strep was upon stone.

As each moment transformed achingly into the next, a deafening roar filled the silence. It built slowly, heralded by the deep, persistent thumping of her own heart: the drumbeat orchestrating the flow of blood through her body, the wellspring of the roar.

Never had she felt so alone. Blackness had cloaked her since Morgana's departure, and she'd nothing but her own churning thoughts for company, thoughts that came and went, flitting through her mind like cautious butterflies pursued by the dragons of nightmare. At times, when she peered out, evasive white lights would dot the void, temporary pinpricks in the black fabric; nothing stayed. She could move—swim through the darkness—but reach nowhere, each place attained was ever like the last.

Then—after eternity—another sound: just a faint, distant whiff of a voice, but in the silence, it boomed like thunder, drowning out the sounds of her heartbeat and the blood rushing through her veins. She felt the pain in her head again, and she focused on it, gathering her other thoughts around it, fighting desperately to regain her will. As she fought, silver sparks began to stream forth from her ring. In the darkness, the silver shined like life itself. The sight heartened her, and she coaxed the magic forth consciously now until she stood in the void, bathed in the light of her magic

She had not *lost. Morgana could not hold her.*

In a burst of brilliance, she filled the void with silver. The magic showered, exploding in the darkness. She poured it forth until she felt cold stone beneath her feet.

She looked down at the stones. Her feet were like mist, insubstantial, without flesh.

Her body was elsewhere . . .Still back at the ship? Never mind, she thought. For this battle, flesh would be useless . . .

A round chamber—how far up the tower, Thyri didn't know. On one side, a spiral staircase wound both up and down. In the center of the chamber was a large table, laden with a feast enough to feed twenty men. On the far side of the table was a woman. When Thyri's eyes fixed on her, the woman rose.

She was tall and slender, perhaps twenty years old, if that. Her gown was dark violet, and her dark hair spilled down well past her waist. She possessed great beauty, but her eyes were cold, impersonal. Thyri looked into them and drew her sword.

"Won't you dine with me?" the woman asked. Her voice was sweet—like honey. With the sound, Thyri felt a hunger consume her; her mouth filled with saliva, and the aromas of the feast on the table assailed her nose. The woman's eyes grew warm, and Thyri began to lose her sense of time.

She forced herself forward, trying to throw off the bewitchment.

"At least speak with me," the woman said. "You cannot kill me. If you do, you can never leave."

Thyri stopped, she felt the tower's walls pressing in on her, crushing her, strangling her, suffocating her. She forced another step.

"I invited your entrance, and only I can invite your exit." The voice was like nectar, intoxicating. *"Don't you see? Look at me. Look at my body. Is it not beautiful?"*

The woman filled Thyri's eyes. Thyri could almost touch her. Scents of honeysuckle and sweat danced in the air. Supple flesh moved sensually under velvet; breasts pushed themselves enticingly toward Thyri's mouth, then drew away, but the woman's soft eyes drew her in. *"I am heaven, and heaven is yours. I will trade, my body for yours."*

Thyri concentrated hard and forced another step.

* * *

Rollo turned on Ottar. "If you suggest again that we follow her, I will kill you!"

"But, Rollo," Sokki intervened, "we must do something!"

"Guard Megan! Those were her orders! We do not know what we face here. You saw Thyri disappear as did I! How do you propose we follow?"

Sokki glared at Rollo, put one hand on the ship's gunwale, and jumped over the side into the water.

Rollo lurched forward and looked down as Sokki splashed toward the beach. He started forward, then felt a hand on his shoulder. He turned to see the face of the archer.

"No, Rollo," the strange man said. "The folly of one man should not tempt that of another."

"Sokki!" Ottar shouted, rushing for the gunwale.

Gerald pushed his way to Rollo's side. "Whatever happens now, Rollo, he shouldn't go alone."

Rollo turned his eyes to shore; Sokki had gained the beach and headed inland without looking back.

"We can't all go," Rui said to Gerald. "This is a witch place. We may see no enemy now, but that is perhaps the greatest danger. Magic and danger fill this air, can't you feel it?"

Rollo looked desperately from Gerald's eyes to Rui's, then to the shore and Sokki. "He can't go alone," he said. "I will follow." He lifted his leg to the gunwale.

"No," Ottar shouted, vaulting overboard. He landed in the water and struggled to keep his feet. When he finally stood, he drew his sword and held it over his head, then turned briefly, squinting up at the faces who stared at him from above. "I will go," he declared to Rollo. "He is my brother."

With that said, Ottar started for the beach.

"My body for yours . . . My body for yours . . ."

Thyri screamed as her bones wrenched. Her vision blacked out, then, suddenly, the river of her nightmares—the river of blood—stretched out from her feet toward the horizon . . .

"My body for yours! I will take your curse! I will take your curse and your nightmares . . ."

Megan stood before Thyri in the river. She held out her arms, but Thyri leapt, her fangs digging into Megan's smooth flesh, ripping into her throat.

"Yes!" she screamed. "Take it!"

"My body for yours . . . My body for yours?"

"Yes!"

The river of blood disappeared, and the woman danced before

her, drawing closer, into her. A cold darkness began to wrap itself around her heart.

Then a brightness flared up through the darkness, and the woman screamed. Thyri felt the clouds around her mind tear away. She felt her blade in her hand again. She opened her eyes, and the room, this time, appeared nearly bare. On the table, where once she'd seen a feast, she now saw only dust—the deposits of years of neglect. The enchantment had broken. Of all the room's ornaments, only the woman looked the same; her transcendent beauty alone had been authentic.

As for sorcery, traces lingered in the air. Streams of light, like errant moonbeams: Megan's ring magic.

Behind the woman, Megan stood, ethereal, silver. Thyri's attacker turned to face the threat of the sorceress.

She watched Megan and saw again the vision Morgana had shown her, the warping of her old nightmares. *I will take your curse! My body for yours!* She tried to press forward, but still couldn't move.

One moment before, they had come within ten paces of the tower's foot. Sokki could see the grain of the granite and its dull polish, the smooth sheen hewn by centuries of pelting, unrelenting sea winds.

Now, he could see only white. Fog cloaked them—they were under attack. He rushed forward for the tower's gate—or where he thought the doors had been. He met only the tower's ungiving walls. And Thyri remained inside . . . He had to help her. Keeping his hands on the tower, he began to move along its face, frantically seeking the feel of wood.

"Sokki!" Ottar called to him.

He pressed against the stone. The door had disappeared! Everything around him was white unless he pressed against the granite. An inch away from the gray stone, the walls were invisible.

"Sokki!"

He couldn't answer. Tearfully, he slumped against the stone. He had failed Thyri. She was lost inside.

"Hello, Morgana," Megan said. "You should not have told me your name!" She stared into the eyes of the ancient demoness, unleashing the remaining potential of her ring toward them.

Her attack was met by a sheet of red fire that sprang up inches from Morgana's face. The silver met the fire and, for a moment, seemed to penetrate the shield. Then, to Megan's horror, her magic began to spread out over Morgana's shield and dissipate harmlessly around its edges.

She dove to the side, using the fury of the conflict between them for cover. In that last blast, she had expended the last of her ring's power, and several hours would be required before the talisman could support even the simplest of castings. Frantically, she searched her memory for some knowledge that might aid her. During all the years she'd spent in study, she'd given precious little time to the contemplation of battle magics. She'd never considered the possibility that the ring's attack could be turned back! She cursed herself—her vanity—for giving the witch the chance to face her, the chance to turn. The first blast of her ring had been meant solely to command Morgana's attention; the attack had been weak, but it had surprised Morgana and bypassed her defenses. Her second, more powerful attack had not, and now she would pay.

Gaining her feet, she whispered a short charm of defense, then another of luck. As the last word of the spell passed her lips, Morgana's fire-shield fell away, and its mistress emerged from the flames. She smiled at Megan, laughing hysterically.

Megan kept her gaze steady on Morgana, though she strained to gain some view of Thyri. On the far side of the room, Thyri appeared now to be moving. She refused to avert her eyes; such an act would alert Morgana to the new threat.

"She knows my name!" Morgana declared, a huge mass of fire gathering around her raised hands. "You know *nothing*, fool!"

The last thing Megan saw was red. It surged through her, consuming her. She had never felt such pain.

"Loki's tits!" Rollo cursed as a hellish shriek behind him tore his eyes away from the pillar of fog.

"Megan," Gerald said softly, the blood draining from his cheeks as the shriek reached its piercing crescendo. He stared at Rollo, his gaze fixed, his legs unable to move until the big man grabbed his arm and pulled him toward the captain's cabin.

Inside, Gerald saw the sorceress, and again he froze with fear. Megan lay on her back, her hands awkwardly tangled on her chest. The blankets that had covered her lay half off the bed, half on the cabin's floor. Her body quivered spasmodically; her face was white, like ivory. As Gerald watched Rollo move toward her, she moaned painfully, and one arm flailed out to the side, bouncing twice on the bed before going still.

Rollo grasped her hand, then dropped it suddenly. "Like ice," he said to Gerald.

Gerald looked away, and the painting over the bed caught his gaze and stole away his breath. Such was the artist's illusion that the full moon over the haunting landscape seemed to possess a light of its own. Gerald shivered and moved forward to help Rollo, who struggled now to get blankets back over Megan's body.

Anger and despair sent power surging through Thyri as Megan's wail filled the chamber. A scream came to Thyri's own throat, but she denied it a voice. She directed the new strength to her legs.

The woman's back faced her as she covered the distance between them with blinding speed. Only as Thyri began to bring her sword down on her target did Morgana turn, grinning wildly.

In an instant, Thyri watched the ecstatic smile melt into fear. Morgana tried to raise an arm in defense; fire flickered briefly in her eyes, and Thyri felt unseen fingers begin to wrap tightly around her sword arm.

But the rune-blade would not be stopped. It bit into Morgana's shoulder and angled in, snapping bones until it ground to a halt in the center of her chest. Black liquid spurted out, and Thyri jumped back, withdrawing her blade. As the shower of black blood struck the floor, fires sprang up on the stones, spewing out small clouds of acrid, choking smoke.

For a moment, Morgana's eyes seemed yet to possess life. Thyri turned from them; she had never seen eyes exude such hate. When she looked back, the woman had transformed into a black, oozing mass no longer resembling anything human. The black liquid poured ever more freely onto the stones, and the smoke that issued from this contact began to fill the chamber.

Thyri breathed a small amount and nearly gagged. She fought to quell the spasms of her lungs, closed her eyes, and pinched her nose shut as she raced for the side of the chamber, feeling along for the opening where she hoped she would still find stairs.

When the wall turned out, she paused. Megan had fallen in this room. When Thyri had seen her, however, she had only *seen*. Her keener sense, her smell, had registered nothing but the tang of magic. She'd assumed that meant Megan had confronted Morgana unencumbered by her body. But if this were not true? If some sorcery in the place had confused her nose . . .

She remembered the assault Morgana had first waged on her, the scents that had filled her like nothing she'd experienced before. One with such a power could easily have concealed Megan's scent. But would she have done so? In attacking Megan, Morgana had dropped her guard against Thyri.

Thyri could have answered the question surely but for the smoke. She dared not open even her eyes now. She could *feel* the smoke against the skin of her face and hands, burning her like weak fire.

But if Megan remained there?

Then she was already dead.

But what if she wasn't?

As she stood there, the pain caused by the smoke grew until she felt as if her skin was aflame. Still torn by the question of Megan's fate, she turned into the spiral staircase and started down.

Halfway down, she was challenged. A growling—some beast—barred her exit. She pinpointed the growl and lashed out with her sword, feeling a dark satisfaction as her blade bit into flesh. The beast howled, and she attacked again. This time she heard a dull thud as the animal—whatever it was—collapsed on the stairs. She stepped over it, and quickly moved on.

Outside, in the fog, Sokki felt something that he imagined as the fiery breath of a fire giant blow through him before the fog suddenly disappeared as quickly as it had come. The sun above dug into his eyes, and he fell to his knees, feeling as if he'd wakened abruptly from a terrible dream.

Ahead, along the tower's wall, he saw the wooden doors that he'd failed to reach in the fog. A moment later, he heard a crash against those doors; as he rose to his feet, they burst open, and Thyri emerged, dashing out into the daylight.

Puffs of dark smoke followed her, then she slammed the doors shut.

"Thyri!"

She turned on him; by the look in her eyes, he felt as if she were about to attack. Her face was red like the skin of one scorched by the hottest summer sun. Blood, and some darker, fouler liquid, stained the edge of her blade. He stared at her, readying himself for death. The moments seemed to slow, then recognition flashed in Thyri's eyes, and her expression hardened into one of simple anger. She exhaled, then breathed in deeply.

"I told you to stay with the ship!"

He stared at her, unable to speak.

"Who else came with you?"

Slowly, he rose to his feet. "Ottar," he stammered.

She looked around. "Where is he?"

His eyes followed hers. His brother was nowhere in sight. He looked back at Thyri. She stood oddly, sniffing the air. "Never mind," she said. "I know. Follow."

Without looking back at the tower, Thyri turned. She led him fifty paces from the tower's base where they found Ottar in a gully. Thyri ordered Sokki to carry his brother, then she raced ahead of him, back for the ship.

Thyri gained the deck, glanced only briefly at Rollo, who helped her aboard, then rushed to her cabin. Inside the door, she stopped, dropping her sword, staring at Megan on the bed, relieved that her friend hadn't perished in flames, but already aware of the chill in the air and the pale, deathlike mask over Megan's features. Hesitantly, she moved forward and pulled back the blankets covering her lover.

Megan's beauty brought tears to her eyes. Thyri bent and rested her head against her lover's breast. The heartbeat within was so faint . . .

"Odin," Thyri wailed. "Not again!" Sobs wracked her body. She clenched her eyes shut and saw Megan, laughing that day Thyri had returned from Castle Kaerglen to winter with the sorceress. *I have something you desire,* Thyri said then. *Several things,* replied the sorceress.

Not death!

Oh, Odin! Not again!

Wordlessly, Gerald, Rui, and Horik gathered around Rollo as all tried to ignore the weeping Thyri did not bother to conceal. Rollo looked at them and frowned. For the time, there was nothing any of them could do. Nevertheless, the tension—the feeling that something *had* to be done—began to grow unbearable. Rollo himself had almost turned for Thyri's cabin when movement on the beach caught his eye and he looked to see Sokki struggling with the limp form of his brother.

Horik's eyes followed Rollo's and he gasped. He looked to Rollo, who nodded, then he jumped into the water to help the pair reach the ship.

Gerald and Rui, likewise, were thankful for the distraction. Together, they went to the hold for rope, fashioning a loose noose that could be used to hoist Ottar aboard. When they returned to the gunwale, the sons of Gunnar were waiting below.

A few moments later, they lay Ottar on the deck and knelt down around him. He yet lived, but showed no signs of reviving.

Rollo felt around his scalp for wounds but found none. He looked at Sokki. "What happened?" he asked softly.

Sokki shook his head. He didn't know.

Rollo stood and looked up at the sail, testing the wind. The air was all but still. He glanced briefly at the tower, cursing softly, then ordered the others to the oars.

As they exited the bay, the sky suddenly darkened anew and lightning flared.

"Ship the oars!" Rui shouted as a terrific wind smashed into the ship, filling the sail. The mast creaked and strained. Fighting sudden swells, they got the oars aboard and headed for the cover of the cabins. Rui alone made it; he tried to grab Gerald on the way, but the ship lurched, throwing Gerald to the deck. Horik and Sokki had already fallen.

Rollo barely kept his feet, dove at the boom, gave slack to the sail, and *Nightreaver* shot out of the harbor into the sea. The rains came again, and lightning struck dangerously near the ship; Rollo hung on desperately, praying that the spears of crackling energy would strike clear of the mast. His muscles screaming, he rode out the wind until the island and its tower became lost in the storm's fury.

And then, as before, the storm subsided as unexpectedly as it had risen.

Rollo unclamped his hands from the boom and fell to the deck. His head ached and his muscles throbbed; pain and exhaustion made every movement an effort. Groaning, he rose and looked around. Gerald, Sokki, and Horik lay flattened against the deck. Rui emerged from his cabin and limped out to the gunwale. Sokki got up and crawled toward his brother. Gerald groaned.

"How's Horik?" Rollo asked, looking up wearily at Sokki.

"He's alive," Sokki said after a moment.

"Where's Ottar?"

Nobody knew. They searched the ship, but Ottar was nowhere to be found.

Avalon

She pulled herself from the water and looked down at her body, running her hands slowly over her chest and her hard, flat stomach. The muscles in her arms responded effortlessly, even after the swim. She felt as if she could rip a tree, roots and all, from the earth.

Already, she felt all her strengths returning . . .

Standing naked on the beach, she gazed musingly at the stark, inland tower where she'd been trapped for so long. Throwing her head back, she laughed. The deep, resonant boom that issued from her throat startled her. She paused, then tested the voice, singing a song she'd once heard voiced by Lancelot.

The poor, ignorant swineherd!

When she finished the song, she chuckled, gazing at the tower. She felt her loins stir; she looked down and smiled, hesitantly touching her rising pillar of manhood. The rippling sensation that flowed from the contact shocked her, and she moved her hand away.

She would have plenty of time to explore this new possibility later. She thought of Eiriksdattir, and her humor grew dark. She had come so close. *The power of this male flesh was nothing compared to the prize she could have won.*

She wondered if Thyri could have known whose soul had perished there, inside the tower. No, she decided. The wolf's friend might have understood, but she fought now a darker foe even than Morgana. The sorceress battled death, and had not the leisure to think of anything else.

Morgana suddenly gripped the twitching thing between her legs and hoped Megan would win. Even though this wasn't the body she'd wanted, it was quite strong enough for now. And Thyri's body could still be hers, in ways more varied than she'd previously contemplated. Revenge would be sweet.

Smiling again, she strode for her tower. When she opened the door, the black smoke of her near-death buffeted her. She coughed, then waved her hand to dispel the sorcery.

On the stairs, she found Ra licking the blood from Vishnu's seeping wounds. She looked at the beast and smiled; he looked up and growled at her, then began to whine painfully.

After a moment, the hound burst into flame. She watched her fire consume him and the body of his brother. When the flames died, she stepped over the carnage.

"You are no longer necessary." *She chuckled absently, continuing up the stairs to the chamber where she'd slept for all those years. There, she went to the window that looked out over the sea.*

A gentle breeze blew in, caressing her cheeks. Merlin's spell was broken, and she was free.

Book VI: THE GODDESS

It's spring, and the warmth and sunshine taunt me with their gentle omnipresence. Looking up into the blue sky, I have asked myself why I do not set down this pen, why I do not lose myself in idle leisure. But I cannot; this task of mine may not be abandoned. But I have made it more easy, at least for a time. No longer do I work in the tower room next to Satan's Chalice . . . The atmosphere there is dark, unbearable at times. And there is a smell—of rot and decay—that will not let me write.

I have moved my desk and my notes to a room off the old library, a room that looks out into the garden with its sparkling fountain. The spring growth there is fantastic: brilliant blossoms dot the branches of every tree and bush; flowers of every color imaginable lie strewn over the yard like gemstones in the treasure trove of some ancient king. So I have great beauty before me when the words refuse to flow. Better than a circle of leering, mocking red. At times in the past, I have stared idly for so long at the surface of that pool that, when I lie down to retire, the red circle remains, hovering before my closed eyes, inviting me into haunted, disturbing dreams.

I no longer need that pool at my side, day in and day out. I write now, finally, of experiences I have lived through, and much of my research now involves recollection rather than sorcery. What questions I have for the sorcery to answer I now may assemble for brief excursions to the tower when they become absolutely necessary. Even then, I have come to question this necessity at times, for have I not reached that point in Thyri's life that captured my imagination completely when I could but see from the outside? Is there not sufficient wonder in that alone? And, in so many cases, such as the sequence of events that led to Rollo's inclusion in our adventures, do I not know enough from the tales of others to avoid sorcerous intrusions into their pasts?

Such are my thoughts now. In ways, what I write now is far less demanding of my spirit than what I have written in the past, for the characters I know, and the places I have seen with my own eyes. And yet I have encountered new difficulties for there seem to me so many ways to present this tale, so many interesting perspectives that conflict, yet complement one another. And I have such a wealth of detail at my command that the formation of *Nightreaver*'s crew might occupy this entire volume if such were my desire. But I cannot desire this, for my story, in fact, is still merely beginning.

I have written before of difficulties I have experienced in attempting my sorcery on those of great power, and within this context, I must admit that Morgana proved no exception to this rule. I desire foremost to achieve accuracy in my telling, but Morgana's entrance into the stream of events has always puzzled me, and it seems now that I may never learn with certainty the real reasons for her involvement. That she drew *Nightreaver* to her lair is fact; that she battled Thyri and Megan as she did is also fact, and that she was awakened or persuaded to these actions must necessarily be fact as well. She surely possessed the ability, at the time of the battle, to escape from Merlin's exile by taking the place of another, and I find it incredible to think that she might have endured four centuries of imprisonment in anticipation of this possibility. For could she not have drawn to her any vessel from the seas of Midgard, freeing herself at the earliest opportunity?

No, Morgana slept. Nothing else fits, and my instincts guided my pen as I wrote of her awakening. It is fantasy, surely, but if another scenario possesses a greater claim to accuracy, let it reveal itself to me. Where I cannot write what I know, I must write what I believe to be likely.

For purposes of clarity, I reiterate here that Megan Kaerglen remains closed to my sorcery. In relating the details of *her* conflict with Morgana, I needed only draw on Thyri's memory for, in time, Thyri learned these details herself.

On the evening after the battle with Morgana, *Nightreaver*'s crew ate in silence. Thyri, in her cabin, had grown quiet. Rollo tried to take her food, but she ordered him out, telling him to do what he wished.

He emerged with her orders and looked out over the sea. He could think of nothing to do but wait until Thyri could contain her grief and give them direction. Grimly, he joined the others, resolved, simply, to get through the night.

* * *

Before I forge ahead, a brief word needs be given the old couple who ran the country tavern that Guthrom's guard burned the day they rode in search of Rollo and Thyri. This word is that they did not perish, but fled to the farm of the old man's sister's son shortly after Thyri, Megan, and I departed. They fled with curses on their lips for the Norse, and some slight fear of the *were*-beasts rumored to roam the vicinity. Passing under the tavern's threshold, the old woman snatched the talisman of protection and carried it with her. Later, she hung it over the portal of the farmhouse where she lived out her days, thankful, at least, that she had some protection from the dangers of the moors.

Ghosts

The morning after the battle fared no better than the night, worse perhaps, because Thyri's sobbing had again grown audible. While the others broke fast, Thyri emerged, red-faced, to fill a flagon with fresh water. As she stood at the barrel, bent to this task, Rollo hesitantly approached, laying a hand on her shoulder, half expecting her to flinch away. To his relief, she did not, but neither did she acknowledge his presence.

"She yet lives, does she not?" he asked her softly.

For a long moment, she did nothing, but in the end, she nodded. "Barely," came her coarse whisper.

After that, she returned wordlessly to her cabin.

Near noon, the inactivity grew unbearable. No wind had risen, so Rollo ordered all to the oars, and, for lack of a better direction, they began to propel the vessel eastward, where Rollo hoped they might reach Frankish shores. He didn't necessarily intend to dock, but sighting land might, in some way, break the monotony of endless seas that did nothing, at present, to boost morale.

At the oars, the amazing effectiveness of each stroke reminded all of the power of the sorceress, and the loss they now faced. And it caused them, also, to think of darker things. Each of them could not but help envision Megan as a goddess, immortal after the fashion of such beings. Yet now she lay near death, making the consolation of faith treacherous, insubstantial and fleeting. Even for the Norse, whose theology necessitated the deaths of immortals, direct confrontation with such an idea was unsettling.

Gerald found himself working an oar next to Sokki. Next to Thyri, the young Norseman appeared most affected by the battle. Gerald studied the man; it was almost painful to watch Sokki's eyes gazing ahead with resigned listlessness. He'd known the Viking for less than two days, but his first impression had been one of implacable vitality and optimism. It had been Sokki's optimism, even tainted by despair, that had propelled him ashore to help Thyri—his optimism that any dangers ahead were surmountable and, thus, not to be taken seriously.

From the sidelines, two nights before, Gerald had understood that Sokki knew Thyri, that Sokki, in fact, worshiped the swordsmistress with a fervor akin to that which Gerald felt within himself, perhaps even a greater fervor, for it had been Sokki who had, upon watching Thyri's disappearance at the base of Morgana's tower, felt compelled to rush to her aid. Such a reaction hinted at a greater feeling of loss, a more deeply seated fear of losing a companionship so recently regained.

And so he had defied Rollo and rushed to Thyri's aid. His brother, who had followed, had fallen, then had gone overboard, unconscious, and had undoubtedly drowned. Gerald suspected that Sokki blamed himself. In Sokki's eyes, Gerald saw something of the same things visible in Thyri's: despair, sorrow, and anger without an object.

Watching Sokki, Gerald found himself fishing for words of consolation. He remembered the death of his mother. He'd been a boy then—eleven in years, scant months away from his uncle's death and his trip southward to join Alfred's scribes. At the time, no one's mere words had been able to ease the pain. He'd long thought that the experience had ushered him into manhood. If he'd remained a boy, he'd simply have perished with her. Only as a man could he accept the fact that life had to continue.

But how did one handle the death of a brother? He didn't know, he'd never had one. Drawing on his sketchy knowledge of Danish customs, he tried desperately to find something to say; the words that came out were stilted, peppered with uncertainty: "He is happy now, Sokki," he said, gripping the Viking's wrist. "He is with Odin in Valhalla."

Sokki didn't look at him. "Perhaps," he said after a time. "But we do not know how he fell, even the nature of his enemy. We do not know that he fought bravely."

"He was your brother," Gerald said. "He could have fallen no other way."

Sokki grunted, but kept his eyes fixed ahead.

In actual fact, Ottar had not fought at all. Morgana had not given him the chance; in the space of an instant, she'd drawn him into her tower as she'd drawn Thyri, then she'd simply plucked his soul from his body as if it had been a grape on a vine. Her exit, after that, had been no problem at all.

Rui rowed with Horik, whose mood, in many ways, mirrored Sokki's. The archer, however, did not try to speak. Instead, he paid particular attention to keeping the rhythm of their oar constant, hoping, in this, to ease the Viking's heart with the consistent, meditative quality of their work.

Rollo, meanwhile, climbed to the foredeck and gazed out to sea. Resting his hand on the haunch of the wooden wolf Megan had carved there, his eyes scanned the horizon, searching for the slightest hint of land.

Near dusk, Rollo began to suspect that something was amiss. Solid ground remained as elusive as the heartbeat of a fly. He had not seen even a gull, something that struck him as strange the longer he reflected upon it. The birds were always a constant fixture of life at sea; now, he could not recall hearing their chatter since before the storm that had deposited them in the harbor of the dark tower. Once that afternoon, he'd thought he'd seen something in the sky in the distance. Yet, even then, it had seemed impossibly huge—far too distant to be a gull or any other bird he'd ever encountered. After rubbing his eyes, the thing in the sky had disappeared.

And the events of the day before, the battle that Thyri had obviously undertaken in that tower, began to nag at him. For all that he'd assumed command of the crew, he still didn't understand why. Thyri had said nothing of her experiences. Nor had Sokki, for that matter.

With the sun setting on one side of the horizon and the waxing moon rising on the other, Rollo called the others to dinner. Over the meal, he watched Sokki and Horik. He needed to speak with Sokki, but he couldn't find words to broach the subject. The entire meal, again, was silent.

After eating, Rollo filled a large plate with dried pork, added an apple in the center, poured two large flagons of mead, and knocked on the door of the captain's cabin. After a minute passed with no reply, he cautiously pushed the door open and entered.

He shivered involuntarily; the inside of the cabin had grown unnaturally cold. He pushed the door fully opened and stoppered it, then stood there, looking at Thyri. She sat on the edge of Megan's bed, the sorceress's right hand sandwiched between hers.

After a moment, she spoke: "Close it," she said without turning.

He paused before answering. "No, Thyri," he said softly. "It is like winter in here, and she needs warmth. The others will not intrude; they have sorrows of their own. Sokki and Horik have lost a brother." He walked to her table and set down the plate and the flagons; then he sat so that he could face her.

Slowly, she turned to him. "Ottar is dead?"

"We laid him on the deck when he was unconscious. After the storm, we could find him nowhere."

She stared at him, her eyes distant, as if they looked through him. "It has begun again," she said sadly.

"You must eat, Thyri," he said.

She focused on him slowly. "How long? How long have I been here?"

"Only a day."

"That's all?" She smiled weakly and rose, squinting as she looked out the open door.

He watched her, noting that, even burdened with sorrow and despair, her every move embodied subtle grace. She tried to smile again when she sat across from him.

"She yet lives?" he asked, glancing at Megan.

Thyri nodded, tears welling anew in her swollen eyes. "I do not know how to care for her, Rollo. I give her water, but her mouth never seems parched. I do not think she hungers. It's as if she is frozen, neither alive nor dead. Outside of time."

"Perhaps she struggles within herself." He reached out for Thyri's hand, turned it so that her palm faced up, and placed a chunk of pork in her fingers.

Thyri absently carried the morsel to her lips, chewed it slowly, and washed it down. "Now and then," she said, "her ring flickers. I do not know whether she causes this, or whether some sorcery within the ring acts on its own to keep her alive."

Rollo watched her, feeling relieved as her hand went on its own to the plate of pork. After eating another chunk, she looked into his eyes. "You and the others should leave us," she said. "Abandon this ship. You are not safe with me. With Ottar's death, it has all begun again."

He looked into her eyes, detecting, in their depths, a restrained, almost childlike pleading. He smiled at her. "Not possible," he said. "I have sworn to myself to serve you, to follow you wherever that may lead me. I cannot speak for the others, but I'm sure they feel the same. And aside from that, we have found no land upon which to disembark. This vessel is more swift than any I have known, and we've propelled it ever eastward since the morning. No land in sight, and I can't explain it. We should have been scant hours from either Frankish or Frisian shores."

She looked down at her hands. "I feared as much," she whispered. "I have some sense for magic, Rollo, and things have felt slightly wrong since the onset of the storm that drew us to Morgana's island. We are not where we should be. It is possible that we are no longer on the seas of Midgard."

Rollo lifted his flagon and took a long draught. Her words didn't really surprise him much; during the course of the afternoon, he'd begun to fear something akin to what she'd just expressed. On the other hand, he remembered the thing he'd seen briefly in the distant sky. If they *weren't* in Midgard, then he wasn't sure he wanted to speculate on the nature of that which he'd seen. If it *was* some sort of bird, he was glad it had flown no closer.

He voiced none of this aloud. Instead, he tried to turn the conversation to what he did need to know. "Morgana?" he asked carefully.

Yes, Thyri thought. That was what Megan had named the woman when she'd entered the battle. "Some ancient demon, I think. Powerful, I know. Perhaps Gerald can tell you more; I believe the Saxons know of her."

Calmly, Rollo reached out again and squeezed Thyri's hand. "What happened, swords-mistress?"

Thyri looked at him and brushed back a tear. She pushed another chunk into her mouth, drank deep of the mead, and related to Rollo what she'd experienced on Morgana's island. In speaking, some small part of her pain began to melt away, and something in Rollo's eyes almost made her tell him of her curse and how Morgana had tried to use it against her, how Morgana had almost won. But this she did not tell.

All of the rest, however, she poured out to him, hoping vainly that she would see some way that it had all been a dream, that she could blink her eyes, turn for the bed, and see Megan rise, smiling her old smile.

Later, after Rollo had calmed Thyri and left her alone with Megan, he went to Gerald and asked the Saxon about Morgana. He did not like what he learned. Gerald said that Morgana had an older name: the Morrigan, he called her. The bringer of death. Morgana was a name she'd earned only centuries before—the name she'd assumed when she'd single-handedly destroyed the golden empire of Arthur, whom Gerald called the greatest and most noble king ever to rule over a nation of men.

In the end, the bringer of death had learned defeat at the hand of the great sorcerer, Merlin of the Seven Groves, but even Merlin had been unable to kill her. He had, however, imprisoned her in a dark tower he erected on a small island, in a sea where normal men, by accident, could not fare . . .

After learning this from Gerald, Rollo sat alone for several hours, staring into the night sky, trying to prepare himself for what might lie ahead. Thyri claimed that she'd killed the demoness in her tower. But if Merlin could not kill her . . . Merlin was a legend among Saxons, but tales of his great power and deeds were such that they traveled far from Saxon shores. Rollo had first heard of the wizard when he was but a boy in Denmark.

His thoughts turned back disturbingly to the strange storm during which they'd lost Ottar, the storm that had raged *after* Thyri's battle. It had felt as unnatural as the storm that had drawn them to Morgana. His most optimistic explanation had Megan somehow, in her battle with death, creating the maelstrom.

This, he hoped, was the truth. If it wasn't . . . What meant a physical body to one who lived for centuries?

In the night sky, he vainly sought answers. Even after retiring to his cabin, sleep eluded him for most of the night.

In the morning, Rollo emerged early, hoping the sunlight would make his fears of the night before less real, less substantial. The sun on his face felt good, but the pleasant warmth seemed false, illusory. He found himself wondering about what sorts of monstrosities might lie below the surface of the sea, and what they might find on land, if and when they ran across it.

As he stood on the deck, he noticed that an easterly wind had arisen. With this discovery, he set to raising the mainsail, grateful for the opportunity to exercise his muscles rather than his mind.

Once the sail was up, he worked the rigging, fighting to keep *Nightreaver*'s course as straight as possible as the others began to emerge from their cabins. One by one, they joined Rollo at the ropes. So passed the morning.

With the sun high overhead, they had their first glimpse of land: another island. As they drew near it, Rollo left the sail to the others and went to Thyri, informing her that they'd sighted land and that he would take two of the others ashore in hopes of learning something of the nature of their situation.

Thyri agreed to his plan but expressed no desire to leave her cabin.

Megan's condition had not changed.

Warriors

Gerald stooped and examined the trail. It was well worn, but bore no signs of human feet or horses. In places, however, the earth was split by long gashes, two to three feet in length. He shook his head as Rui drew next to him.

"Claw marks?" the archer asked, looking down.

Gerald stood. "I hope not." He looked down the slope. Rollo had scouted to the north; he was still halfway down the hill and closer to the beach. Far below, *Nightreaver* rested at anchor in a shallow bay. Gerald caught Rollo's eye and waved to him; the Viking nodded and trotted toward them.

Gerald stooped again to examine the markings while Rollo covered the distance up the slope. He was shaking his head again when Rollo reached his side and bent next to him. The Viking ran a hand along one of the gashes. "Perhaps the earth is weak here," he said. "Perhaps rains caused this."

"They're not all downhill," Gerald countered.

Rui had wandered to the nearby trees. After a moment, he called the others to him, and pointed out the condition of the lower branches. "This can't be a wolf run," he said. "If it was, some of these would be broken. You'd find bits of fur."

Rollo nodded. He stood up straight and rubbed the back of his neck. In doing so, his eyes traveled upward. "Odin!" he gasped involuntarily.

Gerald's eyes followed his. High in the tree, several branches looked as if they'd been pulverized. It hadn't been lightning's work; there were no scorch marks, and the damage was nearly uniform from tip of branch to trunk. It looked, rather, as if some great hammer had smashed into the tree from the side.

Rui had, again, wandered farther away. Gerald could hear him foraging behind a nearby bush. He approached the sound and parted the foliage. Rui looked up at him and lifted what first appeared to Gerald to be a large stick. Then the archer rose, turned, and stepped forward, dragging something behind him.

Gerald backed away and waited for the archer to reach the trail. As he emerged, Gerald and Rollo gaped wide-eyed at his burden.

Trailing behind the archer was a white feather the length of *Nightreaver*'s mast.

"Birds?" Gerald said incredulously, looking at Rollo.

Rollo swallowed hard. Carefully, he began to relate to the others what he feared he'd seen the day before. He related also some part of the conversation he'd had with Thyri—the suspicion that they journeyed now in a world far different from the one they knew.

When Rollo finished, Gerald pointed out that the feather was white. "Maybe they're just chickens," he said.

Rui chuckled. "And what," he asked, "do you suppose chickens that size might like for dinner?" He paused, his expression growing serious. "If we're to explore this place further, we should do so well away from the trail."

Rollo nodded, and turned into the forest. A hundred paces in, he turned north, and the others followed.

As they picked their way through the underbrush, Gerald reflected on the conversation he'd had the evening before when Rollo had asked of the gods of his people. For some reason, his mind had refused then to connect the conversation with reality, but he suddenly realized how he'd been a fool not to understand Rollo's curiosity, to understand why the Viking had dwelt on the Morrigan.

Now, after seeing the feather and knowing that no such bird could be real in the world he knew, he began to grow afraid. The dark tower leapt back into his memory, becoming Morgana's prison. *Her prison on an island, in a sea where normal men could not fare*.

But they'd reached her, and Thyri Eiriksdattir had battled not a mere sorceress, not a witch, but a demoness as old as legend. What amazed him was that Thyri had survived. But had she been victorious? The land upon which they now trod belonged, undoubtedly, to that sea where Merlin had exiled Morgana. And the sorceress that Thyri called friend—she lay near death back on the ship.

These thoughts all confirmed the feeling that he'd had before, the night he'd taken Thyri to summon Megan, the feeling that he'd entered the affairs of the gods. If they *had* battled Morgana . . . He could not now envision the dweller of the dark tower to have been anyone other than Arthur's bane.

So—they meddled in the affairs of gods and walked upon an

island of giant chickens. What troubled him was that he, Rui, and Rollo had forged ahead alone, without Thyri at their side.

After an hour of slow, cautious progress, the sound of waves crashing against cliffs began to grow louder with each step. Shortly, the forest gave way to a grassy strip, about fifty paces wide, that led up to the cliff's edge.

Among the last stand of trees, they hesitated, looking out to both sides in search of danger. Only after several minutes did they venture forth, Rollo in the lead.

Even before they reached their destination, Gerald sensed something was wrong. Amid the crashing waves, he heard a sound he thought was thunder; in looking up, however, he saw barely a hint of clouds, just thin, insubstantial streamers of cottony white. Then, near the cliff's edge, a huge, branchless tree trunk thrust slowly into view.

When they looked over and down, they saw a ship: not a normal vessel—its mast stretched up, high over the deck and level with their eyes. Within its hull, one could fit hundreds of *Nightreaver*s.

And further north, off the bay that harbored the ship, a huge hall constructed of wood and mud rose up from the ground. By its size, it could have been a hall of gods. Its slovenly appearance, however, could mean but one thing: the chickens had keepers.

Before Gerald could get past his amazement to scrutinize in detail what his eyes told him he saw, Rollo grabbed his arm and yanked him away from the cliff's edge. Without speaking a word, the trio dashed for the relative safety of the wood, then continued on in stealth and silence, each struggling with his own fears, each unwilling to voice even a disbelief of what he had seen with his own eyes.

In the end, all their caution, all their stealth, went for naught. Halfway back to *Nightreaver,* a deep, silly giggling roared across the sky. A voice followed.

"I smell little goodies," it said.

Nearby, several trees cracked, and the ground shook under the weight of a heavy foot. Looking up, Gerald caught a brief glimpse of a huge, cherubic face above the trees. His despair brought tears to his eyes. At the same time, he almost felt like laughing. They'd been discovered not by a warrior-giant, not by a master-tracker giant or even an oversized wizard, but by a child.

When the giggle had first rippled through the air, they had frozen in their tracks. When the voice had followed—the words were Norse and thus understandable by all—they had looked up frantically for its source. Now, with the grinning child's face visible, they drew swords and began to run. The heavy footfalls followed, and the chase was hectic, but brief. A massive, stubby-fingered hand appeared suddenly before Rollo. Its fingers wrapped around him before he could dodge out of the way.

As the giant lifted him off the ground, Rollo brought his sword down, slicing into the huge thumb. The blade stopped when it reached bone. The earth shook as the child fell to his knees. The violent motion threw Gerald and Rui to the forest floor.

"Goody stung me!" the giant squealed. "Bad goody stung me!"

The sound was almost deafening. Gerald watched agony crease Rollo's face as the giant began to squeeze the Viking. Leaping to his feet, Gerald dove at the giant's wrist; his sword point met flesh, drawing another horrible squeal from above.

Rui, meanwhile, notched an arrow and sent it whizzing up through the branches. Glancing up, Gerald saw the arrow dig into the giant's eye. As Rollo fell to the ground near him, Gerald dropped his sword and covered his ears. The child screamed and fell back, the impact creating another bruising earthquake.

When the worst of the tremors had passed, Gerald crawled over to Rollo. The Viking sat, shaking his head; when Gerald helped him to his feet, he winced and clutched his side.

"Can you run?" Gerald whispered desperately.

"I'll have to, won't I?" Rollo grimaced. "Let's go," he spat out, "before Daddy arrives and really gives us problems."

Trying to keep close together, they ran for the ship. The ground they had covered stealthily in a half hour, they covered now in five minutes, though those minutes were among the worst Gerald had ever endured. Pain wracked his lungs, and, occasionally, he and Rui had to force themselves to slow so that Rollo could catch up. The Viking, all the while, clutched his side. Gerald didn't even want to guess how many ribs the young giant had cracked. As they ran, tree trunks snapped and the ground shook behind them.

Cresting the hill that led to *Nightreaver*'s harbor, they heard Rollo's fear realized: a voice, far deeper than that of the giant they'd battled, growled distantly behind them. The child had been found by an elder; as they raced down the slope, the rapid approach of their new pursuer sent boulders tumbling down the slope with them, and they fought to keep control of their descent. Below them, Gerald saw Sokki and Horik raising the mainsail.

When they reached the water, Gerald and Rui spun the panting Rollo around and dragged him in backwards, holding him between them as they swam for the ship. A moment later, the sons of Gunnar pulled them quickly aboard and drew in the anchor.

Nightreaver, at first, lurched for shore and almost grounded itself. Rollo, still clutching his side, staggered to the boom and pushed it around until the sail sagged. "Row!" he yelled.

As Gerald ran for the oars, he glanced back. Above the tree line, a huge head appeared. Its eyes were like fire, and Gerald's heart nearly burst when those eyes fell on the ship. He gained the oars with the others, and, somehow, they managed to time their first stroke. Such was their desperation that *Nightreaver*'s hull creaked as it sped out of the bay. The ship jerked then as Rollo let the sail fill, and the easterly wind grabbed them and sent them skimming along the island's southern shore.

They dug the oars in until their speed threatened to crack the blades, then they looked back. The giant raced over the island's southern terrain, but he appeared to be falling behind. Gerald sighed in relief, then moaned as their pursuer shifted course, gained the beach, reached out over the water, and smashed his massive hand down into the waves.

A monstrous swell began to rise up behind them. In unison, they dove under the benches and clutched at the braces as the sea tipped them forward. Gerald felt a painful popping in his ears as the sea lifted them high into the air. He braced himself for a jarring descent, but it didn't come. After a minute, he crawled cautiously from his hiding place, fearing now that he might actually find the ship flying through the air with no water beneath it. Instead, he saw something he'd thought he might never see again:

Thyri, grinning with wild abandon, worked one end of the boom, helping Rollo to keep *Nightreaver* balanced and riding the crest of the swell. The weight of the moment had somehow drawn her from her dark humor.

One by one, the rest of the crew went to aid them. Behind them, the island of the giants receded rapidly into the distance.

As Thyri worked, her fears of the coming night, as well as her fears for Megan, came and went. Meanwhile, the giants' great vessel took to sea and headed after them. Thyri glanced back occasionally to check its progress; there were moments during which she hoped the ship would catch them. Battle would force her fully into the present and chase the clouds from her mind. The huge ship, however, was slow. It gradually disappeared below the horizon.

The swell did not level off until late afternoon.

When their battle with the sea had ended, *Nightreaver*'s crew ravenously pillaged the hold. Thyri, uneasily eyeing the descent of the sun, could not bring herself to join them. Instead, she went to the stern, ostensibly to watch for signs of the giant ship emerging under the coming sunset. Rollo followed her.

Thyri looked at Rollo then and realized, for the first time, the wound he had sustained. He had shut out his pain during their flight; now, with the danger passing, the pain returned. He winced as he returned Thyri's gaze, his hand again moving involuntarily to his side.

"You were right," he said, forcing a smile. "We are no longer in Midgard." He stepped away from the gunwale.

She forced herself to smile back. "I'm sorry, Rollo," she said. Behind him, a full moon began to rise from the sea. She glanced west again; she had two hours of the sun left to protect her, then it would go dark and the wolf would take her.

Desperately, she searched his eyes for consolation, but she found only his pain. A pure pain—physical, unlike that which tormented her. But beneath the pain, Thyri found hope.

"Come," she said to Rollo, taking his hand. "Those ribs need tending."

On the way to Rollo's cabin, she ordered the others to tack north for a while; assuming the angry giant would be slow but persistent, she didn't want to take any chances.

She stopped Rollo just inside the cabin's door, turned him, and took off his shirt. Carefully, she felt around his injured ribs. The Viking looked down at her, gritting his teeth, refusing to voice his pain. After a moment, she stepped back. "If you do not make any sounds," she asked, "how am I supposed to do this?" She moved closer again; this time, as she explored his side, he let her know where it hurt.

When she was satisfied that she'd determined the extent of the damage, she smiled up at him. "You've been worse off," she said. "If we bind you right, you'll hardly feel it." She left his cabin then, returning shortly with several long strips of fabric.

Slowly, she wrapped the cloth around him. He held his arms out, his eyes never leaving her. On each turn of the bandage, when she moved closer to him to reach around his back, he could feel her warm breath on his chest. The sensation excited him, and it scared him as well. He had never thought of her as a *woman*. He had never thought of her as he had of Fandis. She was more than a woman; she did not deserve such thoughts.

And her lover—she lay, near death, in the next cabin.

Yet now . . . Thyri's breasts brushed against him. The hairs on his chest stood out as a chill swept through his body. Underneath the thin cotton of Thyri's shift, her nipples hardened, then her breasts brushed against him again. The pain in his side grew distant.

As her closeness to Rollo filled her senses, Thyri thought of the moon.

That morning, fear of the coming night had overshadowed the pains she felt when she gazed at the pale figure on her bed. Megan grew neither worse, nor better, and Thyri had become accustomed to the melancholy monotony of her vigil.

But with the approach of the full moon . . . Her monthly terror had gripped her. That morning, her mind had replayed each moment of her second change on the *Black Rabbit;* she had relived the death of each crewman, seen their faces, witnessed their fear, tasted their blood.

And when the rush of memories had ebbed, her reality had treated her no better. She would see Megan on the bed and remember the scene Morgana had shown her. She would envision her fangs sinking into her lover's neck, and she would jerk away, only to have the vision linger in the darkness of her mind, awaiting her next weakness, its next opportunity to surface.

Her only hope had been the painting over the bed. On their first night out, while they drank, Megan had whispered to her briefly, promising that the painting would aid her when the curse took her body. But how? It couldn't stop the beast; Megan would have told her that precisely if it were true. And it couldn't be true because otherwise Megan would have lifted the curse from her long before.

Thyri had spent long, idle hours gazing into the picture's haunting, dark corners. It looked so real—if she knew Megan, and knew her sorcery, then the painting would be her window, her gate into another world. A place where she could go . . . a place to hide her, and to hide *Nightreaver*'s crew from the beast's bloodlust.

All this she hoped. but what if the sorcery failed? What if it needed Megan, alive and well? What if it was incomplete, or if it required some specific action from her of which the sorceress had not had time to tell her?

What if she had to *do* something that she did not know how to do? And then—what if it worked, but not in full? What if she could not return?

That fear had kept her on board when Rollo had disembarked to explore the island. She had feared nightfall on land. She had feared her own crew discovering her dark secret and abandoning her, fleeing from her. Either way, trapped on land or trapped in the painting, she would be without Megan again, and that thought she couldn't bear. Not as long as there was hope . . .

Until Thyri could learn how to help her friend—if she could help her—then she could risk nothing. But tonight, she would have to. She prayed that the painting would grant her haven and a safe return. If she could overcome the fear of being trapped . . . But if she couldn't, she would lose all to the beast, and then Megan, Rollo—everyone—would die.

And then, if the sorcery didn't work—if she were trapped on the ship, in the cabin with Meg . . . She would have no choice but to leap into the sea, placing Megan in the care of the others. She refused to consider stocking her cabin with meat from the hold. She had managed that before and succeeded, but just barely. She *had* to be in the cabin *with* Megan to get to the painting . . . if its sorcery failed, she couldn't bear thought of the conflict that would ensue. No amount of dried meat could sate the wolf's hunger when it smelled fresh blood. True, she had defeated the beast's nature before, but always she'd had assistance. On the *Black Rabbit,* she'd had walls between herself and Elaine, the ship's sole survivor. On land, she'd always had other prey. On *Nightreaver,* tonight, she would have none of this.

Whatever happened, she could not allow herself to destroy her whom she loved most. But would she have the strength to do whatever the night might demand of her?

Strength—it was strength she needed. And compassion. The darkness of the recent days had chipped away at her humanity, and she desperately needed that back.

The afternoon had restored something of her old vitality. At least it had made her feel alive. She needed to keep that feeling, she needed to make it grow.

She needed to feel *human*. Now she had her chance.

Cautiously, she reached behind Rollo for the end of the last strip of cloth. She tied it slowly, looking up into his eyes. He had a kind face; blue eyes sparkled even amid his confusion. His cheeks were high and strongly defined.

"Is that all right?" she asked.

He nodded uncertainly. Thyri tried to decode the emotions hidden behind his features. She felt another flash of fear as she recognized something in his eyes—a something she had seen before, in the new land, in Akan's eyes—a sort of reverent disbelief, a denial of the intimacy she offered.

Rollo, like Akan had, thought her a goddess. He thought her above human love. The realization sent her thoughts racing. With Akan, she had overcome this. But she knew already that Rollo was stronger than Akan. He was as strong as any man she'd ever known. What if he denied her?

Never before had she so wanted to be touched, to be held. For the first time in her memory, she grew nervous. She felt a warm wetness spread out over the space between her thighs. *Touch me*, she thought.

"Is something wrong?" she asked.

"No," he said. "Thank you for the bandage." He made a weak effort to step back.

Her hand darted out for his. "Sometimes," she said softly, "I wish I had never seen a sword."

He looked at her oddly. "But . . ." She turned his hand palm up, then ran her fingers over his, over his palm, to his wrist. "Megan," he gasped.

She looked into his eyes. "She would understand," Thyri whispered. "More than you can. More than I can."

She took his hand and placed it on her thigh. The contact sent shivers up and down her leg. Slowly, she moved his hand up, pushing up her shift, then she swiftly brushed it against her wetness. She pulled his hand up between them, the moisture of her passion shining softly in the cabin's weak light.

"I am a woman," she said. "Won't you love me?" She smiled at him, watching his eyes. She pressed his hand against her breast and closed her eyes. "Love me, Rollo," she said. "Don't ask questions. Don't doubt." She reached between his legs and massaged his awakening manhood. He grew harder under her touch.

Slowly, he squeezed her breast.

"That's it," she gasped. She pushed him back, toward his bunk. Once there, she pressed down on his shoulders and he sat. She stood in front of him, moved closer to him, her breasts inches away from his mouth. "Undress me," she whispered.

Hesitantly, he reached out, unclasped the buckle of her war belt, and let it fall slowly to the floor.

"Undress me," she repeated hoarsely.

He ran his hands up her legs, then gripped the bottom of her shift. As he raised it up, her breasts came free and she pushed them toward his face. She threw off her shift and moaned as his hands touched on either side of her waist. His tongue danced lightly over a nipple and she dug her fingers in his hair, pressing him closer, feeling herself grow wetter as he took her breast into his mouth.

After a moment, she gently pulled away and pushed him back onto his bunk. She knelt, lifting his legs, her mouth hovering teasingly over him. She wanted to taste him, but the fire in her loins burned achingly, and his nearness only added to her desire. She forced herself to stand, then she moved onto the bed and straddled him, pressing her knees against his hips.

She bent down and kissed him, teasing his tongue into her mouth. She moved her mouth to his ear; he moaned as she brushed herself against him.

As she pushed back and felt the waves of ecstasy as he entered her, she bit him lightly on the neck. "Slowly now, Rollo," she whispered. "Don't forget your ribs."

Changes

A mist rose near sunset.

Gerald and Sokki stood side by side on the prow, peering out into the mist. The sea lapped hypnotically against *Nightreaver*'s hull, and both men lost themselves in thought long before. Their conversation had been pointless; Gerald tried but could not remember even the subject. They had spoken on everything but the one thing they both dwelt on. Each knew what the other felt; each had been unable to voice it. Meanwhile, time had passed with Thyri, alone with Rollo, in his cabin.

Once, she had cried out. The sound had sent chills up their spines.

For Gerald, what had occurred had been unthinkable. He had known, and understood, Thyri and Megan. Now he felt that he understood nothing. He did not even understand his own jealousy.

Sokki felt simple pain. From the moment he'd met Thyri, he'd seen the woman underneath the hard shell. It hadn't been a difficult thing for him; as a warrior, he'd known many men—commanders—who could cast aside the cloak of authority and become an equal among their charges. Thyri, however dark her moods, had proven no exception to that rule. And part of his pain was that he understood what she'd done, or at least he felt that he did. She mourned Megan, and, in her mourning, her need for comfort had grown unbearable. He had felt much the same since Ottar's death, but, while he had needed her, she'd been lost in her own sorrow. His heart had ached with a desire to go to her, to offer her comfort, but he hadn't known how to do that. Now it didn't matter.

He felt no hate for Rollo—neither did Gerald—but he cursed himself. His was a sorrow of lost opportunity, for the moment that might have been.

In all their churning thoughts, neither man could guess that the real reason for Thyri's actions floated before them: a silver orb behind the mist.

They turned briefly when Rollo's door opened and Thyri

emerged. She glanced at them and smiled, then climbed up to the prow toward them.

As she approached, Gerald began to feel that all, again, was well. What had occurred in Rollo's cabin had not, in fact, occurred. Her smile was too real—too authentic. He shook the dark reflections from his mind.

When she reached them, she placed her hands on their shoulders and spoke softly. "Rollo must rest," she said, gazing out into the mists. "Danger may lurk out there," she whispered. "Be prepared."

She looked at Sokki sadly, then wrapped her arms around him, pressing him close. "I'm sorry about Ottar," she whispered in his ear. "If I could bring him back, I would." She pulled away and looked into his eyes briefly, then she turned to Gerald.

"I must not," she said, "be disturbed tonight. Under any circumstances. Please—if you do nothing else—heed me in this?"

Slowly, he nodded. She smiled again, then turned for her cabin.

They watched her until her door had shut, then they stared back out to sea.

Thyri threw off her clothes, crawled onto the bed, and looked down into Meg's face. In the shadows, the sorceress looked so at peace on the surface, but what did she feel inside? Anything? Did her serenity bode good or ill?

Thyri bent and kissed her, then crawled to the head of the bed. She rose up on her knees, placed her hands on the painting, and gazed in at the moon.

"Oh, Odin!" she whispered. "Let this be real! Do not torture me tonight . . ."

A wave of sensation swept through her body. She felt the hairs on her arms stand out.

It begins . . .

Within the painting, the moon grew bright. Or was it just her eyes?

She blinked. A dull ache ran up her arms from her wrists. The moon drew away from her. Dew glistened on the grass before her eyes. she pushed forward, but the canvas did not give.

She began to cry. Through her tears, something moved. She wiped her eyes. A bird had appeared on the limb of a nearby tree; Thyri couldn't remember it being there before. She glanced down at Megan, then gasped as the claws popped out from the tips of her fingers. For a moment, they pressed into the canvas; she feared she would tear it, then she fell forward, and her hands met the earth.

Her body on fire, Thyri leapt forward. She rolled on the grass and came up on all fours. Pain flashed through her; she screamed, but the sound that escaped her throat was a thin, mournful howl.

She looked back at the place from whence she'd come: a cave in a hillside. Its depths were black, unfathomable. Her hunger was like that—it ached, clouding her thoughts.

She glanced up at the moon and growled. Around her, the forest beckoned.

Silent now, the white wolf turned for the trees.

Avalon

When the darkness came, she smiled. In the orb of Babd, she watched them and fed off their fears, their sorrows. Perhaps, over the next few nights, the chaos in their mistress's heart would show them the full extent of their folly. Mortals in Jotunheim!

She laughed.

No need to offer them an easy death now. Let them suffer. Let them mourn their dead brother . . .

He will return to them soon enough. And they meant nothing compared to the wolf and the witch. She would gain her revenge, however, in her own way.

Rising, she wrapped the orb in a swath of black velvet, then she placed it carefully into the burlap sack where she'd collected the few other talismans she'd felt worth keeping. With twine of twisted goatskin, she tied and bound the sack.

In darkness, she descended from her tower and walked slowly to the moonlit beach. There, she glanced back briefly at the spire that jutted darkly up into the night. She would not miss it.

She looked down at her naked body and ran her hands a last time over her muscled chest; then she whispered the incantation of feth fiada *in dark, menacing tones. Almost immediately, pain shot through her as her bones stretched out. As she felt her jaw push forward, a hoarse cackle bled from the half-formed beak.*

With the spell, she needn't feel pain, but that was the way she'd always liked it.

She screamed as the bones in her arms cracked and stretched. Her skin turned black, stealing the moon's light. Down grew from her body like moss, then feathers sprouted from the downy bed. Within moments, the transformation was complete, and she stood, a huge, black bird-thing.

She tested her wings and opened her beak, sending a terrible, shrieking caw out over the sea.

In her talons, she gripped the burlap sack, and, with this burden, she took to the air, spiraling slowly up into the night.

Wildfire

In the night, she knew harmony. The forest was bountiful; the hunger—she sated it quickly, easily, and without anguish.

The old buck eyed her as she brought him down; in his gaze she thought she saw gratitude, as if he tired of battling the summer heat and the winter snows. Within her, he became strong again, lord of the trees and protector of his brethren from the fangs of the wolf. At least for the night.

After dining, she roamed. Her world knew no borders but the mountain peaks on three sides. Between them, a valley flourished, and mountain streams fed a river that flowed gently out to some distant sea. At the river, she drank deep; the water was cool and clean. Everything felt real, tasted real. And the smells—she'd never imagined they could all fill the air of one place. Some flowers: she knew them only from her childhood in Norway, but the pines recalled to her the woodlands of the new land over the ocean. Behind it all was a sweet tang—magic, but here it seemed real and proper, too, as if it had grown, with the vegetation, out of the fertile soil.

Beside the river, she lay down on a bed of moss. The magic was the earth itself; she could feel it. What small kingdom had Megan gifted her? She felt at home—at peace with the beast as she had not felt since . . . As she had never felt. Even now, with her lover neither alive nor dead. In the air here, she could feel Megan's love.

As she rested, she began to sense the presence of another: a familiar, friendly scent, but its identity eluded her, as if her memory of it had withered, buried itself under layers of other thoughts, other impressions.

She strove to peel back the layers, and as the memory came into her grasp, as deep sorrow wrapped suddenly around her heart, he stepped from the shadows.

Thyri, he growled softly.

She stared at him, into his ancient eyes. The wildness of the beast surged within her, but her sorrow was too great, overwhelming.

How came you here? he asked.

She didn't answer; she just stared at him, unable to believe that her past had so returned to haunt her. And it was a past in which she'd loved—all the more cruel because she could not lash out; she could not destroy it. She could only flee as she had before, except now she had nowhere to go.

He approached her slowly; she felt the warmth and sweetness of his breath. *I sensed your entrance on the pathways. I came here as quickly as I could.* He stopped, gazing at her.

In his eyes, she saw Pohati's. *Akiya toyn,* she heard in her mind, *it has not been long, but it feels like forever.*

The white wolf looked away from the gray. She wanted to run, but she could not move. On the bed of moss that edged the gentle river, the white wolf wept.

Here, my reader, I must intrude and admit failure. Though my heart bids me stop, I cannot omit this part of my telling for reasons that will, in the end, become apparent.

Yet, of the past events that might serve to illuminate this moment, I have written nothing. I had thought to spare myself the memory of what little I learned of Thyri's last, dark months in the new land, but my task has proven me wrong. By all accounts, I should set aside this section of my manuscript, return to the beginning, and tell it as it should have been told. Though this cannot be evident here, I have just spent an entire evening staring at this half-finished page, considering this thought. I feel no better for it.

I cannot go back. I cannot direct again my research to the days of Thyri's deepest pain, for I do not possess the talent to relate them well. Beyond that: beyond this scene with Woraag Grag, those dark days need not be told. The pain Thyri felt then, she came to tame, to hide so well that it could not touch her, so that it could retain no hold on her life. She never thought of it outside those moments when the presence of Woraag Grag summoned up the cruel, treacherous winds of remembrance.

And still I digress. I have written how Pohati fell in Thyri's clash with Aralak, and I have written how Woraag Grag, the ancient one, took the young Habnakys battle-mistress's essence into himself. I have written that, after the war in the new land had ended, Thyri roamed, wintering alone and, near spring, shunning the company even of wolves. One who has read closely this history of mine must ask, "Why? Why was it that she who had gained a peace with her curse, she who had found a new home among the beasts of the wood, would retreat into the darkest of her depressions, for that is how she is described that last day before Astrid's descent from Valhalla and her return to the lands of the Norse. Indeed, upon that return, she desired to die. Why?"

I have the answer, yet still I hesitate to immortalize it in ink. But I have come too far to turn back . . .

Woraag Grag, as written, was a god. Within him, the souls of countless fallen warriors shared his eternity. Pohati was but one of many.

But Thyri had loved Pohati. During Thyri's first changes after Pohati's death, she had sought out the ancient wolf, and they had hunted together, Thyri at peace with Pohati nearby. And, in the pale hour before sunrise one night, they had loved.

Three cycles of the moon past that, Thyri gave birth to three monsters, all dead.

There—it is written. No more! I will not go back to fit this event into its proper place, for it has no proper place. It is neither a fitting end to the tale of Thyri's life in the new land, nor is it a fitting beginning for her departure. It is only a sadness beyond words, and I am yet tempted to strike it from this page. Perhaps I shall do so. Have I not entered fantasy in my presumption to know Morgana's thoughts? Is not my tale already blemished by lack of truth? If Morgana, why not Woraag Grag? Why not leave Thyri at peace with the new land, in love with its people and the families of beasts that ruled its wood? Why not have her flee Astrid, and have her battle her cousin? Have Astrid subdue her and carry her against her will into that conflict with Alfred?

It is late, this night on which I write. By rights, I should sleep, but I know already that sleep will elude me. For now, I shall embrace that which my sorcery has known me to be true.

I move on . . .

Woraag Grag watched her silently as the tears trickled from her eyes, soaking her snout. He let her cry for a long while, then, finally, he inched closer to her, settled down on the moss, and gazed out over the river.

I never thought our union might have caused you such pain, she heard him say in her mind. *Such mortal burdens should not be yours.*

I am a mortal woman, she replied. *This form I wear under the full moon is a curse, not a blessing.*

So I have learned. Once I knew you to be mortal, but through Pohati's eyes you are akiya toyn*—the wildfire. Through the eyes* *of many others you are the same. Do you know that you age? Are you certain that this—this form you wear—does not shield you from the ravages of time? I have sought to understand much since your passing from my land. I sought you on the shadow-paths, to no avail until now. But I found others. I have counseled with your teacher, and she informed me of much.*

For a moment, Thyri felt as if time had suddenly stopped; as his words sank in, her mind caught fire as waves of excitement cut through her despair. *Scacath!* she thought. *You have spoken with Scacath?*

Yes, he answered. *Does this anger you?*

She rose, shaking her head, banishing the last, lingering phantoms. *Where is she? What did she tell you?*

She is where she is, just as you and I. You have not yet told me how you came to this place. He looked up into her eyes. As she studied him, she grew aware that he shared with her the sadness of their past, that he would, if he could, undo their tragedy. Love remained in those eyes. Pohati's memory lurked there as well. *Have you learned to walk the roads of the ancients? I always thought you knew, for by what other road might you have reached my distant shores?*

The shadow-paths, she thought. *No.* She remembered the certain turnings she'd taken to reach Scacath's grove during her years of training under the goddess's tutelage. She remembered how it had always seemed that she'd passed from one world into another, quite separate realm. *I think, perhaps, that I have done so without understanding how.*

It is not difficult, he said. *Some pathways are so open that they may be found by accident alone. Is that how you came here?*

She lowered her eyes. *No. I came here through the sorcery of a friend.*

She is a powerful sorceress?

Thyri nodded slowly. *But I fear she is not powerful enough. She lies near death, and I do not know how to aid her.*

He looked at her sadly. *Would that I were a healer. But I am not, and we are many worlds away from my own.*

What of Scacath? she asked. *How near are we to her world?*

Near, but I cannot promise she is there.

Take me to her, she said pleadingly. *Can you do that? Can you teach one how to find these shadow-paths?*

For a being of power, it is a simple task. But it can be demanding, at times very dangerous, for great evils know the pathways as well. Will you risk this?

Yes, she replied. For Megan, she thought quietly, she would risk anything.

As Woraag Grag led her downstream, Thyri realized that she had not pressed him for knowledge of Scacath's words to him. Now she did not wish to interrupt him with conversation. The night was no longer young, and from wherever he would lead her, she would need to return.

They did speak, or, rather, he did, from time to time pointing out to her the signs that he followed: the curious, unnatural twist of a certain twig; a certain change in the air that she perceived as an eddy in the ocean of magic surrounding them. They had not gone far when he abruptly turned toward the river and stepped off the bank into the air.

She smiled wryly as she watched him walk out over the current, his paws inches off the surface of the water. Fearing to think too critically of what she attempted, she followed him, smiling again when she discovered that she had not plunged into the water's depths. The air around her felt charged; her fur bristled up her spine and along her flanks.

At midstream, he disappeared. When she'd reached that point, when she saw him again, they were in another world.

They walked along a ridge, high above a golden city. A haze filled the air, and the full moon's light was paled by the burnings of countless candles below. Peering down, Thyri picked out roads traveled by what she guessed to be giant beetles marching rapidly in bizarre, chaotic patterns executed with an almost military precision.

Woraag Grag continued to speak, and she forced herself to tear her eyes away from the scene below. As she breathed the air of this new place, she noted many unplaceable scents; their impression overall was one of decay.

Strange trees dotted the ridges. They skirted them, but each time, the gray wolf quickly led the white back to the ridge's peak. He told her that he sought a specific tree and that she too should recognize it when they found it.

Indeed, she did. The overall tang of magic in the air had dispersed completely once they'd fully come into this world, but as they neared the tree of which Woraag Grag had spoken, the tang returned. She was aware of it several moments before he pronounced his discovery.

As they drew close to the next twisting in their journey, Thyri looked to her left and felt her heartbeat jump as she found herself face-to-face with one of the beetles. It was, at most, twenty paces away, and its eyes watched her dully. It smelled of metal, and it did not move. She could see into its belly; it had devoured two people, but they did not seem to care. They were—kissing.

She paused a moment and watched the people. As she did, they paused in their passion and gazed out of the beetle's stomach toward the ridge. For a moment, they did not see her, then suddenly the female's eyes met hers. A muffled scream split the night, and the beetle's eyes came suddenly to brilliant life.

At the edge of her vision, Thyri saw Woraag Grag step again out into open air. To her left, the beetle roared with a fury she'd never heard escape the throat of even the fiercest bear.

She bolted forward and dove into the air, following her guide.

Two worlds later they came to a forest that Thyri recognized immediately. She knew every tree, every trail. Years before, she had hunted here; she still possessed the boots that she had lined with the fur of a rabbit she had slain among these very trees.

Every step forward brought a new memory rushing into her mind: there, under that oak, she had loved with Astrid on a rare, lazy afternoon; here, on this very tree, she had once pinned a lizard of many colors and, in doing so, won her second braid. And, in the distance, she heard the tinkling stream that led to the bear cave full of rainbow stuff where she had won her third braid and her sword.

The memories engulfed her; the scent of her teacher filled her nostrils, and she raced forward, leaving Woraag Grag behind.

The smell of Scacath grew stronger, overwhelming her. She *was* here. All trails led to the common, and that is where Thyri found her. She sat in the clearing's center, her carriage erect, her visage dark, the embodiment of power.

Thyri stopped abruptly before her. Several moments passed before Scacath opened her eyes. "Hello, little one," spake the goddess.

Thyri, watching her, was no longer aware of her wolfen form. She was again the student, fearful of her teacher's presence, yet forever in awe. Only vaguely did she sense Woraag Grag's approach behind her.

"What brings you here?" The goddess's eyes burned like dark fires.

Knowledge, Thyri answered. *I must ask of you many things.*

You cannot ask many things, the gray wolf spoke in her mind. *If we do not depart soon, the dawn will be upon you.*

And Megan's sorcery may fail . . . Thyri looked at Scacath desperately. *I captain a ship now, teacher, and I have found love again, but she has fallen in battle and neither moves nor dies. Will you aid her?*

"I am not a healer, little one. But I fear that, even were I able to help you, I could not. Matters of grave import need attending; the balance of the major worlds is endangered; even now, Surt arms his legions."

Ragnarok?

"Perhaps." Scacath looked away and up into the stars. "On what seas do you sail?"

Jotunheim, or so I believe. We have battled giants.

Scacath raised an arm, pointing to the western sky. "Then follow that star," she said. "Under it, you will find healers. Do you see it? The left eye of the Great Raven?"

Thyri looked up. *Yes, teacher.*

Woraag Grag nudged her flank. *We must go,* akiya toyn. *Do not tempt fate!*

Thyri looked at Scacath; her teacher smiled at her—the mysterious half-smile she knew so well from her youth. Her mind on fire with fear of the future and fear for Megan, she forced herself to turn away. Woraag Grag quickly led her back through the wood.

During their return, Thyri found it impossible to concentrate on Woraag Grag's instructions, even though she knew it meant that she would be unable to make the journey again on her own. Her emotions, her fear that she would be unable to return to Megan before sunrise, spoiled her thinking, which itself turned constantly on one thing: her failure. She had failed to fulfill her dream, that dream she and Astrid had shared of spending idle time with their teacher as equals. She could never be equal to Scacath; the goddess had been as elusive as ever she was when Thyri was young.

Dawn licked the horizon as they passed through the world of the golden city and the beetles. Thyri began to fear she would be trapped in Megan's forest, unable to cross the final portal back into her cabin.

If the sun rose, perhaps Woraag Grag could still usher her back onto her ship. Then again, perhaps not . . .

When they gained the air over the gentle river, Thyri ran with Woraag Grag pacing her at her side. Near the end of their journey, he spoke with her, words she would not fully understand until later, when she'd time to reflect: *I will not seek you again,* akiya toyn, *for I understand now your pains, and I do not wish to deepen them with my memory. However, when you walk the shadow-paths, you may call to me. I will hear you, and I will come.*

She glanced at him only briefly before she dove into the dark cave in the hillside. She felt the wolf flee her as dawn exploded into the world, and she landed on her bed, naked, exhausted, the tentacles of sleep wrapping quickly about her mind.

Jotunheim

When she wakened, well after noon, the past night seemed to her like a dream. She recalled Woraag Grag, but his memory brought back only her pain in the new land, her memory of that night when . . . when . . .

She looked over at Megan.

Scacath pointing up . . . *"The left eye of the Great Raven."*

Healers.

Woraag Grag.

Thyri shook her head, rose, and staggered out into the daylight. Rollo, at the prow, looked back at her and smiled. She remembered the evening before . . . She smiled back weakly. Odin! she thought. *What tortures we might suffer in one passing of the sun!*

She turned back into her cabin, to Megan. She spent the afternoon at her lover's side, trying not to think too deeply on the past day's trials.

As the day grew old, Rollo brought her food. She felt no hunger, and though she tried, she could not eat. He grew concerned, and when he touched her hand, sorrow filled her heart. She looked into his eyes and saw the love there. Part of her wanted to return it, to replay the evening before, the way the actors in a play repeat the same loves, fears, and agonies on consecutive nights. But she could not: Scacath had given her hope for Megan, and she had to cling to that now.

She told him she had had a vision, and she had found for them a haven. The experience had exhausted her, but he needn't fear for her because now she had hope. She needed only rest for a couple of days. He should explain this to the others.

And after sunset, he should set course for the left eye of the Great Raven. Did he know it?

Yes, he answered; then he left her alone.

As the evening grew dark, she fought the turmoil in her mind. Woraag Grag had promised to come at her bidding. The mere thought of that promise pained her. But—his presence again?

Only his mention of Scacath had been able to overcome that agony.

She yet desired Scacath's counsel. Her teacher was wise; Thyri felt that she, of all beings, could help her sort out the tangled mass of emotions that her life had become. Only Scacath could tell her why. . .

Assuming she would.

But to find her again, Thyri would need Woraag Grag. And if she called him once . . . If she weakened and let the part of him that was Pohati through again to her heart?

No. The risks to her sanity were too great. And Scacath had already told her what she most needed to know. Later, when the weight of the moment had lessened, perhaps she would try to reach her teacher on her own. Perhaps Megan could help her; perhaps they would walk the shadow-paths together.

When the wolf came, Thyri roamed Megan's valley, filling her night with the hunt. She ate her fill several times over, but, in doing so, resisted the temptation of a return to Scacath, an act that could leave her either inextricably bound again to Woraag Grag, or hopelessly separated from her lover.

The next day and night were much the same. Another two days passed before Thyri again found herself able to endure the company of others. When she joined them one afternoon at the sail, she saw the joy in their faces as her mere presence uplifted their spirits.

She could understand their reaction—but then again, she could not. Looking into herself, she could not see what they saw. She felt dark and desolate inside. Pohati's face would often surface in her thoughts, and Thyri would realize the cruelty inherent in her rejection of the gray wolf.

All the while, Megan lay motionless in the dim, cold solitude of their cabin.

When Thyri had offered Rollo their new course, some small irony had lingered in the fact that, at top speed, they were yet just under a month from their destination. As *Nightreaver* sped eastward over the immense ocean, the moon waned and waxed again, growing ominously more nearly full with each passing night.

Of that journey, much could be told of small mishaps and near-adventures: near because they were avoided as *Nightreaver*'s captain grew obsessed with her desire to dock under the left eye of the Great Raven. One episode warrants mention, however, but for no reason other than that Rollo had dreamed of it that morning before he woke at Fandis's: On the mist-enshrouded seas, late one evening, *Nightreaver*'s crew fell under the enchantment of a solitary voice that called sadly to them through the mist. Rollo, at the time, recalled his dream and he turned *Nightreaver* for the voice. As they approached, they saw the woman, a wraithlike thing of skin and bones, but at the time, all thought her beautiful, and Rollo began to shout with Sokki, arguing over who should love her.

During that battle of words, Thyri emerged from her cabin, calmly took Rui's bow and quiver, and ended the siren's song with a single arrow.

All other events were minor and of no lasting consequence, even though Horik almost lost a hand during one of the battles with sea monsters. No, during that journey, only small happenings came and went. Sokki and Horik slowly grew to accept the death of Ottar, and the jealousy the others felt for Thyri's attentiveness toward Rollo faded as her seeming favoritism toward the affable Viking came to be accepted as part of the natural order of things. It was to Rollo that the others looked in times of danger, and the perils of the sea left no room for any childish defiance of his command.

And the matter never again grew pressing. Though Thyri occasionally favored Rollo's company while she drove them ever eastward, she remained chaste, and, thus, passing time allowed Gerald and Sokki to build their fantasies anew.

Rui, after his fashion, took all happenings in stride.

Their quest led them to land, the first sighting of any real size. After a brief, southerly diversion, they found a broad river and started inland. After a day and night of struggling upriver, they found what they sought.

Thyri, at the time, was painfully aware that the next night's moon would be full.

fi-Logath

Dawn brushed the eastern sky, painting a mural of red and violet over the city of crystal spires. Several ornately carved vessels, their lines cast starkly in shadow, floated in the waters at the city's foot.

Horik and Rui shipped their oars as the vision loomed larger, stealing their breath away. A spear of sunlight suddenly broke over the land beyond and struck one of the tallest spires, streaking the sky over the river with lights that flashed and flashed again: all the colors of the rainbow. Horik, as a boy, had known well the lights of the North; only against those subtle, interweaving light streams could he measure what he now saw. The rainbows above were brighter, more intense, more dynamic and alive, a concert of rainbow swords lashing out, slicing through the dawn.

As the sun rose, the rainbows settled into the spires themselves. Still, the two men found it difficult to look away. Several moments passed before Rui noticed the figures on the near end of the city's docks: five warriors, armored in gold, stood in a line, watching *Nightreaver*'s approach.

Rui nudged Sokki, pointing at the warriors; he rose, turning to wake the others. Moments later, all stood at the prow as Horik and Sokki brushed the oars lightly over the water, maintaining a slow, steady approach.

"This is it?" Rollo asked, glancing down at Thyri.

Gerald stared across at the golden warriors. Three were male, two female; their armor fit close to their bodies, its contours incredibly faithful; he wondered what smith might have dared such a feat: they looked almost like towering, naked, golden youths. Even at a distance, their height was unmistakable; the shorter of the females stood at least a head taller than Rollo. Their hair, long and golden like their armor, flowed out from under silver, feathered helms. Each wore a sword in a jeweled scabbard; while the males posted spears, the females carried tall, slender bows.

Rui spoke softly to Gerald: "Nothing I have seen—and I have seen much, my friend—could rival this."

"Not giant chicken feathers?"

The archer chuckled. "No," he said, "not even that."

As he spoke, a rich baritone erupted over the river: a steady, wordless tone that suddenly modulated, then soared as if to dance among the clouds overhead. Just before the resolving note, a soprano joined the baritone, following in its steps, mirroring, two octaves higher, each breathless leap, each inflection. They sang in rounds, the melody at once simple yet beautifully ornate, the counterpoint majestic, as if a choir, not two voices, sang a greeting to the morning.

The song's beauty recalled Megan's casting, when she had remade the ship. The singers, if anything, were more exotic and fantastic than the sorceress. The male—the central figure among those on the docks—ended as he'd begun: holding his final note steady while the soprano at his side descended her scale before they jointly dropped off into silence.

Gerald watched the singer's eyes pass over each of them. The gaze was warm, but cautious, guarded. The giant (for he *was* so, in human terms) brought his eyes to rest on Thyri before calling out over the water.

"We greet you, Eiriksdattir," he called. "She of the hidden lightning advised of your coming."

Gerald glanced questioningly at Rui; the archer shrugged. They looked to Thyri as she smiled back at the warrior.

"Then you know of our burden," she called back.

He nodded.

"Can you aid us? I offer you anything in my power to give."

He looked at her oddly, then bent as the woman beside him whispered something in his ear. When she'd finished, he stood straight and called back to Thyri. "That will not be necessary. You are guests."

Nightreaver glided ever nearer the dock. Gerald grew increasingly captivated by their hosts' appearances. At a distance, only their height had confounded their humanity. Upon closer inspection, their skin possessed a blue-gray translucence that seemed both youthful and aged. And their wariness nagged at him; he wondered what *she of the hidden lightning* meant. Certainly not Morgana—and Megan didn't make any sense. Brigid? Had Thyri communed with the goddess that night he'd met her? Much, on the other hand, had transpired since then.

Rollo tossed a rope to the dock; Thyri kept her eyes locked on him with whom she spoke. She too was wary, but only in reaction to the thinly disguised skepticism in the eyes ashore. It demeaned the value of their welcoming song, the beauty of which had been flawless, but, now it seemed, coldly so, offered as an obligation. What had Scacath told them? Threatened them with? Warned them of? If her teacher had not intervened, would these warriors have allowed *Nightreaver*'s approach at all? Surely they were powerful; they lived in a world of constant danger, of giants capable of crushing their fantastic towers under the weight of a single foot, but those towers stood and had stood, Thyri guessed instinctively, for centuries, if not millenia.

And Scacath had said they could heal Megan; there was power, surely, in that, and that thought kindled excitement in her heart. She had reached her destination!

She felt some surprise when a woman's hand was offered to help her ashore. Thyri shifted her gaze, looking up into an uncertain smile. The tang of magic washed over her. Abruptly, she grasped the hand and let it guide her forward. She looked into the woman's eyes and smiled warmly as she felt the magic probing her; she opened herself to it, hoping that whatever darkness it might find would not be one which they feared. She had to gain their trust. They *had* to help her; she hoped they would see that she desired nothing more.

As her foot touched on the dock, she spoke. "I am Thyri," she said into the magic. "Please do not fear us. We come with peace in our hearts."

The woman's smile grew more relaxed. "You bear many burdens," she said.

Thyri nodded. *But they are mine, not yours. I seek relief only of one.*

I apologize, Thyri, if your welcoming seemed less than joyous. These are troubled times when evil often bears a semblance of goodness and familiarity. Odin, himself, we would greet in the same fashion.

Am I evil, then? Or good.

The smile broadened into sad mirth. *Both, as are we all. But you strive to transcend the darkness, and that is all that matters, is it not?* She turned to the warrior next to her. "Go," she told him, "and bring *helfin*, and a harnessed, canopied bed. The ailing Tuathan lies in the rearmost cabin."

The man nodded, then raced toward the crystal spires. The woman turned then to the humans on *Nightreaver*'s deck. "I am Arithea," she said. "We have sung you the ancient affirmation of goodwill. Welcome to fi-Logath."

Slowly, Rollo disembarked and gained Thyri's side. One by one, looking up at their hosts, the others followed.

* * *

What can be understood by mere mortals of such a place as fi-Logath? Crystal spires rooted in the soil not by men, but by sorcery? They reached up into the sky, some straight, some at angles, just as smaller crystals grown by nature. But these were oddly cut, hollowed, melted in places where they resembled the spires and pillars nature fashions in damp caves. They possessed nothing of the symmetry men so value in their palaces and shrines, yet their majesty dwarfed anything envisioned by mortal architects or builder-priests.

Fi-Logath was the essence of that which men strive to capture and edify. Man's works, at best, capture only some small facet of the divine.

Arithea's brother, the warrior with whom she'd sang and he who had spoken first with Thyri, was named Donalu. His eyes were like cool fires, their irises deep blue and flecked with red and orange. When he smiled, as he did now, they were warm, laughing eyes. As Gerald watched him, however, he found himself hoping that he would never have to face those eyes in battle. They had a sorcerous, hypnotic quality: a strange ability to externalize emotion, filling the dining chamber where they now sat with joy and peace. In battle, Gerald had no doubt that those eyes would send real, tangible fear into the hearts of Donalu's enemies.

The foods they ate—strange fruits, nuts the size of small apples, and a sweet, milky liquid—were borne to their table by rosy-skinned, muscular creatures half the size of normal men. *Helfin* Arithea had named them—the same creatures who had come to the docks and carried Megan to the towers of fi-Logath. "They are like us," Donalu had already told them, "a people unto themselves. Their fathers were dwarves, but their mothers were of the fair race. They have some magics of their own, but they use them always in our service. We do not keep them here by force."

His words had rung true. Gerald had watched the *helfin* engaged in their chores. Not once had he seen a face that had not smiled. They seemed to thrive on their work, performing with joy the tasks that human cultures often assign to slaves. Gerald had found this curious, but, in the end, he'd concluded that the relationship between the *helfin* and Donalu's people was a symbiotic one. The little folk found safety under Donalu's wings; manual work was a small price to pay under such circumstances.

Now they ate the products of the *helfin*'s labors. Each bite tasted more delicious than the last. Their drink was heady, like a wine, and it spread warmth through their limbs, yet did not dull the mind or senses. If anything, it made them stronger. Donalu named the liquid *abrosi*. Among the foods, there was no hint of meat or flesh of any kind.

Donalu and Arithea sat across from Thyri and her crew. The table was long, with seating for a dozen along each side. Donalu's people filled all the remaining seats. The chamber was undecorated but for the natural beauty of its walls and arches. In one corner, a trio of *helfin* harpists played sad airs, their instruments resonating hauntingly within the crystal walls.

After introductions had been made all around, it was Donalu, mainly, who spoke. His voice, in conversation, was much like it was in song: smooth, tranquil, and majestic.

"Two millenia past," he said, "when the men of the middle world were yet young, the fates of the elder peoples were decided here, in this world and on these plains. It was then that the sons of Ymir, fleeing some greater, growing evil in the fiery realm of Surtur, came here and did battle to lay claim to their newly chosen land. The wars cost all sides much, for the physical strengths of the giants were great. Only the most noble and powerful of the elder races survived the initial, crushing waves. The *Pharosia*, the eagle people and once rulers of all lands and worlds, were slain to the last warrior by the *fir-Jotun*, Surtur's own sorcerous children.

"They were wars of sorcery against muscle. In the end, the sorcery lost and won. The most powerful warlocks and sorcerers of the elder races cast terrible spells that tore the worlds asunder, thus creating new worlds into which they could retreat, leaving to Ymir's children all the ancient homelands. Into these new worlds fled the children of Danu, the children of Chronos, and of Bor and the rest of the ancient fathers. The homelands became Jotunheim, forever debased but for pockets of light into which lingering sorceries dissuade the Jotun from entrance.

"It is said among the *helfin*—the only race not dislocated during those terrible wars—that Herculon, then the bravest and strongest of the sons of Chronos, had defended this place from the invasions. Herculon alone of the elder warriors was a match for the Jotun. With his sword, he slew twenty of the giants without the aid of sorcery of any kind. In the end, Herculon fell. His blood soaked the earth, and from this joining, we sprang the following spring."

At this, Arithea laughed. "So the *helfin* tell us," she said. "In fact, we are, like them, mongrels. We are called the faer-Jotun, spawn of hil-Jotun, the smallest of the giant races, and a few unfortunate daughters of Danu. We are children of those wars of which my brother speaks, and the blood of both sides runs in our veins. It is said among the children of Danu, whose word in this case I find more trustworthy, that our mothers, before our births, fled here and grew these towers from the earth to house us. They knew then that we could not live among their people or among the Jotun, for both races would see in us their enemies.

"As for the tales of the *helfin,* well, I fear they pity us. We are like them, but worse. True, their blood is tarnished by a mixing of races, but their fathers were not ignoble. One cannot say that of ours. Our mothers all died in childbirth, and the *helfin* cared for us in our youth. I feel that, in their hearts, they yet see themselves as our caretakers. Their tale of Herculon I remember hearing first during my third summer. I have seen countless summers since then, and I feel somewhat wiser."

Such was the tale they heard while dining at the faer-Jotun's table. They also learned that those eighteen faer-Jotun with whom they dined composed the mongrel race of immortals in its entirety. Once, they'd been twenty-five, but seven of their number had perished in various conflicts with the Jotun over the years.

And the faer-Jotun women were of infertile womb. Immortal, divine mules.

Changes

Arithea sat on the floor next to Megan's bed and laid her hand on the sorceress's brow. Thyri, standing next to her, whispered a short prayer to Odin, pleading to the All Father that Arithea would not tell her something she did not wish to hear. Megan *had* to be healed, otherwise Thyri herself would perish from grief.

The faer-Jotun, sensing Thyri's raging emotions, looked up at her after only a moment. *Do not fear, white-hair, she is not lost. Your friend is strong, and though her spirit is gravely wounded, she heals herself even now. In time, she will recover on her own.*

How much time?

Two centuries, maybe three.

We do not have that much time.

Arithea smiled. *I know. I can aid her return to this world. It will take a week, maybe less. You must leave me alone to do this.*

I could not stay even if you allowed me.

The full moon? I know—that is why you cannot stay. Otherwise, your love could aid me. I have seen into you, Eiriksdattir, and I know your pain. You must soon leave fi-Logath and be far from here by sunset. I trust you can fend for yourself no matter what your surrounds. Return when the fullness of the moon has passed, and perhaps, by then, your friend may greet you herself.

"What of my men?" Thyri asked aloud.

"They will think you here with me, will they not? Do not fear, they will be attended. But they are, in their hearts, loyal to you. I do not think that knowledge of your secret would turn them against you."

"No," she said flatly. "That I will never allow."

Arithea turned her gaze back to Megan. "If that is your wish, white-hair, so be it."

Thyri left the dining chamber with Arithea; Rollo, Gerald, and the others stayed. Donalu entertained them with further stories, some certainly half-true or less, of the ancient wars. Spirits among the men rose to new heights when a new, more potent brew was brought by the *helfin* after the eating was done.

After a time, Donalu tired of speaking and asked for a tale in return. The other faer-Jotun joined him in the request, all eyes eagerly settling on *Nightreaver*'s crew. Sokki found his gaze captured by a slender, seven-foot female with an obvious, seductive smile and streaks of red in her golden hair. He felt himself responding to her attentions, surprised that he suddenly could not picture Thyri clearly in his mind.

In their corner, the *helfin* ensemble had grown to ten instruments, and the music had grown wilder.

Rollo smiled. "How can we tell you a tale that you do not already know? We know many tales of Odin and his sons, but I daresay you know them better. Perhaps we have a tale to tell, but she has left the room, and, in any case, she seldom cares to speak of herself."

"You do yourself an injustice, Rollo!" Rui spoke out. "What of your tale? How you threw off the shackles of the Overking of Jorvik?"

"What of it? That is *her* tale in truth, for without her it never would have happened, just as you would not be here, just as none of us would be here. Sokki's tale also, of the battle with Alfred, would be nothing without her. We are but facets of her more brilliant gem."

Donalu laughed. "Well put, my friend! But surely a gem of any worth may be appreciated facet by facet, no? My sister told us little before your arrival, hardly more than to be wary of deception until she was sure you were no Jotun trick. Tell us more."

"I cannot tell without her," Rollo said.

Gerald cleared his throat. He felt elation; the *abrosi* and its successor had more than gone to his head. "I have heard, at least in part, all of our tales. If the others do not object, I will tell." He paused, looking at Rollo. The Viking raised an eyebrow, then shrugged.

And so Gerald spoke. He told of the battle of Ethandune as he'd heard it from Sokki and Horik. He told of Thyri's beheading of Guthrom's guard and how that had drawn him to her, and he told how, later that evening, he had aided Thyri in her summoning of Megan.

Gerald told then of all that had followed, of Rollo and Fandis as the Viking had told it, and of Thyri's reunion with the sons of Gunnar. Then he told of the mysterious island where they had battled Morgana, and he finished with the confrontation on what *Nightreaver*'s crew had come to call the Isle of Giant Chickens, when Rollo's ribs had been cracked (it must be written that, though the Viking had suffered and had, by this time, healed for the most part, he had not shown pain in his features since that evening with Thyri).

Such was the air of goodwill around the table that, when Gerald finished, he was rewarded with spontaneous applause. The reaction brought a beaming smile to his lips.

That smile—his happiness, was, perhaps, his first real mistake.

Unnoticed by all, the morning had turned to afternoon, and the afternoon had aged, turning the crystal walls first a bright yellow that paled and split into oranges and blues as the sun hurried in its descent.

Unknown to them, Thyri had already departed to spend the last hours of sunlight scouting for possible dangers near the mouth of the cave she had chosen as her lair for the evening.

In fi-Logath, all save Arithea had grown consumed with joy and mirth.

Near sunset, Sokki found himself being led by the hand through crystal halls to the chambers of the faer-Jotun with the rosy lips and the red-streaked hair. Her name was Elinta, and his evening with her was long and memorable.

Later, the rest of *Nightreaver*'s crew found themselves similarly matched. For the time, thoughts of Thyri had vanished from all their minds save that of one: Rollo, as the giantess's caresses reawakened the dull achings around his ribs, found that he could not shake the ghosts of that one evening with Thyri from his mind. Caught in his passion, he played it through, but sleep, afterward, was long in coming.

Late that night, Megan Elana Kaerglen heard a faint, distant voice calling to her from far above. For a long time, she listened to it, wondering what it was and what it meant. As she thought, she began to wonder who she was, and, then, what that meant.

After a time, she struggled upward and fell. The voice yet called her; she struggled toward it again.

Slowly, the voice grew louder.

Thyri hunted.

Game in this land was scarce. She'd not lacked sustenance, but the pursuit of small game had led her, by midnight, far from the region to which she'd intended to restrict herself.

She needed something larger than squirrels and rabbits to sate her hunger, but deer—in fact, all hooved beasts—seemed markedly absent. Thyri guessed that unseen, more menacing predators than she were responsible—several times already she had neared patches of the forest that stank of rot and disease, reminding her of the grove of Pye of the Blue Moon on Kaerglen Isle. These blemishes in the forest she'd avoided.

As the night wore on, and as the dark hungers within her grew more demanding, she nearly gave in to the beast, to let it fare where it would, into whatever dangers lay waiting in the forest's darkest, decaying corners. As this thought of resignation played through her head, she caught whiff of a faint, yet distinct scent that sent her thoughts racing anew.

Disbelieving her senses, she followed the scent until she could believe only one thing: Scacath had passed through this wood a mere fortnight before. The goddess had been hurried, unconcerned with covering her passage. In places, Thyri discovered faint traces of footprints.

Her teacher had traversed this ground. She'd been alone . . . Why had she not used her sorceries to inform fi-Logath of *Nightreaver*'s approach? Thyri would never have guessed that Scacath's words to Arithea had been spoken face-to-face.

Unless—*Ragnarok*. Did the final, great conflict truly approach? The warnings she'd heard, from Astrid, from Scacath herself—they were real.

All the Norse knew that *Ragnarok* was the certain destiny of themselves and their gods. But to know that it came *now* . . . How soon? What forces had marshaled themselves for the conflict? Who would perish?

Her thoughts gained urgency. What if it were true? What if the fates of all worlds hung now in precarious balance? What if terrible forces would soon destroy all the lives she knew, even her own? And Megan—did Thyri seek her recovery only to offer her a brief life of warring and bloodshed?

She had hoped, in taking *Nightreaver* from Guthrom's harbor, to travel unburdened by loyalty to all save Megan, herself, and their crew, but this had not come to pass. She had already lost one man, and she'd almost lost Megan. She'd desired to avoid conflict, but now—perhaps conflict was her only destiny . . . perhaps there could be no end to the bloodshed and heartache.

And Scacath: she had spoken with her teacher and failed to gain the answers she so desperately desired. On the last moon, on those last two days in Megan's forest, she had failed to attempt the passage back to Scacath's grove. Now, here, Wyrd, the goddess of fate, had given her a new trail. But to follow it?

Now was the time. In her wolfen form, she could cover more

ground in a few hours than she could hope to match in several days on foot. But what of Megan's recovery and her crew? They were safe. With luck, she would soon return to fi-Logath.

Such was the train of Thyri's rational thought. Beneath the logic, her emotions broiled in a chaotic caldron. Deep within, she knew she could not leave Scacath's trail unexplored. Her decision was never in doubt.

Doubling back on her tracks, Thyri raced to retrieve her clothing and her sword; then, with five hours left before sunrise, the white wolf headed north, away from fi-Logath, into the land the *helfin* had long before named *Atale*—the Reaches of Despair.

Warriors

Rollo wakened, blinking his eyes momentarily against the soft, white light of the room. Hints of silver and blue flickered in the walls; for a moment, he thought himself in a cage of ice, then he remembered the day before.

He sat shaking his head, expecting to feel the dull ache of a hangover. But his mind felt clear and his limbs strong. He felt softness beneath him and tested it with a hand: he had slept on a down mattress. He looked around the room; he was alone.

The faer-Jotun, Ingrit, had left him. Late in the night? No—the mattress next to where he had lain was yet warm, and her perfume lingered strongly in the air, pungent. The smell was sweet, enticing, but as the night came back, he hated it. What had they done yesterday? After weeks at sea, thrust suddenly into the company of a race of gods . . . What of Thyri and Arithea? How fared Megan? When Arithea had made a brief appearance in the early evening, she had told them that she might remain cloistered with Thyri and Megan for as long as a week. They were not to be disturbed.

But what Rollo needed right now was to see Thyri's face. To see himself in her eyes and reassure himself that all was as it seemed. He needed to see that she did not hate him. He knew that she loved Megan; he knew that Thyri could never be his, but he belonged to her nevertheless.

Ingrit, goddess or not, could never sunder that bond. But she had surely weakened it.

As if responding to his thoughts, she entered, bearing a tray laden with fruits and crystal goblets of *abrosi*.

In the morning light, he appraised her. She *was* beautiful, her face perfect, finely chiseled like those of the ancient statues in Guthrom's old hall in Jorvik. Her full, blond mane made him think of the Valkyrie, her lightly rouged lips of his old fantasy memories of Fandis. Flowing silks, violet and white, draped her figure, clinging to her around her breasts, which were full and—he knew—soft and unblemished though she'd told him she was, like the rest of her race, some twenty centuries old.

And yet there was no hint of that age in her eyes. As she gazed at him, offering the tray, she could have been nineteen, for all the girlish nervousness and excitement hidden in her expression.

Seeing her face, Rollo turned away, unable to watch or take responsibility for the pain that his rejection summoned into her eyes. The *abrosi*, the food and drink of these gods, had commanded his actions the previous day. For the faer-Jotun, and perhaps for the rest of *Nightreaver*'s crew, this may have been right, but for Rollo Anskarson . . . Too much weighed on his mind. Danger still stalked them. Somewhere, out there in Jotunheim, Morgana brooded and awaited them. She could not have forgotten them. One amongst them, at least, needed to remember that.

"No," he said to Ingrit. "Today I shall fast. I wish to be alone."

For a moment, she did not move, then he heard her turn and silently exit the chamber.

Sokki's reflection greeted him from every polished surface in the hall of sculptures, his blond hair and brown garb giving their color to each fantastic statue, each etching in the walls of the hall. And the art: nymphs reclined on the floor of a forest of crystal trees while dragons curled around the branches above; fish hung suspended in the embrace of a frozen waterfall; on one wall, a palace of fire and ice topped a distant hill; on another, Odin gazed out over all in the gallery from his throne while, directly before the All Father, empty suits of armor danced a frozen battle with swords and spears that floated free in the air, unmoving, yet unheld by any hand.

As he moved, the colors in the chamber changed subtly—a streak of red here, a patch of bluish silver there. On a low, crystal toadstool at the foot of a lounging wood nymph, Elinta sat, her eyes absorbed by his face, his sense of wonder.

"You're impressed?" she asked, smiling.

He nodded.

"Some pieces," she said, idly looking around, "were the work of centuries."

"Who are your artists?"

She laughed, tilting back on the toadstool. "These are all mine," she said. "We all must have something with which to occupy our time. We can raise no children. You might say that we are willing prisoners of our towers."

"Why can't you leave? Fare out into this world and conquer new lands?"

She raised an amused eyebrow. "Why? What might we find that we do not already have? We are only eighteen, and can be no more. We are comfortable here, and we are seldom threatened. The *helfin* provide for our every need."

"Have you never felt lonely?"

She leaned back, running a hand up the leg of the nymph. "Sometimes. But great beauty can flow from loneliness. You do not like my work?"

She sat up straight, her arms against her sides, her hands pressed against the curve of the toadstool next to her hips. Her long legs stretched out over the floor toward Sokki.

"It's beautiful," he said. "Like she who created it."

She smiled. "Over the years we have had countless visitors, so loneliness does not concern us much. We are a haven for those of the elder races who occasionally pass through these lands. And we entertain each other. Most of us have galleries like this among the towers. I have two others, but this is my favorite. But we all do different things. Ingrit paints. Doranu crafts animate toys to entertain the *helfin* children, and Arithea carves figurines from black stones when she is not practicing sorcery. Did you know that every tune you heard the *helfin* perform yesterday was composed by Donalu? And he has written countless thousands more. You must ask him to play before you leave; he can be quite shy in the company of strangers."

He looked at her distantly. "Is that how you see me, Elinta? Another passing stranger? I have never had a night to compare with the one I have spent with you. Will you choose Rollo this evening, or perhaps Donalu? Surely, we mortals cannot match the passions of gods!"

She eyed him cautiously. "We chose each other, Sokki. Have I rejected you? I too enjoyed last night. A moment ago, as I sat here watching you appraise these children of my heart, I thought of how it might be to capture a moment of our love in crystal so that, centuries hence, another might come here and feel—" She stopped suddenly, her eyes moving to the image of Odin she had carved in the chamber's wall. "There may be no more centuries, Sokki," she said distantly. "This may be the last. Ours may be the last love fi-Logath sees before the first gusts of the final winter."

Slowly, he approached her. Her words, tainted so with impending doom, did not disturb him. Instead, they added a desperate, romantic edge to his presence there. So much had changed in the last day! He stood in the presence of an immortal. He had loved an immortal.

He placed a hand lightly on her shoulder, caressing her skin, brushing back her hair. "I am a man," he said. "I am human, destined to die."

"Yes," she said, gazing into his eyes. "But is your heart?"

With that question, Elinta brought tears into Sokki's eyes. She swam in his vision, her face softened by his sorrow.

For long moments, they stood thus, gazing at each other. After a while, she brushed away his tears and summoned a smile up through her sadness. She rose, and walked slowly to the floating battle of crystal swords and armor.

"We all have a little magic in us, Sokki, even those of us who do not often practice sorcery." She glanced back at him. "I have seldom desired to use enchantments in my art, but this piece would have been impossible without them." Her voice again grew distant. "In this lies the essence of warfare. There are no faces in war, only weapons and death. Without weapons, without armor, a warrior is naked, is nothing in battle. And even at the hilt of a sword, in the space within the armor, the life itself—by itself—is nothing. Formless, and too light to tip the scales of the balance."

She reached out and grasped the hilt of a long, gleaming sword."To the Jotun, of course, that doesn't apply. Their weapon is their size." She turned and strode back to him, holding the sword before her. "Take it," she said. "It is a true weapon, the art would have been meaningless were this not so. It will aid you. With this, my brother Feron slew three Jotun before he died."

He stared at her. "But it was a sculpture," he said, reaching out hesitantly to touch her hand where she gripped the sword's hilt. "Part of a sculpture that you created."

"No," she said. "Before the art, there was only this, in my brother's hand. He died thirty years ago, engaged in the very exploits you just so casually suggested. Only after that, after Donalu returned with Feron's sword, was the art born."

He squeezed her hand and drew close to her. The night before, he had felt awkward when they'd first embraced. She had towered over him, pressing his face between her breasts. Now he longed for that embrace. He looked up into her eyes. "I will take this gift, Elinta, but I will never use it. I will never leave you. I will make this place my home."

"You cannot," she said. As confusion swept over him, she smiled sadly. "Oh, do not fear, we would never ask you to leave. I would never want you to leave, but leave you will. It is said among the *helfin* that no traveler may come once to fi-Logath and stay. For two millenia, that has held true. Something will call you away. When you go, take my brother's sword. Perhaps it will give you the strength to return to me."

He brushed his lips lightly over her breasts. "I have not left yet," he whispered.

She bent down. As their lips met, Horik's voice echoed harshly in the chamber: "Sokki" came Horik's words. "We have found you at last!"

He backed out of Elinta's embrace and looked to the entrance.

"Come," Horik called to him, placing his arm around the back of his companion. "Renta has just told me a remarkable tale of a battle between elves and dwarves! You must hear it as well."

Sokki glanced back at Elinta and sighed. She laughed and pushed the crystal sword into his hand; then she grasped his other arm and led him out of her gallery.

Gerald carefully placed the scroll on Tuathan battle customs back into its slot and returned to the long wall of books stacked from floor to ceiling. He had exhausted the middle row earlier, searching in vain for a script that he knew. Even among the scrolls, he had found comprehensible only the one, penned in a curious mix of his tongue and—something else.

He had spent the morning trading tales with Donalu, and after a lunch as enticing as their feast the day before, Donalu had offered him free rein in his library. He hadn't thought then that this embarrassing clash of language would be the result, and his pride kept him from calling for aid.

And, aside from that, he felt good. The *abrosi* had filled him with warm contentment, and the monotonous results of his explorations through the faer-Jotun's tomes had made him laugh more often than not. He had had worse days.

Chuckling to himself, he reached up for another volume.

Rui squinted at his target—a distant tree—and scowled; his last arrow had struck wood, but a full six inches from the knot at which he'd aimed. He notched another arrow, then paused as he sensed someone approaching behind him.

He turned, and, momentarily, the towers of fi-Logath caught him up. They reached up into the blue sky, their sheer faces gleaming with blues and whites from the clouds and the sun's yellow light. The approaching footfalls came from behind a tall hedge; as they grew louder, Rui lowered his eyes. After a moment, Rollo rounded the hedge and stopped before him.

The archer smiled. "So—you seek solitude in these gardens as well?"

Rollo nodded.

Rui turned, unleashing his arrow. This time, he hit his mark. "You do not care for the pleasures offered here?"

Rollo thought for a moment before answering. "I do not mind pleasure. This just does not seem the time for it."

Rui turned back to him. "Why? What's the point of life, my friend, if not pleasure?"

"These pleasures are illusion," Rollo said distantly. "We are here to heal Megan; then we must go."

"Back to the world we know? Because the sorceress can guide us there?"

"In time. But first, a battle awaits us."

"What do you mean?"

Rollo looked at the archer and sighed. He had never laid out his suspicions about Morgana for the crew; before, at sea, he'd thought it for the best. Now, he wished he'd taken a different approach. The threat was too real. On the other hand, the conflict was Thyri and Megan's—they were the ones with whom the decisions rested. Perhaps they wouldn't leave fi-Logath. Perhaps, after Megan's recovery, she would seek out Morgana—for surely the sorceress knew that Thyri's victory could not have been final—with the faer-Jotun at her side.

In that case, perhaps he was unnecessary. In any case, with Megan healed, Thyri would no longer need him, for she would have again her chosen companion. Perhaps he *should* return to Ingrit . . .

But still that didn't feel right.

"Nothing," he told Rui at last. "Our presence here just does not feel right. My thoughts turn again and again to Ragnarok."

The archer laughed, notching another arrow. "A war between gods? Were it so, Rollo, we would do best to seek refuge far from the battlefield. There are lights too bright for mortal eyes." He turned away and let loose the arrow, which bit into the wood just under his last shot.

"We can do," Rui said cryptically, "only that which we can do."

"Who are you?" Megan asked as the beckoning grew louder.

"A friend. Arithea I am named."

"I have no friends."

"That is untrue. What of Eiriksdattir?"

The voice's words conjured images in the darkness: a face, a sword. A body, burnt by the sun, beaten by the sea. A hand on her breast . . . "I know that name."

"That is good."

"Where am I?" She gazed up at the face of Eiriksdattir; the eyes were familiar, comforting.

"The edge of nowhere. You are close; you must come to me."

"Very well." The sorceress struggled upward. She felt as if she swam through molasses. "It is not easy," she gasped as she swam through the face.

The vision shattered, sending streams of color out through the darkness.

Thyri dove to the side as the giant lizard lashed out at her. She felt the hair on her legs bristle as the huge talons missed her by inches.

As she landed, she struck across with her sword, the blade biting through scale into flesh. The sound of cracking bone split the air, and the monster roared. Its head loomed over her; saliva dripped from its jaws, burning the grass at her side. She swung her sword up into the maw of the beast, slicing off a row of its razor-sharp teeth. She swung back and cut through its neck. Blood sprayed over her. She swung again and rolled away, coming to her feet as the monster crashed to ground.

Staring at it, she bent over, her hands on her knees as she caught her breath. She felt filthy; the day's battles had caked her arms and clothing with blood. She felt exhausted, but she knew the land would not let her rest. She had to keep moving, keep to Scacath's trail.

If her teacher could pass through this land, so could she!

She needed only to stay alive until nightfall; then the wolf would keep her safe, its speed capable of outdistancing any danger. At least any the land had thus far served up.

The afternoon wore on, and Scacath's trail twisted suddenly eastward. She followed the signs carefully, the scent more difficult to follow in the day than at night.

Near dusk, she reached the carcasses. They sprawled over broken trees, their bones green, covered with slime and moss. None were fresh, but the smell, to Thyri's heightened senses, was repugnant.

Giants. All long dead, some with impossibly huge swords clutched in bony, rotted hands. She didn't care to know what had slain them. Scacath, thankfully, had skirted the carnage.

Following her teacher's detour, Thyri felt a nausea take root in the pit of her stomach. Pinpricks of light began to invade her vision, and her sense for magic went wild. Something had again found her; she was under attack!

She cast about for signs of predators but found none. The sun rode low in the sky; the moon had already risen. It glared at her, beckoned to her. Soon it would take her, but what of the transformation? She needed safety if she wished to preserve her clothes and her sword. During those few moments, she would be vulnerable.

The nausea clouded her thoughts; she had to banish it, and soon. Swallowing hard, biting her lip to create a new pain, to distract her from the nausea, she rushed headlong for the magic's center.

Her nausea grew, and she fought the urge to collapse, to spill out her guts onto the forest floor. A wind rose up, and leaves whipped through the trees, into her face, but she brushed them away, forcing herself deeper into the heart of the sorcerous maelstrom. She felt her teeth cut through her lip and tasted her own blood mixing with the bile that had begun to rise on its own into her mouth. The leaves grew wilder, and she resisted an insane urge to battle them with her sword. Just when she felt she had lost, that she would surely die at the hands of this unseen foe, she reached the magic's source:

In a clearing, at the heart of the whirling leaves, it stood, a beast like a bear with tentacles and an extra pair of eyes in its forehead. It watched her placidly; it didn't move, though its tentacles flailed about absently at its feet. She felt an agelessness in its gaze, and the nausea flowed through her now in waves. She bit harder on her lip and rushed at it, bringing her blade down into its neck.

She met no resistance; as she charged, it simply gazed at her. As she cleaved through it, no blood escaped. The wind of leaves seemed to sigh, and then the beast collapsed, and the nausea, the magic, fell with it.

She stood there, panting over the bear thing as the sun began to set and the sky darkened. After a moment, she staggered away, stripped off her clothes and wrapped them about her sword, fashioning a blood-caked bundle.

During this last conflict, she had lost Scacath's trail. After nightfall, she would retrace her steps. Now, she waited for darkness, for the wolf.

Magic

Arithea squeezed Megan's hand hard as the eyes of the sorceress fluttered open. The faer-Jotun smiled; then something like white fire ripped through her and she screamed.

Megan feebly tried to break free of Arithea's grasp; the grip had tightened and remained so as the faer-Jotun's wailing subsided into wracking sobs. She closed her eyes and spoke to the voice that had summoned her from the darkness. *What has happened?* she asked. *What pains you?*

He has fallen, Arithea answered after a moment. *Our northern border is breached.*

Megan opened her eyes and looked around at the crystal chamber. Everything was white. She had no idea of where she was, or even, truly, who she was with. Where was the ship? Where was Thyri? And Morgana . . . Thyri must have defeated her. How else might they have survived to come here?

She waited for Arithea to calm, then she asked of her these questions. How came she here? Arithea, still shaken, told her how Scacath had come to fi-Logath and bade them receive *Nightreaver* and heal its fallen sorceress. So they had done so, though not without caution. Arithea had met Thyri and discovered her curse. As for Eiriksdattir: the moon was full, and she was out in the land beyond their towers. She would return the day after next.

Who was "he" who had fallen?

He had no name—the guardian of the north.

How had come Scacath? Through sorcery, on horseback, or by foot?

On foot—the times were dark, and those of the elder races who traveled did so at grave risk. Powerful sorceries enhanced that risk, so Scacath had come alone, on foot.

From where?

Arithea looked at Megan, tragic realization creasing her brow. "From the north," she said. "Oh, Megan—the wolf was pupil to the dark lady! Would she have tracked her? Could Thyri have done this?"

Megan closed her eyes again. *Yes, Arithea. If she has found traces of her teacher's passage, she could only have followed.*

Even with you here?

Even then.

What have I done!

Megan squeezed the hand weakly. *Will you avenge this—this guardian's death?*

For a long moment, Arithea did not answer. *No,* she responded at last. *She could not have known. But the damage cannot be undone; in a way, it is fitting. Ragnarok approaches, and Wyrd has decreed that fi-Logath will not be spared the carnage.*

She rose. "I can find no hate within myself for your friend, but I must leave you know. You are yet weak. I will send food and drink—you will be attended."

"I owe you my life," Megan said. "If I can repay you, Arithea, I shall."

The faer-Jotun smiled weakly. "I must go. The darkness threatens us all now, and I must perform castings and assess the dangers. When I am done, I shall return."

"What of Thyri?"

"What of her? She has chosen this path for herself. I cannot follow, and you are yet weak."

Arithea turned then, leaving Megan alone with her thoughts.

Rollo stirred in his sleep, then started, sitting up suddenly on the bed.

After his conversation in the garden with Rui, his lack of sleep the night before had overcome him, and he'd retired an hour before sunset. Now—what had wakened him? He sifted through his thoughts, trying to find traces of what he'd dreamed.

Nothing.

He rolled over and clutched the downy pillow. Some ghost, he thought, had wakened him. Some ghost within these crystal walls.

He yet felt exhausted, but again, sleep was long in coming.

The white wolf howled as it circled again the spot where Scacath's trail disappeared.

In the distance, something roared, returning her howl. From another direction came a distant crashing of trees.

At the spot, Thyri collapsed to the earth, tears streaming from her eyes as she forced her own mind up through the fierce, instinctive presence of the wolf. And as she did so, as her senses came to the fore, she found hope:

Magic. In the air, lingering in the trees. Magic in a sheet draped over the space between two bushes.

Woraag Grag, she remembered. *The shadow-paths. Scacath knew them as well!*

Slowly, she rose, sniffing the ground before the sheet of magic. Yes, she thought, through this gate, her teacher had gone. Growling softly, she leapt into the magic.

Still she was in a forest, but now the night sounds were familiar, less threatening. She gained again Scacath's scent, and she followed.

As if in a dream, she found herself on the same path she had walked with Woraag Grag a month before. She passed again the trees she knew, the places full of memories of Scacath, Astrid, Hugin and Munin—the ravens—Mind and Memory. And as she rounded the turn to the common, Munin stood before her.

"Thyri," spake the raven, smiling. "Come, she awaits you." Quickly he turned, leading her away to the huts, to Scacath's hut, inside which she had never set foot.

He entered it, and without pausing she followed. Inside, she found only darkness . . . and magic—it swamped her senses. Scacath's magic, and the magic of someone else . . .

Suddenly, from the darkness a figure stepped. He was young, fair of skin and hair and with dark, fathomless eyes. But for those eyes, she knew him. In his hands, he held a black orb, the source of the magic darkness.

Ottar! she growled.

No, he said without speaking. *I am Morgana.* He smiled, his teeth shining white with their own light. They looked like fangs.

She growled and leapt for his throat, but an invisible hand smashed her down to the bare earth. It crushed her, forcing the air from her lungs, and strands of darkness reached in for her mind. She gasped as they strangled her thoughts. Within her, the wolf growled, then whimpered.

Not again, she heard Morgana insert calmly into the darkness. Then—nothing.

Morgana stood over the still form and laughed. After a moment, she waved her hand, and Munin responded, lifting up the body of the wolf and carrying it back out into the night.

Atale

Arithea did not return to Megan until morning. Once there, she sat silently as the sorceress slowly wakened, and even after Megan opened her eyes, it was long before she spoke.

In her eyes, Megan saw thinly veiled fear, but when she spoke, she asked first only of Megan's health. The sorceress replied that she felt stronger; she had used some of her ring's magics to speed her recovery.

"That is good," Arithea replied. "We may require your skills. An ancient evil has passed through here to a shadow world where, even now, it works its dark designs. As I worked my magics last night, I did not expect this. We must marshal our forces against this threat, and soon. We must banish or destroy it, for if it discovers our weakness to the north and summons our ancient enemies, we will have no defense."

Megan eyed her curiously. "What is the nature of this evil?" she asked.

"The Morrigan," Arithea said distantly. "She is free, and nearby."

Megan started, bolting upright, grabbing Arithea's shoulders. "Thyri!" she said desperately. "Arithea, she wants Thyri! We have battled your ancient evil, Eiriksdattir and I! It was Morgana who defeated me!"

The faer-Jotun eyed her grimly. "And you lived?"

"Without Thyri, I would not have escaped."

"I am afraid that your friend may not do so this time. If the Morrigan has found her, she shall perish. We must strike out, but we cannot ride into battle against such a foe. Our only hope lies in sorcery, in annihilation of that half-world where the evil has taken refuge."

"No!" Megan shook Arithea. "You cannot do that! Let me try! Take me to our men. We shall go after her ourselves. You cannot condemn her."

"You will fall again, daughter of light. She defeated you once."

"I *must* try! My body may be weaker, but my magic is not. My talisman possesses its full power, and in the last battle I blundered, I let her win. I will not make the same mistake again."

"You will need speed, but you cannot spell yourself there, else she will be prepared for your arrival."

"Have you the steeds of my people—of your mother's people?"

"Yes." She paused. "You ask much, but I will grant your wish. They will be readied." She gripped Megan's arm and closed her eyes. The sorceress felt strength flow through her, charging her with energy. "There," Arithea said weakly as she moved her hand away. "I give you that as well, though now I am weakened. You must leave within the hour. If I do not sense your victory by this time tomorrow, I will handle the matter after my own fashion."

Megan smiled at her and stood. "Thank you, sorceress of fi-Logath. Lead me to *Nightreaver*'s crew. We must waste no time."

They gathered in the dining chamber where they had been welcomed by the faer-Jotun two mornings before. Sokki sat next to Elinta, squeezing her hand, staring solemnly at Megan, who sat between Donalu and Arithea. Next to Sokki sat his brother, and next to Horik, Renta.

Rollo sat between Rui and Gerald. He was first to break the silence. "Where is Thyri?" he asked abruptly.

Megan tried to smile at him and failed. Eventually, she lowered her gaze. "She is in danger, Rollo. That is why we are here."

Arithea placed a hand on Megan's arm and began to speak. She told them of what she had seen through her sorcery the night before, how she'd discovered, unexpectedly, sorcerous traces of Morgana's passage through their world, and she told the faer-Jotun how she planned to deal with the evil.

"But first," Megan interrupted her, "I wish to find Thyri. I fear that Morgana seeks her, or perhaps she has found her."

"But she was with you!" Rollo protested angrily.

"No," Arithea said. "She sought solitude in the garden two nights before, and she has not returned. We fear that she found traces of something that she could not ignore."

"What?"

"Scacath," Megan said. "The name will mean nothing to you, but to Thyri it was once everything. From Scacath, Thyri learned her skills. Somehow, Thyri's teacher learned of our plight and came here, to fi-Logath, to plead aid for us from the faer-Jotun. She came on foot, and Thyri is well capable of identifying scents in the forest, even those months old."

"So"—Rollo stared at her—"you're saying that she left us here, to chase after this Scacath?"

"Yes."

"Perhaps into a trap? Laid by she whom you battled on that island?"

"Perhaps."

Rollo rose. "Then let us follow her!" He glared down at his companions. "Why do you not rise with me? Did you not hear!"

Slowly, Rui stood. "I will come," he told Megan, "though I do not know what use I will be."

"If you encounter the Morrigan," Arithea said darkly, "probably no use at all. You are welcome to stay."

Rui looked at Rollo, then shook his head. "I will go."

"And I," Gerald said simply.

Sokki glanced at Elinta, then, silently, he rose. His brother followed.

Donalu cleared his throat. "I also will go."

Arithea turned on him, glaring. "No! You are our strongest warrior, and I will not risk your death in this. If the Morrigan emerges victorious over a foe with you among their number, she will turn her wrath on our people."

"But—"

"No!" she said flatly, turning to Megan. "You and your people must go alone. You have one passing of the sun to complete this task."

Grimly, Megan nodded.

The Tuathan steeds awaited them in the garden: six great black stallions, bridled in silver and shod with gold. As they stamped the earth, the ground shook, and their fiery eyes fell on their riders with cold intelligence.

Twenty *helfin* milled about the horses' hooves, running their hands through the thick coats, jumping up on the horses' necks to whisper in their ears. Slowly, Megan and the others approached.

"They will take you where you wish, sorceress," Arithea called from behind them, "but they will not leave this world. If you abandon them, they will wait for you one half-day, then they will return here."

Megan paused and turned. "Thank you, Arithea. We *shall* return."

"Perhaps," the faer-Jotun said indifferently. "Be wary of your sorcery. Let not the Morrigan sense your approach."

But how might I track Thyri?

Your steeds will follow her path.

Megan smiled and nodded, then turned back for the others. Silently, they mounted. After all were seated, without a word, the horses carried their riders swiftly northward.

Gerald, like the others, spent the majority of his time clinging to his mount's neck. When he did look around, the land was little more than an alarming blur. At times, they were pursued by creatures he could not have imagined, even in his nightmares. But the Tuathan steeds easily outdistanced all dangers, and after a time Gerald began to fear more for the pains he would know when he dismounted than anything else.

Rollo's thoughts revolved around Thyri, and his rage came and went. He would not lose her! Not like Fandis! He would face Loki himself if that was Wyrd's demand for Thyri's life.

Sokki found his hand moving often to the crystal hilt of the sword he wore at his side. He thought of Elinta, then of Thyri. At times, he wished he had stayed at fi-Logath; and with that thought, he felt ashamed.

Meanwhile, the sun made slow, relentless progress on its westward trek.

Near dusk, Megan's steed came to a sudden halt. As the others drew next to her, she dismounted, examining the ground. She looked around desperately. Why had they stopped?

Wait! she thought. A gateway . . . Cautiously, she cast a minor magic, and a place in the nearby air grew suddenly substantial—a faint, silvery latticework, like a spider's web. Behind her, she heard the others dismount.

"What is it?" Rollo asked, shaking the stiffness from his legs.

She turned to him. "From here," she said, "we must continue on foot."

Horik kicked out the ache and felt spears of pain shoot up his back. He stamped his feet against the ground and staggered away from his steed, into the bushes.

As he relieved himself, the whispering began in his mind. *Come,* it said. *They do not need you. Come and rest.* To his horror, his foot stepped forth on its own. His other foot followed. Out of the corner of his eye, he saw a dark thing in the trees—a raven, watching him.

Come . . . His pace grew more rapid. He wanted to call out to the others, but his mouth wouldn't open. *Sleep,* said the voice. The sky grew dark, and his limbs heavy. He collapsed to the ground and felt something alight on his back, talons digging into his flesh, pulling him upward.

Sleep!

The darkness enveloped him, and his thoughts faded away.

As they gathered about Megan, Sokki looked about desperately. "Where's Horik!" he whispered. "Where is my brother?" He turned for the wood, but Rollo grabbed his arm.

"Quiet!" the Viking told him. "He knows where we are—he will find us."

"We cannot wait!" Megan said.

Sokki turned on her. "We cannot leave him!"

"We cannot embark on a search either, my friend!" Rollo seethed in his ear. "If some ill has befallen him, it would then find us, one by one. Your brother is a Viking, we will wait a few moments, then go on. If you wish to wait longer, here with the horses, you may!"

Megan closed her eyes and risked another spell. Sokki's brother, she discovered, was nowhere near. "I do not sense his presence," she said after a moment. "Perhaps it is he who has gone on without us."

Sokki lowered his eyes. "No," he said. "He is dead. I have lost another brother."

Rollo squeezed his arm, but Sokki shrugged him off and drew his crystal sword. "Let us go," he seethed. "And let the evils of this place beware, for the last son of Gunnar shall not so easily be vanquished!"

Megan smiled sadly, then asked for each of their hands on her arm. As they clutched her, she stepped through the gateway, pulling them through behind her.

Ice

. . . into a raging snowstorm. The flakes pelted against them like tiny shards of ice; the cold burrowed through to their bones, freezing out the aches of their journey, replacing them with a duller yet more alarming pain.

"Fimbulwinter!" Rollo shouted over the whipping winds.

No, Gerald thought, as weariness flooded through him. It was his dream—that dream he had had that morning after he'd joined Thyri. It was all here: the snows, the cold, the weariness, and the feeling of eternal hardship. And Megan's voice now, calling to him, urging him to move forward. Something horrible, he knew, awaited them out there in the snow. He forced another step . . .

The sky was dark, the clouds and the storm blotting out the little sunlight that remained. Megan's voice came to him distantly. He hurried to reach it.

While the others rushed after Megan, Sokki heard Horik's voice calling him from the side. He turned for it, his mind filling with memories of his youth, of his long days in weather like this, playing outside the family hall, in the snows, with his brothers . . .

In the distance, he saw a figure. As he drew near it, the storm fell away, and his feet touched down on grass. In the waning sunlight, Horik awaited him.

The Viking stood, his blade drawn, smiling at him. "Come to me, Brother," Horik said. "See what I have found."

Sokki watched his eyes; they were hollow, vacant. They stared past him. "Horik!" he cried. "Look at me!"

"I am, Brother," he said. His eyes did not move, did not focus.

Sokki raised his sword and moved cautiously forward.

"I have found Ottar," Horik said. "We are three again."

"Ottar is dead," Sokki said softly. He crouched, then lashed out at Horik's sword, seeking to disarm him. But their blades did not touch as Horik danced back, then whirled into an attack.

Sokki fought him silently, tears streaming down his cheeks.

Horik had the strength of a demon, his attack forcing Sokki ever back, back toward the blizzard. At first, Sokki sought only to disarm; he was ever the better of both his brothers, but never had Horik possessed such strength! His attacks, even blocked by Elinta's crystal blade, sent waves of jarring pain through his arms. But the crystal blade held under an onslaught that iron could never hope to withstand.

Even so, Sokki could not force himself on the offensive. Horik fought demonically for blood, to the death, his eyes vacant of recognition. Once, as they locked blades, Sokki's cheek grazed his brother's, and the contact stung him, so cold was his brother's flesh.

Then, Horik's sword bit into his side. Sokki backed away, and the battle fury possessed him. Horik's face melted into a featureless head, and his body became a shadow. Only the sword in the air before him was real. At it, Sokki lashed out, matching his opponent stroke for stroke, Elinta's gift whirling, glinting with the sun's waning light.

And then—blood. Red streams flying off the end of the blade. He struck again and again until the lifeless figure before him collapsed to the ground.

Only then did the face again become Horik's. When Sokki recognized it, he fell to the blood-soaked grass next to his brother and cried.

A brilliant, silver explosion filled the sky before Gerald, and suddenly he could see.

No trace of the blizzard remained, not even snow on the ground. Ahead, he heard dark laughter. As the shower of silver faded, he picked out figures: Megan, Rui, and Rollo faced—something that vaguely resembled Ottar. Megan and the others had reached a clearing; Gerald raced to join them.

The thing that looked like Ottar had dark, scarred skin. Ottar's features were twisted by the demonic forces behind them. From the thing, came the laughter. In one hand, it held a dark globe from which writhing, black strands escaped like tortured, nightmarish snakes.

It spoke to Megan. "You've come to try again?" it asked derisively. "You did not learn?"

On the ground, next to it, Thyri lay. At first, Gerald thought she was dead, then, he noticed her head move slightly to the side.

On the western horizon, the sun began to set.

* * *

Rollo glanced from Ottar to Thyri, roared, and began a charge. As he moved forward, one of Rui's arrows whizzed past his ear; as the arrow neared its target, it exploded in a burst of flame. As Rollo flew at Ottar, an unseen force smashed him to the ground. Pain seared through his sides as his ribs cracked anew. But he kept his eyes forward, and he struggled to crawl closer to the thing that wore Ottar's body.

Megan answered Morgana's questions with her magic. With a wave, the silver streamed forth. This time, instead of fire, her assault met the black power of the orb of Babd.

From her ring, the silver flowed effortlessly, engulfing the black. She poured it out as resistance mounted.

You cannot defeat me, Morgana sneered in her mind. *I am eternal*.

So, Megan returned, *am I*.

Deep within her darkness, Thyri heard the summons of the moon. The beast joined her in her prison, howling in her mind, clawing its way out to the surface.

She felt no pain, but she pressed forth with the beast. Perhaps, together, they could escape the evil that had defeated them the night before. But, as she thought this, she didn't believe it. Only when the wolf opened her eyes, when she saw the cascading silver, did she know true hope.

Megan! she thought. Again, confronted with the evil from the dark tower, Megan had joined her side. Did she dream? No—Arithea must have healed her friend. Then, this was real. But real also was her inability to move. Before her, she saw the whiteness of her foreleg. She looked up at Morgana; around the demoness, arrows flared and fell harmlessly to the ground. The archer was with her. The others as well?

She couldn't tell; she couldn't move.

Rollo heard his own silent scream in his mind as he watched Thyri's transformation. What had Morgana done to her? He pushed forward, every muscle on fire. Slowly, he inched closer to his goal.

Gerald watched the scene unfold with mounting horror. Megan's sorcery met Morgana's and the two forces clashed like juggernauts in the air. All the while, Morgana laughed. The demoness toyed with the sorceress, but Megan was undaunted. She fought back with fury, exploiting every opening in Morgana's black cloak.

Then flames began to spring up from the ground at Megan's

feet, and the earth beneath her rocked and buckled. She dodged away from the fires, struggling to keep her footing. Streamers of black fire surged through the sudden gaps in the silver, and Gerald heard Megan gasp as a black flare lashed across her leg. His eyes opened wide as he witnessed Megan's blood flowing from her wound.

If the sorceress fell, he knew, so would they all. Drawing his blade, he dove into the fray; Morgana brushed him aside and down as if he were a fly. He found himself, like Rollo, pinned to the earth, unable to move, able only to watch Morgana methodically turn back Megan's weakening assaults.

And to watch, also, Rui exhaust his supply of arrows against Morgana's impenetrable shield.

Growls escaped Thyri's throat as what silver she *could* see gradually grew black. Megan was losing, and this time, Morgana would not be careless, would not give Thyri a chance.

Still, she struggled, and then a thought came to her—another hope. *Call to me when you walk the shadow-paths,* someone had once told her . . .

Scacath's world lay at a crossroad of those paths; this she had learned all too well. If ever she were to summon him . . .

Woraag Grag! she screamed in her mind. *Pohati! Aid me!*

She looked up at Morgana, wondering if she had heard. But no, the demoness, enshrouded in black, was too intent on her battle.

Thyri, trapped at her feet, was harmless.

Megan stumbled to the ground, quickly drawing her magic around her in a shield, using it to douse the fires that Morgana ignited constantly around her feet. And still the black fire pounded against her, consuming her silver. Though she had been careful to conserve, her ring had scant power left.

Especially if she desired to use it to attack. If she ever got an opening.

She crouched behind her dwindling defenses, desperately seeking another tactic, hoping, vainly, that Morgana's talisman would exhaust itself as had her ring before.

But there seemed no end to the black onslaught. And even were there one, Morgana retained all the other powers at her command.

Bravely, Megan rose to her feet and lashed out anew, drawing on the strength Arithea had gifted her. For a while, it would aid her. After that, she would have only what was left in her ring, and the simple magics that had proven useless in her last—

Suddenly, a howl erupted in the air. Thyri! Megan thought. She lashed out again, clearing the black from the space before her. The noise had startled Morgana; Megan could see her now, looking around for the howl's source. Thyri yet was pinned at her feet.

As Morgana looked away, a streak of gray flew through the air behind her head. The gray met the source of the black magic; then a deafening scream split the night as the black orb, and the hand that held it, was ripped from Morgana's arm.

The gray streak landed. For a moment, Megan recognized it as another wolf, then the black engulfed it and a horrible howl emerged from the darkness to join in chorus with Morgana's scream.

As for the demoness, she looked at Megan, dazed. Motion erupted at her feet; Thyri dove at her, tearing out her throat with her fangs. Rollo's sword cleaved through her legs, and she began to fall.

Then began the true battle: Morgana, given a brief respite, would again escape. Megan poured her magic forth, bolstering it with the last of Arithea's gift. She wrapped her fallen enemy in a silver cage and squeezed it shut, trapping the horrible soul. Even now, it fought maniacally, and the battle raged on as Megan emptied her ring of its power.

The others watched in terror as agony creased the brow of the sorceress. Rollo struck the silver mass with his sword, but the impact did naught but throw him back to the ground. Morgana's struggling inside was plainly visible as the magic contorted and pulsated, and an eerie wail filled the night.

They watched, waited, and prayed.

Megan fell to her knees, and still they watched. Morgana's struggling grew wilder. Then, suddenly, another was among them; Gerald turned to see Sokki charging into the clearing, his crystal blade held high. He dove at the silver cocoon, slicing through it with the blade that had slain three Jotun before Elinta's brother had fallen.

The wail grew in intensity, and the contortions of the magic grew more erratic, but Gerald, watching Megan, saw her smile.

Sokki struck again. And again. And again. Slowly, the wail subsided, and the silver ball shrunk until, at last, Megan squeezed it into nothingness.

The sorceress collapsed back then, panting, onto the charred grass.

For a while, all stood still. Gerald's eyes strayed slowly, from the spot into which Morgana had disappeared to the beast that, earlier, had been Thyri. The white wolf, whining softly, sniffed around the charred remains of what had once been one of its kind.

What had once been Pohati. What had once been immortal.

Thyri looked up into Gerald's gaze and whined again, then turned and bounded into the wood.

Thus perished Arthur's bane, and thus did *Nightreaver*'s crew learn fully of Thyri's nature. With the deaths of Horik and Woraag Grag, there was little cause for celebration.

Though we did not wish to stay in that place, we spent the night in Scacath's clearing, awaiting Thyri's return in the morning. She arrived among us as if it were she who had been defeated, as if *she* had perished in the battle the night before. And she mourned, as well, for Woraag Grag. Of all among us, only Megan truly understood.

Another appeared that morning as we prepared to leave. A dark-skinned warrior—Munin, with whom Thyri had trained in swordplay in her youth. He *had* been there; his appearance before Thyri (and his abduction of Horik) had been no illusion. Munin told her that Scacath had abandoned her haven two weeks before to join Odin's host in Valhalla, to await the coming of the end. He had returned only to gather the last of their things, but Morgana had surprised him and stolen away his mind.

From then, until this morning, he had thought no thought of his own.

Necessity bade us depart quickly, else the Tuathan steeds would be gone. Thyri said her farewell to Munin, solemnly covered the remains of Woraag Grag with a blanket of leaves, and came with us. The day's ride back to fi-Logath was exhausting, and, when we arrived, we spoke hardly a word, not to each other, nor to anyone else.

During our stay, the faer-Jotun treated us well, but they remained distant. True, we had defeated the Morrigan, but we also had drawn her there. And they all knew by now how Thyri had laid open their northern frontier. When Arithea told her what she had done, Thyri apologized, but the damage had been done. Thyri offered to stay and fight for them, but Arithea did not welcome that suggestion warmly.

Two mornings after that, *Nightreaver* set sail, Megan again at the foredeck. Once past the mouth of the river, into the sea, she spelled us out of Jotunheim, back onto the seas of Midgard, the seas which we knew.

By then, we had lost all the sons of Gunnar. Sokki, bereft of his brothers, remained in fi-Logath with Elinta. He shed tears the morning we departed, but the tears were as much for himself as for us. The burden on his heart was heavy, and long in lifting.

As for us—well, the world, for a time, was ours. Our new knowledge of Thyri's dual nature did nothing to sever our loyalty to her. Indeed, it made us stronger, for we were now able to understand her moods, to understand when she left our company at first light of a full moon.

Later, when we docked at a Frisian port, we learned that, while scarcely more than a month had passed in Jotunheim, several years had come and gone in Midgard. The year was now 884 by the calendar of the One God. Much remained to transpire.

Here, briefly, I set down my pen.